JUST
FOR
TODAY

JUST FOR TODAY

NELL HUDSON

TINDER
PRESS

First published in Great Britain in 2022 by Tinder Press
An imprint of HEADLINE PUBLISHING GROUP

1

Cataloguing in Publication Data is available from the British Library

Hardback ISBN 978 1 4722 8398 6
Trade paperback ISBN 978 1 4722 8399 3

Designed and typeset by EM&EN
Printed and bound in Great Britain by Clays Ltd, Elcograf S.p.A.

Headline's policy is to use papers that are natural, renewable and recyclable
products and made from wood grown in well-managed forests and other
controlled sources. The logging and manufacturing processes are expected
to conform to the environmental regulations of the country of origin.

HEADLINE PUBLISHING GROUP
An Hachette UK Company
Carmelite House
50 Victoria Embankment
London EC4Y 0DZ

www.tinderpress.co.uk
www.headline.co.uk
www.hachette.co.uk

For my mum and dad

'Bear with me,
My heart is in the coffin there with Caesar,
And I must pause till it come back to me.'

William Shakespeare,
Julius Caesar, Act III Scene II

Prologue

Ever since we began our tradition of swapping notebooks, I've written with you in my mind. It's as if you were sitting in some high-up seat at the back of an auditorium inside my head. I hear you. I wonder if it will always be so; if everything I ever put down in words will invoke that echo.

I hope so.

If I write it all down, everything that's happened over the last year, perhaps I'll understand it. As I lull in the gusset between Christmas and New Year, life is quiet. I've little else to do, and little else I can do now but write. It helps; it always has. The kiss of pen to paper closes the electrical circuit within me; connecting head to heart, connecting myself as I am now to the girl I was one year ago.

The last twelve months come to me in dreams of salty water and the smell of sun on skin. In flashes: a constellation, my head on unfamiliar pillows, a stage, a warm body upright against my own. I ricochet between landscapes: fields and cliffs give way to the glimmering of city lights at dusk. All the houses. All the rooms. The fun we had.

Remembering is painful. I turn over one stone and find others, and, beneath them, many wriggling things that have long since seen the light. An event from just a few months ago will summon up one, if not several, older memories, appearing with such clarity it takes my breath away. I writhe. Every scene my mind presents points so clearly at what was to come, what has now been.

There is one shivering crab apple tree visible from where I sit. Sometimes a robin visits. I am forced to look up from my memories. He looks me in the eye and I feel something familiar, something like joy, and I return to my page with renewed determination.

1

I was lodging in the house of a therapist, a stuffy attic in North London, while working as a nanny for a family a few streets away. I walked to and from work. Every Friday evening, I would buy myself a particular Italian chocolate from the local deli – the kind that has a little fortune on wax paper hidden inside the wrapping – and wander home texting friends to make plans for the night. There was always something happening, and if there wasn't, we would make it happen: moonlit swims in a Hampstead pond, improvised picnics in the park, ending up in an uncharted nightclub at 4 a.m. on a Wednesday.

It didn't matter; nothing did.

Back in my cluttered studio, I'd change out of my conspicuously sensible nanny attire and into something appropriate for the night in store. Shoes that allowed me to move with the same mobility and speed as our nights out did. But not trainers, just in case. There were places in town that didn't let you in wearing trainers. These places were designed for the rich and famous, but we found ourselves swept in with the crowd from time to time, feeling slightly fraudulent as the attractive hostess (who dealt cocaine to guests on the side) checked us in to the guestbook. Behind these secret doors, you entered different worlds. You could find yourself in a country stately home: shelves full of books, log fires, and wallpaper that cost a hundred pounds per square metre; or you might walk out into a Florentine palazzo, tanned hipsters vaping around a fountain. You could find yourself in a riad full of sweet-smelling plants, a speakeasy straight out of the 1930s, a neon basement filled with golden light and the latest pop star in the booth next to you. These places never closed, and I hated to leave. Once the wee hours of dancing turned into day, you could walk into a restaurant for breakfast, pick up a newspaper and spend a few hours reading and crunching toast. Someone you knew might show up, and you'd kill a few more hours with gossip and coffee. Maybe you'd decide to order food, and before you knew it, it was cocktail hour once more.

This rhythm came all too naturally to me, this never-ending weekend. Cornwall last summer was the same: the cyclical hedonism, the constant company. You were never alone; even if you were in the bath, someone would come and sit on the rim of the tub, their feet in next to you, makeshift cocktail sloshing into the water, nattering away while they waited their turn. Time lost its grip. The summer sun seemed barely to have set before reappearing again. Sleep was optional. Nobody ever knew what day of the week it was.

In the city, life was quick. There was no time to waste: you had to find fun and pin it down. If you weren't careful, you missed it, that giddy euphoria, impossible to conjure from nowhere if the air wasn't already ripe. You could decorate yourself in paint and precious metals, and go out, willing and alert, and find you'd been stood up. You'd laugh loudly, you'd drink spirits or take something stronger in an attempt to resuscitate the night, but *it* wasn't there, and so, like a ghost disappearing back under the stairs, you'd go home.

On New Year's Eve, there is a surplus of this energy; so much so that things can go wrong as quickly as right. It's nuclear: volatile, unless channelled correctly. Maybe this is why we gather together in parties or hide away in an attempt to tame it.

I was lucky: I hadn't come up for air since Christmas. It had all been one long hibernation. For my less fortunate friends, offices stayed open. Work didn't hibernate. They were the first to come over, direct from work to my flat – where I, in flannel pyjamas, had been scribbling and snacking all day with the heating turned up too high. They were so grateful to see me: those brave emissaries into the real world, returning thirstily with loosened collars.

Niall arrived with champagne. Mila contributed four pre-rolled joints in neat straws. Jess was supposed to come, too, but she was doing the PR for a celebration hosted by *The Line*, a London weekly culture magazine, and had to make an appearance there before she could discreetly slink off.

Mila and Niall were flirting in insults, as they did back then.

'All that money spent on your education, Niall, and you still don't know when I'm being sarcastic.'

Niall was the most grown-up of us. He had a boring, high-paid job and was unfalteringly generous with his earnings. He had old-fashioned manners and spoke the same way to anyone aged two to one hundred and two. He understood interest rates and could change a tyre. He was a good person to have on your team.

We sipped the champagne as I finished my hair in the bathroom mirror, giggling and speculating about who would be at the party. We forged rescue plans in case any of us got stuck with someone undesirable. People like Sylvie: a doughy, technically very nice waitress-by-day-slam-poet-by-night, but simply the type of conversationalist who gave you the feeling the fun was definitely happening on the other side of the room. Then there was the more actively irksome company: those who managed to not ask you a single question, yet acted like you were boring the crap out of them. Girls on too much coke, older men with bad jokes and worse breath.

Inevitably, five minutes before leaving the house, I was visited by the familiar desire to stay home. The room was baking. My half-empty glass of flat champagne had started to taste sour. Lethargy tugged at my hand and invited me to take off my uncomfortable high heels and bra, to slip back into my still-warm flannel pyjamas. The exclusivity of Mila and Niall's nascent frisson was making me feel alone and bitter. I fretted about how I could break it to them that I wasn't coming. Mila would kill me. At the party, Paddy would see the other two show up without me, add this disappointment to the index of offences against my name, and stop bothering to invite me out. I couldn't have that. I let the momentum of my friends' excitement carry me out into the icy air, and found that there it was: the promise of a night to remember.

Premature fireworks sputtered in a corner of the sky. We teetered as rapidly as we could, passing one of Mila's sweet little joints between us, sucking it up outside the station before plunging into the stale heat of the Northern Line. Everyone on the tube was dressed up and rowdy. We got talking to a group of young women, their modesty hanging on by sequinned threads.

'You girls going to watch the fireworks?'

'No, just a small family gathering.'

Above ground, Starbucks was still open, wafting out the smell of nutmeg and coffee. Arm in arm, we sang 'I'm in the Mood for Dancing' as we walked down the Holloway

Road. Niall gave a homeless man a fiver and a pair of new socks. (He carried them around specifically for that purpose: 'It's just so rubbish not having clean socks.')

Paddy answered the door. 'Thank *fuck* you're here,' he said.

Paddy was an actor, and not one of the introverted quiet types who only come alive when in character. He kissed us all and bundled us inside like fugitives.

'Hannah made me get here at fucking lunchtime to help out.'

Hannah, our hostess, had been at school with Mila, Jess and me, and now worked as a set designer. She had adopted Paddy as soon as she'd met him at Mila's eighteenth. Paddy now handed us four Marie Antoinette glasses from a side dresser, each half-full of pink fizz.

'Joni!' he said, holding me at arm's length. 'This dress. I might have to borrow. Take that coat off immediately – cloakroom is the first bedroom on the left.'

Mila and I left Niall chatting to Paddy and went to put our coats away, scanning the room from above as we climbed the stairs.

As we entered the bedroom, someone ran in behind us and slammed the door. Jess. She squeezed us both and fell back on to the bed, firing off questions about our Christmases and families, filling us in on her own without a pause.

'I had the worst argument with my mum,' she said. 'The whole *single* thing. It's like she can't not bring it up.'

'Oh, God,' I said.

'I know. It's like Mum, calm down, my biological clock is still around midday.'

'My mum's the same,' said Mila, adding, in a strikingly accurate impression of her mother's Nigerian accent, 'When you going to meet a nice boy and stop this nonsense?'

Jess and I laughed.

'Ugh, anyway,' said Jess. 'I've got some top-notch MDMA from the *Line* party. Let's get fucked up.'

Every Boxing Day, Hannah's parents would fly away to Malaga, not due to return until we were comfortably into January, allowing her time for complete redecoration and subsequent clear-up. Her New Year's Eve parties were notorious: everyone was invited, the drinks never ran out. She was rumoured to spend a whole two days prepping the house, locking away any valuables, embellishing the interiors to resemble a theme she had chosen months in advance. This year, she had really outdone herself. The garden was alight with red Chinese paper lanterns and paraffin torches. The whole house smelled faintly of cigarettes and narcissi, which stood in a plethora of glass milk bottles dotted on windowsills and mantelpieces. The entire place seemed to shimmer and cast a golden light upon the furnishings and guests alike. Hannah always quipped that she only invited good-looking people to her parties; which was only half a joke. By rights, everyone should have been double-chinned and bloated with holiday gluttony – but no, here were the beautiful people, in their finest silk and leather.

We smoked in the garden.

'Where's Niall gone?' asked Mila.

We spotted him talking to Cecily Simmons, a girl who possessed all the ingredients of prettiness but none of the flavour.

'Ugh. Rather him than me,' said Jess. She took a deep drag on her cigarette, then placed its moist, lipstick-stained butt in my mouth. 'Here, it's making me feel sick.'

Jess was one of very few people in the world I'd accept a soggy cigarette from. Not just because I loved her, but because the girl was ridiculously clean. More than clean:

groomed. She'd always managed to be effortlessly chic. Even at school, when Mila and I were wearing Primark and the wrong colour foundation, she'd opted for second-hand clothes and minimal make-up. Now, in her role as sophisticated PR girl, she dressed mostly in black, and believed trainers were exclusively for the gym. She washed her hair with a shampoo that cost twenty-five pounds a bottle, and left a perpetual trail of petitgrain in her wake.

My phone buzzed. A text from Dyl.

You here? I'm upstairs.

Telling the girls I was running to the loo, I slithered off through the party, heading for the small room on the top floor to which I knew Dyl was referring. He wouldn't have meant the first-floor games room, where two strangers were nursing a guitar, singing a sickly, faux-ironic acoustic cover of a Beyoncé song; nor the next floor up, where the druggy crowd were snorting lines off old *Twilight* books in Hannah's childhood bedroom. No. He meant the solitary, undecorated room at the very top of the house, occupied by a single wooden table and chair. There he was: smoking out of the window, the crisp air of the turn of the year filling the room like a spell.

'Hello,' I said.

He turned his whole body to me, a trail of smoke curling around his face as he exhaled.

'Phil!' He beamed. His name for me. My real name is Joan, but after discovering Joni Mitchell in my teens, I adopted 'Joni' and never looked back. Though the iconic singer-songwriter may not be aware, she shares her surname with a fat, bald, middle-aged soap-opera character: Phil Mitchell. Hence Dyl's nickname for me. It used to drive me mad; my adolescent idealisations were severely threatened by this association. But my irritation only fuelled his persistence, and eventually I allowed myself in on the joke. We were Dyl and Phil. Dyl is short for Dylan, who was actually named after Bob. His parents are much cooler than mine. My mother met his at an antenatal class, and was taken in by her 'wild hair' and disregard for the preciousness of the other pregnant women.

'"Ring out, wild bells,"' said Dyl, '"to the wild sky, the flying cloud, the frosty light: The year is dying in the night."'

'Byron?'

'Tennyson.'

'Come downstairs,' I said, refusing to let him suck me in. We had seen each other only a couple of days ago, but if left to our own devices we could spend the entire party up here, just talking. There was always something to discuss, some new revelation that needed dissecting. Almost telepathically, we knew where the other was going, could simultaneously weave multiple threads, skate through sudden changes of subject, only to return to the coda in full synchronicity. Silences were comfortable but short-lived. And, my God, he could make me laugh.

'Come on, Dyl,' I repeated. 'What are you doing up here anyway, you weirdo?'

'Mate. I'm pranging. Had a couple of lines before I left the house and they're not doing what they're supposed to.'

'Well, come and have a drink then. Balance you out.'

'Is Niall here?'

'Yes, he came with me.'

'Good.'

Music hummed below us.

'Have a fag with me,' he said.

'I don't want one. I feel a bit sick. Mila makes her joints too strong for me.'

'Has she got any MD?'

'No. But Jess does.'

He smiled, and I smiled back. He came over and gave me a hug.

'Alright, then,' he said, and gave his hair a deliberate jumble with his fingers as we made our way back down into the thrum. 'Let's do this.'

Halfway down the final flight of stairs, Dyl froze. I turned to see what he was looking at, or rather, whom. Between the banisters, I spotted a mass of coarse, slate-coloured hair, piled Edwardian-style above a face wearing an expression of extreme self-satisfaction. A breast lolling free from a too-small blouse, a huge, dark areola visibly dripping creamy droplets. Marla. She was busying herself extracting a breast pump from the bag on the sofa next to her.

'Oh, God.'

'Is it incredibly un-progressive of me to think she should be at home with her baby?' said Dyl.

'Is it incredibly horrible of me to suggest we don't go over?' I said.

Too late.

'Joni! Dylan! Come say hi!'

Marla Taschen was the resident fuck-up; the yardstick by which we measured our own debauchery. (*On a scale of one to Marla, how drunk was I?*) She was a touchstone of chaos. We reassured ourselves that we were not *that* bad. There were several possible candidates for the paternity of her child.

The first time I'd met her was at a warehouse rave. She was by herself in the makeshift toilet, taking cocaine while drinking from a large plastic carton of 'orange juice drink'.

She told me, with cartoonish pupils, that the vitamin C in the juice would 'balance the Charlie out'.

'You know my brother?' she'd said, grabbing my chin and coming so close to my face that I thought she might kiss me.

'Do I?'

'Henry!' she'd shouted, apparently not in control of the volume of her own voice.

'Oh right, yeah. Sort of.'

She placed a finger over her lips, and then mine.

'Shh,' she said. 'Don't tell him about the Charlie, will you?'

I'd kept her secret that night, and learned over the years that Marla's drug habits were as well-known to Henry as they were to the rest of London.

'Hiii.' She looked piously up at us and reached out her hand to take mine. 'How are you kids doing?'

She was only a couple of years older than us, but since becoming a mother had taken on the sanctimony of a cringeworthy teacher. My lips stiffened; apparently I was too mature to be called a kid, but not mature enough not to mind.

She stroked her thumb back and forth over my hand like a painfully slow metronome, dragging out the time in her company. I shot Dyl a meaningful glance.

'Oh, you know,' Dyl said. 'Crushingly disappointed about how little I've achieved this year. How about you?'

She giggled. 'You make me laugh, Dylan.' She prised the suction cup off her teat. 'I'm doing good, man. I love being a mum, when Bear lets me get any sleep.'

'Surely you're used to being kept up all night by a juvenile male sucking your tits?' Paddy butted in. 'Right, you two, Hannah needs us to help set up the dancefloor.'

Dyl and I didn't need asking twice. We three strip-the-willowed our way through the shoal of lovely bodies in the garden and into the studio, where the dancing would take place.

The studio was a double-height space with whitewashed brick walls. There were large plants everywhere, and the south half of the roof had been cut out and replaced with glass, so the general atmosphere was that of half greenhouse, half circus tent. From an iron cross-beam wound in fairy lights hung a two-seater swing. People were taking photos of each other on it, posing with their legs in the air. Some tall girls were arguing over the choice of vinyl, only to be outdone by Frank Ford, who was banging out some eight-bar blues on an old grand piano in the corner. The dancing hadn't started yet, but you could feel it coming like the electric fizz of a tuning orchestra. Somewhere along the way, we had lost Dyl. Perhaps one of the others had found him. Paddy and I flopped on to a large divan and began to judge everyone in the room.

'She asked me if I had any pills earlier,' he said.

'Who?'

'Marla.'

'Jesus,' I said. 'Doesn't that, like, poison the baby's milk or something?'

'God knows,' said Paddy. 'But she seemed pretty rabid.' He imitated her posh, little-girl croak: 'Paddy, Paddy, darling, you got anything on you? Mama wants to party!'

'Christ,' I said, shuddering. 'Who d'you reckon's the baby daddy?'

'Probably one of her brothers. The Taschens are far too snobbish to breed with anyone outside the immediate family.'

'Ew.'

'Speak of the devil.'

And there was Henry. Standing in that hunched, concave way that the very tall adopt, holding a bottle of beer and talking to a good-looking red-headed man whom we all called Rusty. Henry didn't look much like his sister, bar the thick, near-black hair. His eyes were blue like hers, but less vapid — or maybe he'd just taken fewer drugs. He was beautiful like a child is beautiful: unselfconsciously and almost supernaturally. Henry had been one of the notoriously 'fit' boys at Mosshead, the nearby boys' school that Mila and I had been obsessed with growing up; and I, specifically, had been obsessed with him. He'd never paid me much attention until last summer, when we'd hooked up after Notting Hill Carnival. I couldn't believe it; my inner teenage-self was doing backflips when he kissed me. Afterwards, when I didn't hear from him, I was mildly wounded but not in the least surprised. I hadn't seen him since. Word was he had a girlfriend now – Imogen, an intimidatingly beautiful content creator, someone more in his league than me.

'You know she dumped him,' said Paddy, following my gaze.

'What?'

'That gazelle, Imogen. She met a model in Australia. She's gone all clean eating and yoga and crap.'

'And become a lesbian?'

'A male model, you fool.'

Jess came and dived over Paddy and me, causing enough of a commotion for a few people to look over – including Henry. We caught eyes, and – did I imagine it? The effervescent hint of things to come.

'Would you like some drugs now?' asked Jess.

'Yes.'

We gathered in the upstairs bathroom, Niall and Mila sitting side-by-side on the edge of the bath, their hands threatening to hold each other's, Dyl curled up on the windowsill with a cigarette. Jess and Paddy formed little MDMA dim sum out of Rizla papers and handed us one each.

'This bathroom's bigger than our flat,' said Jess, swallowing.

'Legit,' said Mila.

'It's very anti-Semitic, you know,' said Paddy, chasing his bomb down with some water from the sink.

'What is? MDMA?' asked Dyl.

'New Year's Eve. In the Gregorian Calendar, New Year's Eve is Saint Sylvester's day, who was the most awful anti-Semite Pope.'

'Oh, fuck off.'

'It's true.'

'Oh my God!' said Jess. 'Yeah, there's a street race in Brazil, the Saint Silvester Road Race. My cousin's always posting about it on Facebook. Annoying.'

'Of course there is,' said Paddy. 'Brazil is where all the Nazis went to hide before Nuremberg.'

'Are you saying,' said Dyl, 'that because I am one of the chosen people, I shouldn't celebrate New Year's Eve?'

'In Belgium, women who don't finish their work by sunset on New Year's Eve are cursed to not get married for the whole year,' said Niall.

'Like that's a curse,' said Jess.

'Why do you know that?' said Mila.

Niall gave her a sad smile. 'Lina.'

Lina was Niall's ex; she had dumped him out of the blue six months ago with no explanation.

'Maybe that's why she left you,' said Paddy. 'Because

she hadn't met her deadline and didn't want to wait another year.'

We all got hysterics, chemicals kicking in.

Fig candles burned here and there. I remember fleeting snippets of shallow conversations, all the time aware of Henry in my orbit, Henry across the room, everyone I spoke to just a time-filler before Henry.

'Hi.'

Finally.

'Hi,' I said.

Somehow, we decided to go and take a line of cocaine together. I let him lead the way to the downstairs loo and shut the door behind me. His arm curved around my waist to turn the lock, his body above mine, his mouth level with my eyes for that split second.

'Rusty gave me this,' he said. 'Hope it's alright.'

'I need to dance,' I said, coming up from my line.

He smiled down at me through long eyelashes. 'Cool.'

Back in the studio, there were somehow three times as many people as there had been fifteen minutes before. The music was louder, conversations had to be shouted at close range and people had begun swinging each other around the dancefloor.

The Rolling Stones' 'Brown Sugar' was playing. Henry and I edged into the fray. We'd done this before; we moved well. A flash of him pulling me up to stand on a wall by his side, somewhere along a crowded Ladbroke Grove, dancehall beats thrumming.

He was the perfect dance partner: sporadically taking my hand and spinning me, then giving me space to move, and as we went on he would draw me right into his arms and up close to his body. His smell, a flicker of his hand in my hair.

The drugs snaked through me; I was floating. Lights around the room lost focus. All I could see was him.

At some point, the music stopped. Hannah stood on a chair and shushed everyone. We raucously counted down from ten, nine, eight . . .

'ONE!'

'HAPPY NEW YEAR!'

The familiar and uncanny feel of Henry's lips. I lost him briefly as Mila and Jess pulled me over to dance until my heart was beating so hard I could feel throbbing in my chest.

I came out to the garden to find Henry talking to Dyl, who was puffing on a joint and creased up laughing.

'What's so funny?' I asked.

Dyl was too much in pieces to answer, and Henry merely shrugged. I tweezed the joint off Dyl and dragged on it hard, trying to mellow myself out a little.

'I'll take you there if you like,' Henry said to Dyl.

'Where?' I asked.

'My family have a place down in Cornwall. It's very remote and quiet. I was telling Dyl he could go and do some writing there.'

Dyl attempted to gather himself. 'I would absolutely love that. Are you really sure you're not just saying it?'

Henry pulled on his cigarette. 'I don't do that.'

'You're the best, Hen.'

Explosions in the distance; the smell of gunpowder in the air. A few white stars were visible from this pocket of London.

Inside, the pulsing beat changed distinctly from the shoulders-and-hips cymbals of rock 'n' roll to the head-and-hands throb of house music.

'Oh, God,' I said.

'Come on!' Dyl yelled, and darted into the studio to join the throng.

Henry drew me to him and enveloped me into his jacket, kissing me more urgently now. Ecstasy spread warm and easy through my body.

'Oh, shit.' Dyl was suddenly calling over to us from the studio door. 'Henry, you don't wanna see this.' Everyone was laughing and cheering inside at some spectacle. The terrible thin music was suffocating. Unable to see what was happening, I looked to Henry, who, at well over six feet tall, was something of a human periscope. There was something wrong.

'Hen? Henry, what is it?' I shouted.

His jaw constricted. 'It's Marla,' he said.

'What?'

I managed to cram my way into a gap in the bodies, and saw Henry's big sister, stark naked, clearly high as a kite, writhing almost gymnastically around with Rusty, who looked utterly wasted himself.

I turned back to Henry and yelled, 'Do you want to get out of here?'

'Yes.' He nodded. 'Yes, please.'

*

In the taxi, he lay across the back seat with his head in my lap, unable to see me failing to keep the giddy grin off my face. He moaned a little into the folds of my dress.

'I'm just so embarrassed for her,' he said. 'She'll regret it so much tomorrow, and she can get really depressed about that sort of thing.'

I knew the feeling. Thank God it was her and not me.

'Don't worry,' I said. 'It's New Year's Eve, everyone's fucked. No one will remember.'

'Except me.'

'Well, yes. That image will probably be burned into your retinas forever. But no one else will remember.'

He laughed. We were both still fairly high.

Henry told the driver here was fine thank you just seconds after passing the electric billboards of Piccadilly Circus; the lights of Coca-Cola and the latest Apple technology dancing colours over the skin of my bare legs.

'Are we going to the club now?' I said, tumbling out of the car just off Regent Street.

He took my hand and pulled me face to face with a black metal door, sandwiched between shop fronts at the foot of Savile Row. He was jangling a wreath of keys.

'Henry, is this where you live?'

I must have walked past this doorway dozens of times en route to see exhibitions at the Royal Academy, and had never noticed its presence before. Perhaps it only appeared on New Year's Eve.

The black door closed heavily behind us, and I found myself in a small lodge. A uniformed doorman, as Christmas-card perfect as the giant teddy bears outside Hamley's just yards away, greeted Henry as 'Mr Taschen', and I smirked. Henry wished him a happy New Year and dragged me onward into a vast courtyard, flanked on each side by stone and timber stables.

'Sorry, did we just go back in time?'

'Relic from the eighteenth century,' Henry said. 'The old bachelors who lived here needed somewhere to keep their horses.'

'Right,' I said. I was fighting to suppress a sort of mad cackle.

More keys. Three flights of carpeted stairs. A slightly damp, musty smell.

'Here we are,' Henry said, and I followed him through another door.

I had stepped into the London of a bygone era. The ceilings were impossibly high, the huge windows framed with yard upon yard of heavy velvet curtains. The antique furniture was a showcase of English trees: walnut dressers, cherry bookshelves, oak tables. The only reminders of the present day were scattered gracelessly around the place: the frayed wire of an overused phone charger, a strewn line of running shoes, Bose music speakers.

I looped from room to room, taking it all in, directing a bewildered line of questioning at Henry.

'Why do you live here? Are you a spy? We're in our twenties; no one lives here.'

Henry explained that we were in a building called the Albany, built in the late 1700s as prototype bachelor apartments. Henry's mother, Christiane, had inherited the flat from her aunt, Beatrice, who had married a confectionery tycoon but had no children with him. Christiane preferred to live in the countryside, so Henry was given free rein of the flat, for a sickeningly nominal rent.

'Well, fuck you,' I said.

'I thought that was the plan,' Henry said, stuttering into laughter halfway through at the seediness of his own line.

'Yeesh,' I said, pretending to mind.

In the bedroom, Henry switched on just one lamp, casting our shadows long up the wall. He landed himself on a daybed in the alcove of the window, unlacing his shoes. I watched him for a moment, then walked over and climbed on top of him, my knees either side of his hips. I took his head in my hands and kissed him. *This is how I would want to be kissed.*

*

I don't remember falling asleep. I do remember the phone ringing.

Henry didn't seem to hear it. After the third time, I nudged him awake.

'Henry,' I croaked. 'Answer the damn phone.'

He sucked in a great lungful of air and stumbled his way out of the bed, still naked. I reached for my own mobile from the marble-topped bedside table and tilted the bright screen towards me; the blue light of reality hitting me in the pale new-born hours of the first day of this new year. Henry answered the call, his voice hoarse from sleep. I had five missed calls from Paddy – he was probably drunk-calling to tell me off for leaving the party. There was a thud. The phone had fallen from Henry's grasp.

'Marla's dead,' he said.

'What—' I began, but he interrupted me.

'My sister's dead.'

He started pacing, his breathing jagged, his hands over his head; his nakedness suddenly exposing and absurd.

'No, you're joking—' I tried.

'Fuck.' He was shaking. 'Fuck.'

I wanted to go to him, to press my own warm, naked body against his, to save him, but I found I was sandbagged to the bed.

'No,' I said. 'No. No.'

'I need to go to her.'

I nodded.

'Stay here.'

He had pulled on his clothes from the night before: his party clothes.

'I'll be back,' he said, and he was gone.

2

God knows how I fell back to sleep. The cold woke me. I felt it in my spine, the ache of it. I pulled on Henry's dressing gown and went to the window; the light already fading. Gazing down into the cobbled courtyard, I half expected to see him, returning to me just as I'd happened to look out.

It couldn't be true. It just couldn't. We had seen Marla a mere few hours ago. Had seen too much of her, in fact: her bare arse upturned on the dancefloor, her heavy breast dripping with milk on the sofa, her hand – warm, *alive* – in mine. Dead? No. Marla had overdone it before and always bounced back. She had partied hard her whole life. It would take a lot to stop her – or some extremely dodgy pill. *Paddy*, I thought. *I've got to call Paddy.*

He picked up instantly. 'Where the fuck are you?'

I'd heard him shout before, but there was an infantile raspiness to his voice that made the back of my nose prickle.

'I'm at Henry's.'

'Congrats,' he said, meanly.

'Paddy, is it true?'

'She's dead, Joni. She's fucking dead . . . she was lying there on the bathroom floor, everyone just crowding round not doing anything.'

'Oh, God.'

'I know.'

'Oh, Jesus.'

'Where's Henry?' asked Paddy.

'He's gone, he left. I don't know how long ago.'

'What are you doing?'

'Nothing.'

'Come to Hannah's, you should be here. Come now, we're all here. Except Dyl, he went in the ambulance with her and I can't get hold of him.'

'Why did *Dyl* go?'

'Dyl was the one who found her.'

I found I was unable to speak. An image of Dyl holding Marla's limp hand in the back of a blaring ambulance.

'Joni?' Paddy barked at me.

I shut my eyes. Time, which had felt so protracted in this antiquated building, was suddenly moving much too fast. I was nauseated and disoriented.

'Henry – he asked me to stay here.'

'Henry's going to have much bigger things to worry about than your whereabouts, darling. Come back. Come be with us.'

'I have to stay here. He asked me,' I said. It felt imperative that I do as he'd said.

'Fine,' said Paddy. 'Keep your phone on loud.' He hung up.

I stared at the phone screen: it was 4.20 p.m. Outside, the light had become a bruised indigo, and Henry had not come back. The tall china-based lamp on the dresser was still on, keeping its dingy glow to its own corner of the room.

The stiff brass taps of the bath hurt my hands as I turned them, the old pipes wheezing and clunking into gear. I drifted over to my reflection in the bathroom mirror for company. My eyes were caked with black smudges, my lips swollen and raspberry-coloured. Minuscule flecks of glitter winked at me from across my chest and shoulders. I could see the veins in my breasts, forming a sort of map around a central loop on my sternum. *Around my heart*, I thought, and then I remembered that the heart lives under the left ribs. I lowered myself into the scalding tub just as the last hints of colour in the sky were swallowed by blackness.

I tried not to think of Henry having to see his sister's corpse. I tried not to wonder how long she'd still be lactating for, whether they would pump her addled milk one last time for her child. I tried not to think of Dyl – in the ambulance, and now God knows where. *Think of Henry's face smiling, Henry's blue eyes looking down at me through those long lashes.* Dear God, I wished he was with me in that moment, reclining opposite me in the steaming water. On a New Year's Day in some happier, parallel universe, we'd be ordering takeout from the tub, eating it in two clean pairs of his pyjamas, washing it down with the hair of the dog. I sank down under the surface and held my breath, savouring the soundless space, the feeling of being held in by the pressure of the water all around me.

*

On the second day of the year, I woke up very late. Messages had poured in from everyone except Henry and, perhaps more worryingly, Dyl. I switched off my phone.

The kitchen must have enjoyed its most recent refurbishment in the 1960s: all linoleum and Formica. I inspected the contents of the fridge: some wilted rocket, an open tin of anchovies, and a brown paper bag of coffee beans. The cupboards yielded little more: a couple of protein bars and a sticky bottle of soy sauce. A true Bachelor Pad indeed. I made myself some coffee, and realised I hadn't eaten in nearly two days.

The stillness was unendurable. I flitted around the flat, cradling my mug, taking in some of the more peculiar features: an unpolished samovar that smelled of rotten fruit, a brocade jewellery box filled with nothing but radiator keys, a small porcelain statue of a jolly parrot. Above a doorway, on a small section of wall only just big enough to even mount the picture, hung a crude painting of a horse. The colours were muddy and red, the dimensions of the creature charmingly wrong – its body too long and eyes too humanoid. In the lower corner of the frame, blobby letters had been mashed on with a fat brush: the initials MT. Marla must have done this painting when she was a little girl. I needed a drink.

In the living room was a well-accoutred, old-fashioned drinks trolley. Among the no-doubt priceless vintage cognacs and ports was a bottle of amber bourbon, which I seized, proceeding to swallow one fiery gulp straight through its neck to mine. The sweetness both soothed my throat and burned in a pleasing, reviving way. On my empty stomach, the alcohol hit me quickly. Bottle in hand, I buried myself back in the bed.

The third day: my chemical comedown. I lay on the bed, bawling. Huge, loud, heaving sobs that echoed through the empty apartment. Poor, poor Marla. I called out her name, as if her ghost would materialise before me. I phoned Henry again and again, but there was no answer. I wanted desperately to speak to Dyl, but took his silence as a warning not to. I would have to call Paddy and admit that I had been abandoned.

The world felt closed to me. Only a couple of streets away throbbed the sounds and smells of Soho: frying chicken and ice rattling in cocktail shakers; people rollicking before it was time to go back to work. I might as well have been in a different universe. The sumptuous surroundings now seemed to mock me, as though I were a princess stuck in an ornate painting.

Hunger came and tore at my stomach with a profound urgency. I scoffed down both of Henry's protein bars, choking on their sweet chalkiness and my own sobs, when the sound of the phone ringing made me jump out of my skin. *Who even has a landline anymore?* I thought wildly, as I ran across the hallway to the old telephone.

'Hello?'

'Joni? Good, you're there.'

'Henry, oh, God, Henry. When are you coming back?'

'This evening.'

'Tonight?'

'Yes.'

'I'll make food, what do you want?'

'Whatever. I'll see you around seven. If you need to go out, there's spare keys under the doormat.'

'Alright.'

And he rang off.

The only thing I had to wear was my party dress from New Year's Eve. I couldn't help but laugh idiotically as I put it back on. Christmas lights were still up on Regent Street: cut-out reindeer leaping over the buses as they carried tourists down the wet tarmac. Brightly coloured SALE signs hung in every window. People were out shopping. I spotted a bright yellow jumper in one of the stores and found myself drawn in, the yellowness of it professing a cheer that I yearned for. A solid wave of central heating swept over me as I entered. Rails of sad party dresses that hadn't been asked to dance this holiday. A mother shouting something in Italian at her sulking daughter over a white coat. Piles of discarded clothes littering every surface.

I lifted the jumper off the rail and tried it on in the nearest mirror. It felt static and cheap, and my reflection in the harsh light was fiendishly clownish. The music suddenly seemed very loud over the women rowing, the air too dry. I yanked the jumper off and stumbled my way out of there on to Glasshouse Street, closing my eyes and letting the wind whip the hair off my face, trying to recalibrate my senses. Breathe: in for four, hold for four, out for four. Like my therapist landlady had shown me.

In the supermarket, I loaded my basket: mostly fresh, healthy items, as well as some insalubrious, decadent ones. I wanted Henry to return to a feast, to a sense of abundance and safety. For supper, I bought steak and potatoes, spring greens and a bottle of red wine. I knew I didn't have enough to pay for it all. Maybe I could just take a hundred quid from my savings account; surely the situation was an emergency. A few taps on my banking app. Problem solved. I could replace the money when I got back to work, and my parents would never know that my inheritance from Grandma Helen had been disturbed.

The desolation of the empty flat assaulted me upon my return. Things appeared squalid: the bedsheets tangled and a certain dampness over everything. Food packed away, I unearthed Cif and sponges from under the kitchen sink and set to work: hoovering, scrubbing surfaces. Bed made and cushions plumped. Darkness had fallen around me, and I turned on all the lamps. *Look how nice I've made everything, Henry. Look what a great girlfriend I would be.*

By the time Henry arrived, I was just getting out of the bath.

'You're back!' I said, his looming figure appearing in the doorway.

He looked ashen; unshaven and even thinner than usual.

'I didn't hear you get in,' I said, reaching for my towel.

He silently moved towards me, took the towel from my hands and swaddled me in it like a child, before pressing me into his body.

'Hi,' I whispered into his shirt.

'Hi,' he said. I looked up at him. He took my face in both hands and kissed me, softly at first, and then more insistently. He pulled off his coat and started unbuttoning his shirt.

'You don't have to say anything,' he breathed, and we didn't.

A little while later, we were lying on the bathroom floor, Henry apparently calmer now. I kissed his nose and got up.

'I bought steak. For supper,' I said, pulling on Henry's shirt; the warmth of it felt like tenderness.

'Mm,' he murmured, his eyes still closed.

'I'm not leaving you on the floor.'

'I might get in the bath, actually,' he said, flopping over on to one side.

'Alright. I'll get dinner going. Do you want a glass of wine?'

'Yes.'

I left Henry to soak with a glass of Rioja as I chopped vegetables and sipped my own. Only one station was static-free on the old kitchen Roberts: a piano concerto, allegro but inoffensive. Steam filled and warmed the whole room. The oil in the steak pan caught fire, and the flames made me shriek and then laugh. I went to open the window. The cold night air smelled of rain. *Petrichor* – I had taught the kids the word for that smell (Jem, the younger of the two, called it *Pet-treacle*). As I leaned out on the wet ledge, the smell ran away from me with each searching breath. The kitchen faced north, and I looked across the rooftops in the direction of my flat, where the champagne glasses would still be standing unwashed in the sink, my tights still in a ball on the floor. *Couldn't I just never go back?*

'Smells good,' Henry called out.

He came in in his paisley dressing gown and buried his face in my neck.

'Close that, it's freezing,' he said, and slid the window back down.

We ate without speaking, immersing ourselves in the business of cutting up and chewing the food. The scrape and clink of cutlery on china made me horribly aware of the sound of my own mastication. When he'd finished, Henry stood and took the plates over to the sink; his back to me, the wine run out.

'How was it at home?' I asked.

He paused and bowed his head. His shoulders began to shake a little. He was laughing. He wiped his brow with the back of a wrist and groaned.

'Fucking awful,' he said.

'I'm so sorry,' I said, staring at the back of his head. 'In what way?'

He didn't answer at first, but set about doing the washing up. I picked at a cuticle.

'I hate my parents being in the same house,' he said, eventually. 'It's like they're in a competition of grief.'

I released a laugh. He didn't.

'Were your brothers there, too?' I said.

'Yeah,' he said, and craned his neck to half-face me. 'Get us a fag, will you? There's stuff in my coat.'

'Oh, sure. Yeah.'

I went and retrieved his coat from the floor of the bathroom, hung it on the corner of the kitchen door, and pulled out tobacco, papers and filters to sit down and roll us each a cigarette.

'You'll have to be my hands,' he said.

Side by side with Henry – him facing the sink and me the kitchen – a lit cigarette in each hand, I smoked my own and raised and lowered his for him.

'How are your brothers coping?' I asked.

'I don't know. Nick, my older brother, he's so weird and repressed.'

'And your little brother, what's his name?'

'Ed.'

I knew that this Taschen was the youngest, born almost a decade later than Henry. Rumour (Paddy) had it he had been a last-ditch attempt to save Henry's parents' marriage.

'Ed came into my room on the first night crying,' Henry said.

'Fuck.'

'He said he didn't feel like he knew her. She was twelve years older than him, you know. By the time he was able to walk and talk, she was pretty much living in London.'

'Oh,' I said.

'Yeah.' He gave me a side-jerk of the head to indicate he wanted another drag. 'Marla—' He stopped, audibly cleared his throat: a sound that was almost aggressive. 'She was expelled from school at sixteen and no one knew what to do with her. Dad was pretty much entirely absent by then, and Mum just sort of gave up. I think she was tired of being the bad cop. So they just let her come and live here.'

'When she was sixteen?'

I looked around the stark kitchen and tried to imagine a teenage Marla inhabiting this space – cooking for herself, reading magazines, painting her toenails.

'The only times we ever saw her were when she'd turn up, unannounced, needing money. Usually stoned and always with a different bloke.'

'Shit.'

'Yeah. So Ed comes to my room in floods in the middle of the night.' Henry sighed. 'And I calm him down, and he tells me he's crying because he feels guilty.'

'Guilty?' I said. 'What, like, survivor's guilt?'

'No,' said Henry, impassive. 'Because he didn't really like Marla.'

I didn't know what to say. It seemed like the ultimate sin now to admit that none of us really did.

Henry's front and sleeves were soaking, and he kept wiping his face with the back of his wrist, smearing dish-water across his cheek.

'He told me he used to wish she would overdose.'

'What?' I said. 'Jesus. What did you say?'

'I told him I understood,' Henry said, switching off the taps and finally taking his cigarette; the smallest of griefs swimming over me that I wouldn't be his hands anymore.

'She made all of our lives a nightmare, Joni. She shagged half my friends. We used to get phone calls from hospitals and police stations in the middle of the night. It basically broke my parents' marriage.'

'But, I mean, it wasn't her fault?'

He sucked the butt of his fag hard and said nothing. We stood like that for a while. I didn't know whether he wanted me there anymore.

'Let's go to bed,' said Henry.

I looked up at him, droplets of water flecked on his dark stubble. I really, really fancied him.

'Cool,' I said.

3

Henry fucked me like a soldier home from war. That's almost all we did for the next few days. I was ashamed to admit to myself how much I enjoyed the feeling of being needed by him. I called Terry, the kind and eccentric mother of the kids I nannied, and asked if I could start a day late as I had to go to a funeral. When I told her it was a friend's, she gave me the week off. I texted everyone, except Dyl, and told them I'd see them at the church. I had heard nothing from Dyl and, with a sickening guilt I did my best to ignore, kept telling myself this was a sign that he didn't want to talk. The truth was, I couldn't face reaching out in case he did, in case he drew me away from Henry's bed – sleeping, screwing, occasionally getting up to make toast – and the blissful pedestal of his desire. Henry cried often – proper, guttural sobs – and I didn't know what to do. Sometimes I would just hold him and stroke his hair, saying nothing. Other times I would kiss him, and the kissing, more often than not, would lead to sex.

The night before Marla's funeral, Henry and I were drinking hot chocolate in the kitchen, wearing pairs of his boxer shorts we'd had on-and-off all day.

'Everyone's coming here tomorrow morning, before the service,' he said.

'Who is?' I asked, swallowing a scalding mouthful too quickly.

'My family.'

He was looking down into his cup, not meeting my eye.

'Oh, right. OK,' I said, folding my arms across my naked chest. 'I'll go home, then.'

'You don't have to. You can stay here, they won't mind.'

'I'm sure they will mind, Henry.'

'No, it's—'

'It's fine, I have to get something to wear anyway.'

'Can't you wear your dress?'

'My New Year's dress, you mean?'

'It's black.'

I smiled. 'It's fine. I should go home. You should all be together tomorrow, without me here.'

'I suppose.'

I left my cup in the sink and went to gather my things. Henry followed me into the bedroom.

'I'll get you a cab,' he said.

'You don't need to, I can jump on the tube.'

'No.' He had his phone out and was ordering me one already. 'What's your address?'

I swallowed. '7 Quadrant Grove.'

'It'll be here in seven minutes,' he said.

'Great.'

We stood waiting on the street, me feeling like I'd been spat back out of Narnia, without talking. My feet already ached in my worn-out heels.

'Henry?' the cabby inquired out of the window.

'Yes. Thank you,' Henry said, opening the car door. 'See you tomorrow.' He bent down to kiss me. A quick, perfunctory kiss; Henry stretching forward as if to keep his body as far away as possible from mine.

'Bye,' I said.

He shut the door. The car moved off down the street.

'How are you this evening, love?' said the cabby.

'Fine, thanks,' I said, looking out of the window, tears obscuring the names of the jeweller's on Bruton Street. I got out my phone and finally texted Dyl.

See you tomorrow?? Hope you're ok. Phil xx

'D'you get anything nice for Christmas, then?'

I looked up and caught the driver's eye in his rear-view mirror. 'Oh, not especially. The usual. You?'

'The Mrs got us a, uh, what d'you call it? Prime membership. Got hundreds of things on it.'

'That's lovely.'

'Yeah, it's good. You got it, then?'

'Me? Er, no, I don't.'

'You should get it. It's good,' he said again.

I smiled in response to this and then realised he couldn't see me, so I stopped.

London glowed. I rolled down my window as we drove up Park Lane, and from behind the trees I heard the screams from a fairground ride at Winter Wonderland, still going in Hyde Park until the twelve days of Christmas were up. We passed the impressive, cake-icing houses of Regent's Park; wealthy families curled up watching films, tummies full of chocolate. I lost myself in the windows of other people's homes: a wicker lampshade, brimming bookshelves, perfect lives. Traffic was sluggish on Haverstock Hill.

'Nearly there.' The driver sighed, as if I wouldn't know that we were just streets away from where I lived.

Patients with dressing gowns over their shapeless smocks stood smoking outside the Royal Free Hospital. Is this where the ambulance had taken Marla? I wondered if it would have been the nearest A&E. I looked up at the looming block of it, yellow wards visible in patchwork. I hoped that no one had had to spend their Christmas here.

The house was warm and silent. My landlady, Fiona, was visiting her daughter in Australia for some of the winter. I headed to her kitchen, which was large and tidy (unlike the tiny kitchen corner of my studio, with its microwave and minibar), and spent a couple of minutes gawking inside her fridge, my hand gripping the door. The funeral was tomorrow. My sixth. Most recently, Grandma Helen's, whose bequest to me I had disturbed just a few days ago. Before that had been the funerals of both of my grandfathers. (My mother's mother was still alive, in a care home in Harrogate.) Then there had been a girl in my year at school, who had died of cystic fibrosis, but I didn't really know her. And, the first, Dyl's little brother. I closed the fridge again. On the table was a neatly wrapped, perfectly symmetrical Christmas present that could only have been chocolates. I took them upstairs with me, planning to replace them before Fiona got back – not that she would mind either way. I showered and got into bed with the chocolate box and an American sitcom playing on my laptop for company, scrolling through my phone at photos of people either on drugs or white sand beaches, people having a wonderful time, until I must have fallen asleep.

When the doorbell rang, it was still dark outside, the people in the sitcom had had facelifts, and my phone was still in my hand. The buzzer went again. I looked at my phone: four missed calls from Dyl. It was 3.25 a.m.

I hobbled out of bed to the intercom on my wall. 'Dyl?'

'Phil, hi. Sorry to disturb you, can I come up?'

'What the fuck?'

'I called you, but you weren't answering.'

'I was asleep.'

'Sorry. Can I come in?'

'Are you high?'

'No. Not anymore. It's really cold out here. Phil?'

I groaned and buzzed him in, pulled the door ajar then got back into bed. I could tell by his spasmodic gait as he climbed the stairs that he was definitely high, or at least drunk.

'Phil!' he stage-whispered as he crept in.

'I'm asleep, Dyl,' I said, not opening my eyes.

'Sorry, sorry,' he said. He was shuffling from foot to foot. 'I was at Niall's, and then I decided to walk home, but I walked here instead.'

'You've just walked here from fucking Vauxhall? What happened?'

'Nothing. We were drinking and he went to bed. But I couldn't sleep, you know, all the thoughts. So I let myself out. I left him a note. It was a beautiful walk, actually.'

'Come to bed,' I said.

'Yeah. OK, hang on.'

I heard him pad into the bathroom and shut the door, switch the shower on and then swear at its temperature as he got in. I was drifting back to sleep again when he clambered into bed with me, taking long, held breaths as though trying not to disturb me by the very act of respiring. The inane stiffness of his body, tense with his effort not to wake me, made me take pity on him. I wriggled around and into the nooks and crannies of his shape that I knew so well. His stringy body was still hot from the shower, and he smelled of booze and my jasmine shower gel.

'Phil,' he whispered.

'What?'

'How's Henry?'

'I'll tell you tomorrow.'

'OK.'

'Are you OK?' I asked.

He swallowed. He kissed the top of my head. 'I'm alright.'

*

The next morning, I hopped around the room, pulling clothes on and off again while Dyl sat on my bed drinking strong coffee.

'The first one was good,' he said, stretching.

'No, it's slutty. I want Henry's mum to like me.'

'It's not a date, Joni.'

He never called me by my actual name. I took it as an indication of the depths of his hangover.

'What the fuck are you going to wear anyway?' I asked, unzipping the jumpsuit I had on. 'Did you bring anything with you?'

'It doesn't matter,' said Dyl. 'We're invisible, dude. No one's going to be looking at us.'

'They'll be looking at you if you show up in your bloody jeans.'

'You know, Henry's mum just completely blanked me, at the hospital. Like I wasn't even there.'

I stopped trawling through my tights drawer. 'Seriously?'

'Seriously.'

'She probably didn't realise who you – I mean – what you'd done. Plus' – I let out a dry sound, somewhere between a sigh and a chuckle – 'her daughter just died. Give her a break, maybe?'

'She didn't thank any of the NHS staff, either.'

'Well,' I said, going back to my clothes, 'I mean, Marla was dead already – what was there to be thankful for?'

'They tried to save her, though, didn't they? She was just—' Dyl shrugged. 'They're all like that. Entitled. Not Henry, but the rest of them. Posh twats.'

I went and put my hands on his shoulders. 'Today's not the day, comrade.' I was smiling at him, but he was refusing to catch my eye. 'You should at least wear a black coat. Fiona's probably got something that would fit you.'

We chewed down some dry cereal before leaving the house; me wearing too much make-up and Dyl an eighties black woman's coat with padded shoulders that, to my annoyance, looked great on him.

The funeral was a bus ride, two underground lines and a walk away, in a pretty square in Chelsea. On the journey over, I found myself monologuing about Henry; Dyl making non-committal grunts in response and apparently trying not to throw up. On the walk to the church, we passed other people in black; I exchanged a few sombre greetings with them while Dyl scowled on my arm. Smoking on the pavement outside were Paddy and Niall, looking handsome in their long coats and scarves.

'Hi, darlings,' Paddy said, kissing me on the cheek and gripping Dyl firmly on the shoulder. 'Hell of a party.'

I hugged Niall.

'Giss a fag,' I said.

'What happened to you last night?' Niall asked Dyl, handing me a Marlboro.

'Bad dreams,' said Dyl, smiling weakly.

'How are you?' I asked no one in particular.

'*Bit* hungover,' Niall said.

'Here.' Paddy pulled a silver hip flask from the inner breast pocket of his coat. We each took a swig before stepping inside.

Mila and Jess were already in there, sitting halfway up

the aisle; Mila looking extremely grave and Jess extremely glamorous. I sidled in next to them, giving them each a one-armed hug in the narrow pew. A flat dirge began to play on the organ.

'You OK?' asked Jess.

'Fine. You?'

We smiled feebly at each other, huddling together to keep warm.

I looked around for Dyl and saw him sitting with Paddy and Niall in a row further back. At the front of the church, I could see Henry's mother, Christiane, sitting poker-spined next to an elderly lady who I assumed was Henry's grand-mother. On the other side of the aisle, Henry's father stood with his pretty second wife. I observed him for a while – shaking people's hands with both of his own, thanking them for coming. In my (admittedly limited) experience, Henry had rather painted his father as the villain of his childhood. To me, he had the look of a kindly, if slightly camp, maître d'. Familiar faces were dotted in among the hats. Hannah was there, in a pretentious little veil, sitting next to Cecily Simmons, who was drawing the attention of a lot of leathery older men. Clustered in the rear few pews were a motley bunch a little older than us, who I guessed must have been Marla's 'party' friends. They were all slightly jaundiced-looking, giving off a certain seedy romance in their Afghan coats and fishnets. I wondered if one of them was Bear's father.

The dirge stopped. Everyone stood and faced the open doors. I turned with the direction of the crowd and saw Henry, standing in formation with his brothers and a couple of other men I didn't recognise, heads bowed and each with one arm raised to balance the coffin they shoul-dered between them. Wreaths of white roses and lilies trailed in the gaps between the men. Another adorned the top of the coffin – a word spelled out in flowers, though I couldn't read it from where I stood. *Ave Verum Corpus* played as the procession began to make its way forward. Henry was positioned on my side; he would be walking straight past me. I squirmed at the prospect of catching his eye while he performed such a sacred duty.

'Can we swap?' I whispered to Mila, and shuffled around her before she had time to answer. As they passed us, I saw that Henry had shaved. He kept his eyes lowered to the ground in front of him. As they set the coffin down in front of the altar, the effort of keeping it level became clear, and with a lurch I became suddenly conscious of the weight of it: that dense, lacquered wooden box; the human being within. Once it was safely in place, I could see the word spelled out in roses on top: MUMMY. Henry and his brothers took their seats next to Christiane.

The music stopped. The priest rose. 'Let us stand for the first hymn, "The Lord is My Shepherd".'

We stood and the organ started again; the meagre collective voice of the congregation fighting weakly against it.

> *The Lord's my Shepherd I'll not want*
> *He makes me down to lie*

Mila's voice next to me was beautiful. I sang more quietly.

> *Yea though I walk in Death's dark vale*
> *Yet I will fear no ill;*
> *For thou art with me*

From her still, square shoulders, I could see Christiane Taschen was not singing, but holding on to the arm of her eldest son, Nick, and staring straight ahead.

Goodness and mercy all my life
Shall surely follow me,
And in God's house for evermore
My dwelling place shall be.

The priest stepped down from his pulpit and took his place in front of the altar, facing us all. His arms hung limply at his sides. He composed his face into an attempt at sympathy.

'We are here today to celebrate the life of Marla Lucy Taschen, taken from us much too soon. God needed her with him.'

He carried on in this way, making euphemistic references to Marla's sybaritic lifestyle and repeating how it was 'God's will' that she was dead. I picked at my cuticle until Mila nudged me hard to stop.

'And now, Marla's brother, Nicholas, will remember her.'

Nick prised himself from his mother's grip and made his way up to the lectern. He should have been handsome: he was tall and had the Gaelic Taschen complexion, but it was as if his features belonged on separate faces, the expression of each one not quite corresponding with that of the others. I'd met Nick on a few occasions, during the latter of which he had claimed not to remember me. His voice was almost parodically plummy.

'I stand before you today the representative of a family in grief,' he said. He took a deep breath. 'Marla. Today is our chance to say thank you for the way you brightened our lives, even though you were only granted so little time to do so. We will always feel cheated that you have been taken away from us so young, but we must learn to be grateful to have known you at all.'

Christiane muffled a sob into a handkerchief.

'Only now that you are gone do we truly appreciate what we are now without. Your joy for life transmitted wherever you took your smile and sparkle. Your boundless energy, which you could barely contain.'

There was a loud cough from behind me with a familiar timbre. I turned and saw Paddy wheezing, his head down, busying himself with unwrapping a tissue from its plastic sheath.

'Marla and I were the two eldest in our family, and we spent an enormous amount of time together as children. Fundamentally she never changed from being my naughty little sister, fighting with me at school and keeping me entertained on long car journeys. She always remained true to herself.'

The pew was hard and only just deep enough to perch on. I could see the back of Henry's head, which twenty-four hours earlier had been between my legs.

'I would like to end by thanking God for the small mercies he has shown us at this dreadful time. Marla leaves behind her a son, who will never know his mother. I ask that all of you who knew Marla endeavour to teach him, as he grows, what an amazing human being she was. Thank you.'

A wave of sniffs moved through the church. My make-up sat heavy on my face, and whatever I'd swigged from Paddy's hip flask was making me sleepy.

The priest spoke again. 'Thank you, Nicholas. What a loving tribute. We will now hear a poem, written by Marla's dear friend, Sylvie, for this sad occasion.'

'Christ,' whispered Jess.

Sylvie took the stage and cleared her throat.

'Life!' she exclaimed, loud and urgent. She paused, and eyeballed the room. 'Gone.' She was turning towards us.

I looked down.

'Love!' Sylvie shouted. 'A note that plays on.'

The room had palpably stiffened.

'Daughter, Sister, Mother, Friend. A light whose beam shall never end.'

There was a strange whimper on my left; Jess had buried her face in one of her hands, her chest quivering. She turned to look desperately at me, hysterical tears lapping at the bottom of her eyes. She had the giggles. It was utterly contagious. I kept my head down and began to laugh in total silence, my stomach hurting from the effort. Mila's jaw tensed, but she continued to give Sylvie her full attention.

'Fly on, certain butterfly,' Sylvie said, face tilted upwards and eyes darting around the ceiling.

'Flap!' she shouted, her nasal voice catching. She seemed deeply moved by her own words.

Mila's face contorted.

'Flap your wings!'

We were all three hunched over now, giggling so hard the entire pew was juddering.

'I'm so sorry,' Jess gasped to the couple on her left.

The poem then took on a sort of beat style; Sylvie half-rapping the words and using her hands a lot. Mila clutched my wrist so hard her Shellacs left a mark. When the performance finally ended, there was a small ejaculation of applause from Marla's party friends at the back of the church.

'At least someone liked it,' said Jess.

*

The reception was at Henry's father's flat, a few streets away; we huddled together and smoked on the walk over there. The day was crisp and bright, the sun bouncing off the white houses of Chelsea. I squinted up at them, taking a drag of my cigarette, and in the glare, I remembered Henry's face beneath his sister's coffin; unbidden tears sprang to my eyes. Marla's death had been a tragedy, without question, but the sorrow I felt was for him, for Henry, who I knew would never put that coffin down – not really.

Paddy was sipping from his hip flask. 'Excuse me,' he said. 'But did no one else notice the flagrant plagiarising of Nick Taschen's eulogy?'

'What?' said Dyl.

'I thought it was sweet,' said Mila, taking the flask.

'No one recognised it?'

We all shook our heads.

'Heterosexuals.'

'Oi,' said Jess.

Paddy gave the air a kiss in her direction. He went on: 'That speech was taken practically fucking verbatim from the one Charles Spencer made at Diana's funeral.'

'As if,' said Mila.

'As if you even know that,' said Jess.

'Mark my words, he must've googled "brother eulogy for sister" and copied and pasted that shit.'

'Well, it's not like he had an easy task,' said Niall.

'Oh fuck off, Niall. Don't go jizzing pathos all over the situation.'

We'd caught up with some of the other guests from the funeral, who now turned to look coldly back at us.

At the house, spotty teenagers in white shirts stood with trays of red and white wine, and a table had been laid out with soft sandwich triangles and mini sausage rolls.

Rob Taschen's flat was on the first floor of a four-storey Georgian terrace, light and modestly decorated. A childless home. An open arch divided the kitchen at the back from the large living room, where tall sash windows faced the street. I looked around for Henry, but couldn't see him – or any of the Taschens, for that matter. Dyl handed me a glass of red – he knew I preferred it – and we settled into one of the plush sofas.

'What a load of bullshit,' he said.

I let my head rest on the high back of the sofa and gazed idly round the room. Cecily Simmons kept looking over at us.

'I can't stand all that stuff about God's will,' Dyl went on. 'She was twenty-nine. This wasn't God's will – it was just a fucking disaster.'

'Where's the baby?' I asked. 'I haven't seen him all day.'

Dyl shrugged. We lolled there, sipping from our glasses, the warm side of his body against mine. Cecily caught my eye and started to make her way over to us.

'Look out,' I said to Dyl behind my hair.

'Hi, Joni, hi, Dylan.' Cecily leaned in and kissed each of us on the cheek before perching down on the ottoman opposite us. 'Sad day, huh?' she said.

'Yup.'

'I feel so bad for her parents.'

'I know.'

'Their only girl.'

'Yeah.'

'How are you?' Cecily turned her full attention to Dyl. 'It was so brave of you to go in the ambulance.'

Dyl shifted his weight on the sofa, uncrossing his legs and sitting up. 'Nah, come on. Didn't have to think about it.'

'Not everyone would have gone with her, though. Was it horrible?'

'I don't really remember, to be honest. I just remember thinking she shouldn't be alone.'

'Wow.'

Dyl was now leaning forward, resting his elbows on his knees. The room felt cold without his body next to me.

'I'm just going to the loo,' I said.

In the bathroom, I held my hands under the hot tap for a long time, trying to get the warmth to spread all over me; the low din of voices droning on the other side of the door. I sat on the toilet seat and checked my phone.

A message in the group chat from Jess: *Can we go get some food plz.*

And a text from my mother: *Good nature doc on telly tonight! BBC One, 9pm.*

Someone jiggled the door handle of the bathroom.

'Sorry, just a sec!' I checked my face in the mirror and wiped some residual mascara out from under my eyes before opening the door.

It was Christiane Taschen.

'Hi,' I blurted out. 'I'm so sorry, for your loss. I saw Marla at New Year's. The service was just lovely.'

Christiane went into the bathroom and shut the door.

I drifted back to the living room, searching for a friendly arm on to which I could latch. Cecily had now joined Dyl on the sofa and was giggling behind her hand at something he'd said. He'd be getting his Moleskine of poetry out next. I spotted Henry talking to one of the leathery old men, and with a jolt realised he looked entirely unfamiliar to me. Henry had a face so beautiful it was often illegible, but in this moment some emotion was clearly commandeering his features. It was emanating from his eyes, his very pores;

what was it? I was about to turn to go when he caught my eye and jerked his chin up sharply, beckoning me over in that equine manner of his. I glugged down the rest of my wine and joined him.

'Joni, this is my Uncle Lachlan,' he said.

'Hello,' I said, reaching out my hand to shake his. He ignored it and went in to kiss me on both cheeks. He reeked of sherry, and I could feel where he'd left a cold wetness on the side of my face.

'Friend of Marla's, were you?' asked Uncle Lachlan. His voice reminded me of my old headmaster at school: a pedantic voice, the sound squashed out through the nose.

'Um, yes. More a friend of Henry's, really, but yes.'

'Just friends, are you?' he said, elbowing Henry, who appeared to have completely switched off.

'I'm so sorry for your loss,' I said. 'Are you on the Taschen side of the family, or . . . ?'

'God, no,' Uncle Lachlan barked. 'I'm Chrissy's brother.'

'Oh, right,' I said. I could have guessed this; he had the same yellow-grey hair as Christiane, and none of the warmth that Henry's father seemed to possess. I looked to Henry; nothing.

'Well, you've got fabulous tits,' Uncle Lachlan suddenly added, chuckling into his sherry glass, a look of rebellious pride on his face, as if he'd bravely spoken some unsayable truth.

'Christ, Lachlan,' said Henry, his eyed glued to the floor. I tried to laugh, but it sounded more like a yowl.

'Just going to get a top-up,' I said, gesturing pointlessly at my empty glass.

I abandoned the top-up, and Dyl – who was still flirting on the sofa – and slipped out. The others were all outside, passing round one of Mila's thin spliffs.

'There you are,' said Paddy.

'There *you* are,' I said. 'Dyl's trapped with Cecily Simmons, and I just got deeply perved on by Henry's uncle.'

'Yuck, was it that old guy with Henry?' asked Mila. 'I did not get a good vibe from him.'

'Yeah,' I said. 'Ugh. Anyway, shall we go eat?'

'Shouldn't we wait for Dyl?' asked Niall.

'Something tells me he doesn't want to be waited for,' I said. 'Come on, let's go.'

We ended up back at Niall's place. He ordered us all takeout curry, and we picked up a couple of bottles of whisky on the way. Niall came from, and made, more money than the rest of us, which meant he was the only one without flatmates (unless you counted my studio – which you didn't, because I was a lodger). His apartment was completely devoid of taste. That is, he didn't have bad taste: he simply didn't have any at all. He lived on the sixth floor of a modern glass tower block, where residents enjoyed shared use of a gym, garage and roof garden. As far as I could tell, the sparse, functional furniture he possessed had come with the property. The walls were bare – save for a couple of black-and-white photographs of the African savannah – as were the poured concrete floors. The kitchen was granite, the living room leather, and the bathroom limestone. The floor-to-ceiling windows faced north-east, over the river. He had a cleaner who came once a week, twice if he was entertaining. All in all, it was the last place I would have chosen were I on Niall's salary. Today, however, it was reassuringly clinical and unobtrusive.

'What a grim old day,' Paddy said, as we all traipsed inside.

We kicked off our shoes and spent the evening working our way through huge portions of dahl and naan breads, nursing tumblers of whisky. Someone turned on Niall's giant plasma widescreen, and put on the same sitcom to which I'd fallen asleep the night before. Paddy googled Charles Spencer's eulogy to Princess Diana and read it aloud to us all in a cutting (and accurate) impression of Nick Taschen. Above the panoramic view of London, the sky went from blue to milky lavender to eerie tangerine-black. Dyl never showed up.

Somewhere close to midnight, Jess and Paddy stretched and got up to leave.

'Some of us have work tomorrow,' said Jess. 'Night, loves.'

'Ciao, my dears,' said Paddy. 'I'll see you all at my play, yes?'

Niall, Mila and I were left with each other and the canned laughter of the TV. Her body had sagged gradually deeper into his over the course of the evening, and they were now comfortably snuggled up on one of the sofas.

'Let me clear this up,' I said, standing and stacking our bowls.

'Don't worry,' Niall said, allergic as ever to anyone helping when it was his house.

'Mate,' I said, heading for the kitchen, 'sit down. You paid for it all. Least I can do.'

Over the running water, I heard the sudden soprano of Mila's laugh, followed closely by the bass notes of Niall's. Maybe tonight would be the night they finally crossed the threshold from the platonic to the romantic. God knows it was time. Mila's feelings for Niall were so blatant, and yet so deep that we had never mentioned them; as one never mentions the knowledge that one day we will all die, or the

shared dislike of a friend's parents. In turn, Niall's recipro-
cal feelings for Mila had been, we all suspected, the reason
for Lina's mysterious exit. For my part, I was afraid. Mila
was my second-oldest friend, after Dyl, and something
inside me said that if she and Niall were to break the seal
of their pact of friendship, she would be his forever; his
in an all-encompassing, spiritual way that I was yet to
experience, and one that would leave me behind.

'We're turning in.' Niall appeared by my side, a brotherly
arm on my shoulder.

'Cool.' I smiled. 'Night night.'

I gave him a hug – my blessing. He seemed to understand.

'There's a spare duvet on the sofa for you,' he said.

'Thanks, mate.'

I settled on to the sofa, wrapped in a synthetic fleece
blanket and thumbing mindlessly through my phone, when
Henry messaged, as if the power of my thoughts had willed
it so.

*Sorry about my uncle. Wanted to punch him for saying
that. You do have great tits tho.*

I laughed.

Punching family member at funeral = always great, I
typed, but then deleted it.

*Thanks, I'm especially proud of the left one. Hope
you're ok x*

I waited twenty minutes for him to reply, but he didn't.

*

Big Ben, live from across the river, woke me up on the stroke
of eleven, January sun filling the silent room. I made myself
a coffee using Niall's fancy machine and took it to the
window, where the muddy Thames sparkled below. With

the others already departed for work, I couldn't resist the opportunity to snoop around the apartment: Niall's bedroom smelling of Mila's coconut oil, the mirrored cabinet in the bathroom rigidly organised with no tantalisingly named prescriptions, garment bags from the dry cleaner's, covering half the items in the wardrobe. No dirt, in either sense of the word. I pressed the button for more coffee and called Dyl.

''Ello, 'ello, 'ello,' he answered.

'Well, you're awfully chipper.'

'I got laid.'

'Shut your face.'

'Yep.'

'Not Cecily Simmons?'

'Yep.'

'For God's sake.'

He laughed.

'You weren't the only one,' I said.

'You shack up with Henry again?'

'Nope. Better than that.'

'Who? One of the old Taschen men? You got yourself a sugar daddy?'

'Yuck, no, not me. Mila and Niall.'

'Stop it.'

'It's true. I'm at Niall's now.'

'Not a threesome, Phil?'

It was my turn to laugh.

'Well, that was a while coming. Good for them.'

'Yeah.'

'Something in the water,' said Dyl. 'Do you think it's the mortality thing? Supposed to make people horny, isn't it? Like the people in Auschwitz, famously at it like rabbits.'

'Fucking hell.'

'I'm allowed to say that, I'm Jewish.'

I thought of Henry, arriving back at the Albany and just wanting to screw. Dyl had a point.

'Let's go for lunch.' I said. 'I want every detail about Cecily.'

It was freezing but dry, and I decided to walk into town, crossing the river at Lambeth Bridge. I put on *Blood on the Tracks* as I walked. Dyl had once told me that 'Simple Twist of Fate' always made him think of us, in particular the line about being twins. I stood looking downstream, at the Eye on the South Bank and the Palace of Westminster on the north. Walking in the city always had this effect on me; it gave novelty to the streets and buildings I knew so well. It was fun, sometimes, to see London through the eyes of a tourist.

The water below me was choppy and opaque. *Would you die if you jumped here?* I doubted it.

*

As ever, seeing the kids again was grounding. The job itself had been an accident. I had seen the advert in a coffee shop after a walk with Dyl on the Heath one hungover weekday morning.

'Go for it,' Dyl had said, ordering us each a cheese toastie. 'You've been meaning to quit the pub for months.'

'Do I even like children?' I had wondered aloud.

Dyl had shrugged. 'Who cares? But it's something, isn't it? We can't keep doing this. I'm at the pub every night with you – my wallet needs a rest. And you're never going to have time to write anything if you just sleep all day and work every night.'

I think Terry and her husband, Raf, had hired me purely because I could start straight away; that, and the fact that the kids were enamoured with me in the immediate, unsubstantiated way I have since learned is their custom. What I hadn't been prepared for was how easily and instantly I would love them back.

They ran down the hallway to envelop me as I arrived, crying 'Nanny Jo! Nanny Jo!' Clara was seven and Jem was five. He still gave off that sweet, babyish smell from the crown of his head. Their mother hugged me.

'Hi, darling,' she said, holding on to me.

'Hi, Terry, how are you?'

'Fine, darling, fine. I'm so sorry about your friend.'

'Oh, it's OK,' I said.

'How absolutely dreadful for you.'

'I'm OK. Thank you for giving me the week off.'

She released me from the hug but continued to stare intently into my eyes. 'Kids,' she said, 'you'll be extra good today, won't you? Nanny Jo's had a hard week.'

Jem gasped. I winked at him.

'Why did your friend die?' Clara asked.

I turned to Terry for my cue, but she just stood smiling sadly at me.

'Well, it was a terrible accident,' I said.

'How old was she?' said Jem.

'Too young. She was twenty-nine.'

'That's old.'

'It's not old enough to die.'

'Our cat died, and he was only eighteen!' said Clara.

'Cats don't live as long as humans, Clarabear,' said Terry.

'That's eleven less years than your friend,' said Clara.

'Good maths, Clara!' I said.

After Terry left, the kids took me upstairs and showed me what they'd got for Christmas: Clara an iPad and Jem a Lego castle, complete with drawbridge and dragon. Clara got annoyed because I seemed much more interested in the castle, which I was.

We decided to go to the park. Jem let me wrap him up in a bundle of thick coat and scarf, but Clara insisted she'd be warm enough in just her jumper. I pushed Jem so high on the swings that he squealed with fear and delight. Clara stood around chatting with some girls she'd bumped into from school; hands on hips and tossing their hair. I always got cold and wanted to leave before the kids did, so to entice them away I promised them both 'babyccinos' from the café – little cups of frothed milk with hundreds and thousands sprinkled on top, which they loved sipping in miniature takeaway cups 'like Mummy does'. Back at home, they drew pictures at the kitchen table while I boiled broccoli and baked chicken Kievs.

I loved sliding into their lives: the routine, their pretty bedrooms, Clara's neatly plaited hair and Jem's podgy little hands, the vibrancy of their home, with its mismatched paintings and antique furniture everywhere. Terry and Raf seemed to have it all figured out. They both worked high-powered, creative jobs and still found time to enjoy each other's company, as well as that of their kids. They were still so in love. Sometimes I'd swing by the house before picking up the kids from school and witness the evidence of their previous evening: the stub of a spliff in the fireplace, two tumblers left by the side of the bath. They were both as effortlessly stylish in their attire as they were in their décor: she no stranger to animal prints, and he with his signature fringed suede jacket over his broad shoulders. They were just cool. They made being a young family look fun.

After supper, I gave the kids a bath – bubbles and toys and giggling about bottoms – and put them to bed: Clara first, then Jem. Sometimes I would read them bedtime stories, but they liked it more when I made one up. I'd name the hero or heroine after them, and slip in details I knew they'd love. Anything about dragons for Jem, especially if the dragon gruesomely ate the mean king; while Clara liked being taken in her imagination to a concert of one of her favourite pop stars, miraculously being asked on stage to dance with them. They'd snuffle off to sleep, I'd go downstairs to clean up until one of their parents got home, and then slip once more out of their cosy, constant existence, and back into my own more ambiguous one.

4

Dyl's brother's funeral had been in November. It was a cold, cloudy day. 'Nothing-y' my mother called it.

'It's a bit of a nothing-y day, isn't it?' she said to my father in the front of our old Volkswagen.

I remember my uncomfortable black dress. It was too small for me; Mum had bought it in a charity shop the day before. I fiddled with the toggles of my coat and looked out of the window, counting the telegraph poles as they flashed by. A cassette of *Sweet Baby James* was playing. My father had explained to me what had happened a week ago, when I'd come downstairs ready for school.

'Dad – guess what? I had a dream I was on a boat, like the one in "The Owl and the Pussy-Cat". It was so weird!'

'Really?'

'Yeah, it was me and Dyl on it. Out at sea, and the waves were so big it was crazy.'

'Oh.'

'I thought we were gonna get shipwrecked!'

'Joanie, come and sit here for a moment, please. I've got something to tell you.'

I did.

'You don't have to go to school today.'

'Why?'

My father was pulling a face that I knew meant he had something very serious to tell me. I actually found this expression funny, and had to look down at my shoes so as not to giggle.

'A very sad thing has happened,' my father said. His right hand was resting on the table, as if he were trying to hold it in place. 'Little Ben has died.'

I said nothing. I didn't really feel anything, but I knew I should be sad. I tried to arrange my features appropriately.

'It was a very sad accident. Dylan and Ben were in the bath together, and Dylan got out and left Ben by himself. He was too little to be left alone in the bath, and he drowned.'

I found this hard to believe. Yes, Ben was just a baby, but a bath was hardly big enough to drown in.

'You know you must never leave a little baby alone in a bath, don't you?'

'Yes.'

'Even in six inches of water a baby can drown and die.'

How much was six inches? I thought you measured water in millilitres.

'Yes,' I said again.

I wondered why Dyl's parents had left him in charge of his brother in the bath, when Ben was obviously so useless. He couldn't even stand up by himself; you couldn't leave him alone for a second. Dyl and I had been playing with him not that long ago and he'd fallen off the side of the bed when we weren't looking, and we'd got in lots of trouble. It was very annoying having to look after him.

'Dad?'

'Yes?'

'Is it Dyl's fault, then?'

'No. It's not Dylan's fault. But he shouldn't have left him alone, should he?'

'No.'

'As you can imagine, David and Sharon are very upset. Your mother's very upset. I am, too.'

'I am as well.'

Dad put his hand on my shoulder. It was surprisingly heavy there.

'We're going to have to be brave,' he said, returning his hand to the table and patting it like a dog. 'I know it's a terrible thing that has happened, but when we see David and Sharon and Dylan, we have to be brave for them, yes?'

I nodded. I tried to think of what I would say to Dyl when I saw him.

'But, Dad, I don't have to go to school today?'

'No.'

After breakfast, I went up to my room, passing my parents' bedroom on the landing. Through the door, I could hear a horrible moaning. It was an animal sound, as if someone was in physical pain, muffled by something thick and soft. I had never heard my mother cry like that before. I wanted to open the door to see what it looked like, but I was scared; something about the noises she was making seemed private and embarrassing. I went to my bedroom and retrieved my old toy doll, Pepper, and took her to the bathroom. I hadn't played with Pepper for ages. Dolls were babyish and girly-girl. I ran a bath and got into it with Pepper; cradling her, washing her with soap. And then I turned Pepper face-down in the water. She floated.

*

After I lost count of telegraph poles, somewhere around one hundred and forty-eight, the car pulled up at someone's house. Only it wasn't a house – it was a prayer hall.

'We're here,' said my mother.

It was too soon. I didn't want the journey to be over. The inside of the car was warm and quiet, and outside the world was unfamiliar and cold. I hadn't seen Dyl yet, and suddenly I didn't want to. I felt embarrassed by my too-small dress, my childish frilly socks.

'Can I stay in the car?' I asked.

'No, love,' said my mother. 'Come on, Dylan will want to see you.'

I lingered close to Mum and Dad as they spoke to some other grown-ups, my bare legs turning purple and blotchy in the cold wind. Spitting rain. A wet animal smell emanating from the wool of my coat. We stood around the grave. Dyl and his parents were on the other side of the small cavity, each with a tear in the front of their coats. I gawked at them; why had they come out in ripped clothes? Maybe they couldn't afford new ones. It made me feel better about my charity-shop dress. Dyl didn't look at me. His mother could barely stand up, she kept tottering sideways into Dyl's father, who was openly weeping. This fascinated and horrified me – to see a grown man crying in public. I felt ashamed for him, his nose all red and snot running down his chin. Why didn't someone give him a hanky? Lots of the other grown-ups were crying, too; the sounds of their whimpers and sobs occasionally punctuating the speech of the man in the funny hat. It seemed to go on forever.

Eventually, people started shuffling into a line around the grave, taking it in turns to throw some soil down into the hole. I was delighted when my father said, 'Do you want to throw some earth on the casket, Joanie?'

I nodded. He scooped some dirt from a bucket into my little cupped hand. It wasn't enough, I wanted a bit more to throw, but he'd already passed the bucket to the people behind us. I looked down into the grave. The coffin was very small, no bigger than Pepper's old crib, and covered with a white and black shawl. I tried to throw the soil so it would scatter prettily over the white part of the shawl, but it fell down the side of the coffin. I wanted another go, and thought about asking my dad if I could do it again, but I didn't.

When we got back in the car, my mother said, 'What a thing.'

On the short drive back to Dyl's house, I asked why he and his parents had rips in their coats.

'It's what Jewish people often do to show their mourning,' said Dad.

*

There were sheets over all the mirrors. I remember the smell of eggs. Dyl said, 'Come on, let's go to my room,' and I felt glad to get away from the weird atmosphere downstairs.

'Are you sad?' I asked him as he closed his bedroom door.

'Yes.'

'Why did you leave Ben alone in the bath?'

Dyl shrugged. 'I got wrinkly granny fingers. I wanted to get out.'

'But you're not supposed to leave babies alone in the bath. They can drown and die in six inches of water.'

Dyl was crying.

I tried to make him feel better. 'My dad said it wasn't your fault.'

'That's not what my mum said,' cried Dyl. 'My mum said, "Look what you've done!"'

'But you didn't do anything, did you?'

'I just wanted to get out of the bath!' he choked. 'We'd been in it for ages, and no one was coming to get us.'

I picked up his favourite bear from his bed and took it over to him.

'Don't cry, Dylan!' I made the bear say in a low voice. Dyl scowled. I made the bear give Dyl a kiss.

'Let's play the Film Game,' said Dyl.

I looked at him – we hadn't spoken about the Film Game in months.

It had started about a year before. We had been left alone to watch videos at my house, while our parents ate dinner in the next room. I chose a tape that looked very sophisticated to try and impress Dyl – he was going through a 'girls are stupid' phase. The film was very boring. It involved people in suits talking about money and walking urgently down corridors. Neither of us really understood what was going on, but we weren't about to let the other know this. Then out of the blue, the main man in the film started kissing a woman, who was wearing just a bra and knickers. Then he took off her bra and knickers and kissed her in her private parts. Then he took off all of his clothes and they wrestled around on a bed together making funny noises and sweating. I knew that this was called sex.

'They're having sex,' I told Dyl.

Dyl was giggling.

'My willy's gone boingy!' he said.

I felt scared. 'Show me,' I said.

'No!'

The film had now gone back to the men in suits talking about money.

'Rewind it,' said Dyl. And I did. I rewound the film several times so we could watch the sex scene again and again. I remember feeling very hot.

The next time Dyl and I saw each other was at his house. We were playing with the trucks up in his room when he said,

'Remember that film we watched?'

'Yeah.'

'Let's play a game where we pretend that I'm the man and you're the woman, OK?'

'OK,' I said. 'But I don't have a bra.'

Dyl looked perplexed. 'I'll get you one of my mummy's.'

We snuck into his parents' room and opened his mother's top drawer. It was full of very exciting things and smelled faintly powdery. He chose a black bra, like the one the woman in the film had been wearing, and we ran back to his room in hysterics.

I put the bra on, but it was too big, so we stuffed it with some of Dyl's socks. Then he said, 'OK. Now I'll be the man.'

'OK.'

I think we even improvised some dialogue before we started kissing. And from then on, this was known as 'the Film Game'. For a while, we played it every time we saw each other. It would become the sole purpose of a visit: I would deliberately ask if I could go and play at Dyl's house when I wanted to play the Film Game. Then, about a year ago, we had been playing when Dyl suddenly said, 'I don't want to play this game anymore.'

I was surprised that he wanted to play it now, on the day of his brother's funeral.

'We don't have the bra,' I said.

'We can just pretend,' said Dyl.

He took of all his clothes first, and then I took off mine. We kissed standing up for a while before going and lying down on the bed. I was feeling hotter and hotter in my face, and my body was becoming more and more tense, when the door flew open. It was Dyl's mother.

5

A few weeks had passed since Marla's funeral, and I hadn't heard from Henry since that night. I grew more and more hesitant to commit to weekend plans with my friends in case he got in touch, needing me in his bed as urgently as he had done at the start of the year. Friday afternoon would eventually come with no word from him, and I'd frantically scramble to attach myself to whatever fun the others had in store. Once in their company, I would bore them with questions about Henry: how he must be feeling, why he hadn't called.

'Enough' said Jess, one Friday night, shouting over the music of the club. 'Forget about him. Come and dance.'

Dancing I could do; forget about Henry, not so much. I downed my shot of tequila and joined the girls and Paddy in the crowd, our sweaty bodies packed close in the strobe-lit basement. A fairly good-looking boy in a baggy T-shirt kept trying to dance with me, catching my eye and falling into time with my rhythm. I smiled back. Paddy gave me an exaggerated eyebrow raise in approval. I turned my back to Baggy T-shirt and let him come up behind me, our hips swaying together, his face in my neck.

'Shall we smoke?' I yelled to anyone who could hear me. Paddy nodded and we extracted ourselves from the throng, Baggy T-shirt sidling up to Jess to try his luck. *No hard feelings, then.*

Out in the smoking area, Paddy called a spade a spade. 'You're fucked,' he said, lighting my cigarette.

'I know,' I said. 'Bugger.'

He smiled. 'It's fine, you fool. He likes you.'

'No, he doesn't,' I said, inhaling. 'It's Notting Hill Carnival all over again.'

'He likes you. I know.'

'Shut up.'

Paddy's voice changed, his accent switching from his native Port Talbot poetry to a crystalline RP. '"Everyone knows,"' he said, all of a sudden grave and commanding. '"The world knows. It knows. But they'll never know, they'll never know. They're in a different world."'

'What the fuck?'

'Pinter,' he said, returning to normal in a heartbeat. 'From my play. When are you coming, anyway?'

'Oh my God,' I gasped. I had just checked my phone. *Meet me outside the Albany in half an hour.*

'That's him, isn't it?' said Paddy.

I nodded, trying to hide my elation.

'Just go,' he said, waving his cigarette at me. 'Enjoy your beautiful man.'

Mila appeared beside us.

'Just in time,' Paddy said. 'Joni's off to get the D.'

'Where's Jess?' I said.

'Chirpsing some girl at the bar,' said Mila. 'You going to meet Henry?'

'Yes. Sorry, am I the worst?'

'Yep,' said Mila, hugging me. 'S'alright. I'm gonna bounce soon, anyway.'

We exchanged a look that told me she, too, was off to enjoy her beautiful man.

'Love you,' I said to them both.

I arrived on Burlington Gardens half an hour later. Henry was pulling up in an old Mercedes.

'Get in,' he said.

It was nearly 1 a.m., chances were he'd had a drink, but being told by Henry Taschen to get in a car with him was something I greedily accepted without question.

We drove all the way out of town, through the suburbs and past signs for Legoland and Windsor Castle. The world outside became thick with the dark, as if we had travelled deep underwater. I could see no discernible buildings or road signs, just hedgerows and darkness. I was curled inside Henry's coat, my cheek resting against my hand, elbow propped up on the windowsill. I had no idea how long we'd been driving. I shut my eyes and buried my face deep into the warmth of his cashmere, his smell.

'Jesus, Henry, can you slow down a bit?'

I hadn't realised how close I was to sleep until I was pulled abruptly out of my stupor, the sound of the engine deafening as we overtook another car.

'It's fine,' said Henry, his eyes unblinking on the road. I saw now the shadows that still hung beneath them, how gaunt he looked.

At last we turned down a narrow country lane, a tall brick wall running past us on one side. It seemed to go on and on, until: 'We're here,' Henry said.

We had arrived at a break in the wall: a pair of tall, wrought-iron gates, guarding a long, tree-lined driveway. I rolled down my window. The country air; it was markedly colder here than in London.

'Shit, Henry, where are we?'

'My mum's. We can sneak in. Definitely can't be bothered to see anyone until tomorrow.'

'But she knows you're coming, right?'

'Kind of. I was meant to come back for this dinner party she was having.'

'Why didn't you?'

'Not my idea of fun.'

The drive was a single-lane track dotted with sheep poo and potholes. As we got closer, I could make out a vast brick edifice in the moonlight.

Only that particular breed of old-money eccentrics leave their houses unlocked, I've noticed; with a mile of private driveway, I suppose there's no need. Henry took me in via a side door, which opened into a warm and untidy kitchen. Tin trays charred with rosemary and garlic sat stacked on the table, the sink was full of plates, and every other visible surface was laden with red-stained glasses. Laundry hung from a creel above the Aga. The stone floor was covered in muddy footprints and dog hair.

'Come on,' Henry whispered.

He took me through the kitchen and down a small corridor, past more doors than I could count. We emerged into an enormous hallway with a marble floor and paintings of horses on the walls. Through an open door, I caught a glimpse of the remnants of the night's dinner party: stalactites of creamy wax dripping from candelabras, chairs pushed out from the table, smoke still hanging thick in the air, like a party guest unwilling to leave. On the second landing off the staircase, Henry took my hand and tugged me through three more consecutive doors into a large room with a four-poster bed. He set to work building a fire in the grate.

'Well,' I said.

'What?'

'Is this where you grew up?'

'Yes.'

'Well.'

'What?'

'It just must have been tough, you know, adjusting from here to the Albany.'

He smirked. 'Fuck you.'

*

Christiane Taschen was not exactly pleased to see me. She mostly ignored my presence, which was, in a way, the best possible outcome. It wasn't so much that she intimidated me: I just couldn't think of a single thing to say to her. Quotidian, polite chit-chat grated pathetically in the face of her grief.

By the time Henry and I made our way downstairs on Saturday, the dinner party guests had all left – except Uncle Lachlan, who boomed at us across his kippers and tea.

'Wouldn't leave without seeing you kiddies!'

Henry became palpably strained around him, which seemed only to provoke Lachlan into being as lewd and belligerent as possible.

'Looking awfully tired, hen,' he said, when Christiane had left the room. 'At it all night, were you?'

He chortled into his fish. I sawed bread.

'Do you want some toast, Henry?' I asked.

'No, thanks.'

I kept my back to the men as I slathered on butter and Marmite in equal ratios.

'What are you two up to today, then?' asked Lachlan. 'Fancy coming out with the guns?'

Henry didn't answer him.

'Do you shoot, Joni?' Lachlan bared his sallow teeth at me.

'I don't.'

'Not a bloody vegan, are you?'

'No.'

'Good girl.' He stood and carried his plate to the sink, leaving it soiled in the basin. When he passed me, he muttered, 'So you swallow then?' and wheezed into the back of my neck at his own hilarity.

I looked to Henry, who was petting Dolly, the family dog, and hadn't heard. Lachlan left the room, chuckling.

The day was spent reading *Anna Karenina* on the sofa, Dolly across my feet. Henry was hunched over a formidable hardback biography of a man I'd never heard of. The fire cracked and purred. Lachlan had, as promised, gone out shooting, so I was safe to go to and fro from the kitchen with cups of coffee and biscuits. Stiva and Levin were having a boring conversation about the serfs that went on for page after page; my attention untethered from the book, I landed it gently upon Henry's profile, that dark forelock of hair hanging over his brow, which was creased in concentration. From time to time, he would silently mouth the words he was reading, a practice so intimate I felt embarrassed for noticing.

'Henry,' I said, stretching. 'How do I get back to London tonight?'

Dolly looked affronted at this interruption. I scratched her big soft head.

'Hm?' said Henry, coming up for air.

'How do I get back to London from here?'

'Oh,' he said. 'Do you have to?'

'Well, no, I suppose I don't *have* to. The kids are away for half-term.'

'Well then, why don't you stay?'

'I don't have any of my stuff with me.' This wasn't strictly true; on instinct, I'd stuffed a spare pair of knickers and my travel toothbrush into my bag before going out last night.

'I'd love it if you did,' said Henry, reaching up from where he was sitting on the rug and gripping my ankle.

'Yeah?'

'Yeah.'

For supper, we ate a rabbit which Lachlan had shot, skinned and gutted himself earlier that day.

'Better when you've let it hang for a couple of weeks,' he said, his mouth full, stabbing some brown meat with his fork.

'It's delicious,' said Christiane, who had barely touched hers. 'Clever you.'

She chopped her food up into very small pieces on the plate, washing down her sporadic mouthfuls with red wine. She and Lachlan drank a lot. Henry and I had a glass each, but by the time the meal was over, four bottles had been opened.

'Thank you so much,' I said, taking everyone's plates, scraping the cold, fleshy leftovers into a pile on the top. I had started to wash up when Christiane said, 'Don't do that. The cleaner's coming tomorrow.'

'It's no trouble,' I said.

'Let's go for a cigarette,' interjected Henry.

We left them to finish off the wine.

Henry walked me to the edge of the garden. A crumbling brick wall shielded a steep decline on the other side. He pulled himself up in one movement, sitting like Peter Pan with his legs crossed as he lit the cigarettes. I hoisted myself up next to him, he passed me a fag, and we looked out into the caliginous landscape.

'What's down there?' I asked, more to break the silence than anything else.

'The river,' said Henry. 'I'll take you there tomorrow. We'll go for a long walk.'

'Sounds good,' I said.

The air was scented with something deep, primal, and I fancied I could smell the river I could not see.

'Don't worry,' said Henry. 'He's leaving in the morning. I asked Mum earlier – he's got to get back to town for meetings.'

'Oh. Cool.' I wasn't sure if I was allowed to express my relief and pleasure that I would no longer have to walk about the house in a constant state of tension, afraid of bumping into Lachlan, with his reptilian grin.

'He's got a pretty colourful sense of humour, but he means a great deal to my mum.'

'Of course.'

'It's just a different generation, you know. Less woke.'

'Yeah,' I said. 'Different generation. It was totally fine to comment on a stranger's tits back in Victorian times.'

Henry didn't even smile; he just stubbed his cigarette out on a brick and put the butt in his pocket.

'Don't leave your fag-end on the ground,' he said. 'Mum hates it.'

We didn't have sex that night, but read our books side by side until he switched off the lamp and fell promptly asleep, in that way men seem to be able to. I lay awake for a while. The rabbit – unfamiliar to my digestive system – had made me feel simultaneously too full and totally unsatisfied. On the bedroom wall opposite hung an oil painting of a snowy landscape, depicting a bundled figure on a horse-drawn cart trundling through a field, yellow lights glinting from a row of cottages in the distance. It brought to mind a scene in *Anna Karenina*: Levin seeing Kitty pass by in her carriage. He sees her by sheer chance – he's been thinking of her for months, trying to get over her, and then there she goes. It's the moment he realises he still loves her.

I could hear Henry's deep, slow breaths next to me.

What seemed like five minutes later, I sat up, suddenly aware of a weight at the end of the bed. I assumed it was Dolly, but no – there was a man sitting there, in the dark. It was Dyl.

'What are you doing here?' I said.

'I've come to get you,' said Dyl.

'Go home, Dyl,' I said.

Dyl got up from the bed and walked to the door. 'Come on,' he said.

'No, Dyl. I can't come with you,' I said.

He turned to me, and I saw that he was crying.

'Please don't cry, Dyl,' I said, glued to the bed. And he left.

I woke up, Henry still breathing softly beside me, the room ringing with silence. The throb of my pulse made lying still unbearable. I pulled on Henry's jumper and tip-toed my way downstairs, gripping the cold banister in the dark.

The kitchen light was on, and I could hear a man's voice. Standing mutely in the doorway, I peered in. Lachlan was standing over Dolly, his foot pressed down on her tail so she couldn't get up.

'You stupid fucking beast,' he said. 'Shut up!'

Dolly was whimpering, her paws scratching on the flag-stones as she tried to get out from under him.

'What the fuck are you doing?' I blurted out.

Lachlan's eyes darted up at me and he lost his footing. Dolly made a run for it.

'Hello,' he said. He was drunk.

'I came down to get some water,' I said.

Lachlan took a step back and swept an arm grandly in the direction of the sink. 'Be my guest,' he said.

I took a glass down from the shelf and was filling it from the tap when he came up behind me.

'You're a very sexy girl,' he breathed. He stank of port. He placed his hands on the sink on either side of me, penning me in. I turned off the tap.

'Maybe you should have some water yourself, Lachlan,' I said, twisting around to face him. His eyes were watery and bloodshot. I held the glass up as a barrier between his face and mine. Up close, Lachlan's face was wrinkled and weak. He was a complete stranger to me; an old man.

'You feed it to me,' he said.

I couldn't believe what I was doing, but anything to stall him, anything to sober him up a bit. I tilted the glass to his mouth and he swallowed, but I didn't withdraw at the right time, and some of the water spilled down his chin. He staggered backwards, mopping himself up and laughing. I raced out of the kitchen without saying a word.

'Mustn't keep Henry waiting,' he called after me.

On the second-floor landing, I paused at the bedroom door before bursting into tears. This house was so big, so old, so indifferent. How many generations of silly girls had it witnessed crying in the middle of the night? The grandfather clock kept ticking; the eyes of the paintings gazed out at me with superior nonchalance. I stood in the dark like that, the sleeves of Henry's jumper muffling my crying, until the sound of Lachlan drunkenly coming up the stairs startled me back into the bedroom, where Henry lay fast asleep.

*

Dolly seemed by far the most excited about our walk, ricocheting backwards and forwards from Henry to the door until he said, 'Alright, alright, we're going,' and put her lead on. I was issued gumboots and a wax jacket, and we set off just before lunchtime.

We followed the river for a long while, trailing its sinuous curves. Dolly remained a consistent twenty feet ahead of us, sporadically stopping to turn and make sure we were bringing up the rear. Henry had brought along a picnic rug and some food, which, after walking for an hour or so, he laid out on a wooden fishing jetty. A weeping willow hung over us, its long trailing fingers just beginning to bud. The smell from the river rose up, earthy and deep. I sat down and lit a cigarette.

'Are you alright?' asked Henry. 'You're being a bit quiet.'

'I'm fine,' I said.

He was peeling an orange and looking at me.

'I had a weird dream about Dyl,' I said.

Henry paused. 'What happened?'

I tried to remember.

'It was just one of those really real ones, you know? I woke up, in the dream I mean, and Dyl was there. Just sitting at the foot of the bed.'

'Weird.' Henry swallowed a mouthful of orange.

'And then he told me to come with him. He was crying. And then he left.'

'That was it?'

'Yeah.'

'Hmm.'

I exhaled a plume of smoke, and watched as it danced and then dissolved over the surface of the water.

'It sounds really stupid, but sometimes when I dream about Dyl, it's like he's trying to tell me something.'

'Come on,' scoffed Henry.

'Honestly. I once had a dream where he rode a fairground ride until he was sick, and I called him the next day and he told me he'd had food poisoning the night before.'

'Spooky,' said Henry, sarcastically.

I quietly sang Dyl's favourite lyric from 'Simple Twist of Fate' to myself, gazing at a reed arcing its head down to meet the river.

'What's that?' said Henry.

'Nothing.'

A bird, tiny and assiduous, dipped and drank from the water a few feet away from where I sat, close enough that I could hear the beat of its wings.

'Let's get in,' I said.

'What?' said Henry. 'You want to swim? It's Baltic.'

'I don't care.' I'd already taken off my wellies and was beginning to undress.

'We don't have towels.'

'Come on. It'll be fun. You'll feel great afterwards.'

'You're nuts.'

Lowering myself into the water from the jetty, I drew breath; it was painfully freezing. Silty mud oozed between my toes as my feet touched the riverbed. There was nothing for it – I kicked off, out into the middle of the river, the iciness of the water burning. I realised I was making involuntary yelping noises and started to laugh.

'Get in!' I called to Henry. 'It's wonderful.'

Dolly stood on the edge of the jetty and started to bark.

'She thinks you're drowning,' said Henry.

'Dolly!' I cooed to her. 'It's alright, I'm having a nice swim, darling.'

She wasn't quite convinced, letting out a distressed whimper and sitting down: an exhausted mother surrendering to the will of her lively young.

Henry was standing on the jetty, filming me on his phone. 'You're completely mad.'

I whooped, enraptured, keenly aware that the elements that made up the air and the river and my body were all the same. I swam upstream, away from our camp, feeling the silken water rush through my outstretched fingers. Branches on the opposite bank came down to greet me, and I could see flashes of white through the woods: a carpet of snowdrops overwhelmed the forest floor. I couldn't see Henry anymore behind the weeping willow, and there I floated on my back, ears submerged: soundless and secret.

'You missed out,' I said, approaching the jetty again.

Henry gave me a hand up and wrapped me in his coat. Dolly helped to dry my legs with her rough tongue.

'Here.' Henry handed me a Thermos and I took a deep gulp – it was hot whisky and honey. We made love on the picnic rug, my pale body goose-pimpled and charged. On the walk back to the house, I felt clean and vivid, and feverishly hungry.

Christiane found us eating crumpets and jam by the stove.

'Oh, hello,' she said, crossing the room to unload some shopping into the fridge.

'Joni just got in the river, Mum,' said Henry.

Christiane stopped, turned and looked me in the eye. I realised it was the first time she'd done so since I arrived.

'Did you?' she asked, half-raising an eyebrow.

'Yes. It was lovely.'

'Good for you. I swim all year round. Very good for the heart. Did you get in, Henry?'

'God, no.' Henry took a large bite of his crumpet. 'There is no part of me that would enjoy that.'

'Do you need help with that, Christiane?' I asked.

'Don't bother. You don't know where anything goes.'

'Henry does.'

She actually laughed at this. We both looked at him.

'Fine,' he said, trudging over to the fridge to help her. 'What are we having for supper?'

'Well, see for yourself. There's some fishcakes you could have, pork chops, lasagne . . .'

For a woman so uninterested in food, she had yielded a multifarious bounty.

'Why don't I make dinner?' I said.

Christiane didn't look up. 'If you like.'

I made a pasta puttanesca, which we ate in front of the TV with the fire lit and Dolly squeezed on the sofa between Henry and me. Christiane only ate a tiny portion, swamped in a bowl of rocket leaves, but she thanked me for making it before going off to bed.

*

On what was to be my final night in the country, Henry and I had the house to ourselves. Christiane had gone to stay at the Albany for a few days to look after Bear. 'Your father and the child bride are gallivanting off to Saint Petersburg!' she had told us testily, though it was clear she was excited about spending time with her grandchild.

How isolated this house felt from the real world. I couldn't imagine anyone growing up here, passing from infancy through adolescence, for time seemed to stand still. For me, the opportunity to completely abandon contact with reality was more than welcome – I decided to zip my phone away into the side-pocket of my handbag.

Something nestled there in the corner of the lining. A little parcel. I picked it up and carried it through to Henry, who was in the bath, his biography propped on his knees.

'Henry,' I said, dangling it in the air for him to see. He looked up. 'I've still got some MD left from Friday night. Just enough for two.'

As well as boasting a library and more reception rooms than could fathomably be put to use, the house had a billiards room, and this was where we set up camp. Steely Dan on the record player, drinking rum and half-committing to a game of snooker. Henry was surprisingly brilliant at the game, which, more surprising still, really turned me on. We dropped our little bombs around eleven o'clock. Henry put on *Hunky Dory* and we danced around the room, screaming the words to 'Life on Mars'. Henry said he'd always wanted to have sex on the snooker table, so we did. Afterwards, I got up and pulled my robe back on, swigging my rum and singing along to 'Queen Bitch'.

'Hey,' said Henry, still lying on the green baize.

I sang with Bowie, dancing around the room.

'Joni,' he said. 'I've got an idea.' He sat up. 'Joni,' he said again. 'Let's go up on the roof.'

Up here, the river was visible; an iridescent silver ribbon snaking its way through the darkness. We sat on the parapet, legs hanging over the side. Henry looked up at the clear night sky – that luxury of leaving the city.

'We're very high,' I said.

'Yeah, I'm tripping.'

I looked at him. 'No,' I said, starting to giggle. 'I meant high up, on the roof.'

'Oh,' said Henry, 'we're high *and* high!' He laughed delightedly.

'High and high,' I said. We had utter hysterics. The drop stretched out below my feet; I was soaring. I swayed on the edge of the parapet. Henry started singing 'Life on Mars' again. I joined in.

We sang. The chorus was approaching, so I stood up and belted at the sky. Henry stood up, too, and climbed up on to the parapet, arms aloft.

'Henry, shit, get down,' I said.

He craned his neck back and closed his eyes.

'Dude, get down. You're gonna fall.'

He spun around on the parapet, dangerously close to the fifty-foot drop on the other side.

'Stop it!' I shouted, and grabbed him hard, pulling him back down on to the flat part of the roof behind the low wall.

'Chill,' he said.

'You were scaring me,' I said, my heart thumping in my chest. I moved my body closer to him.

'I'm sorry,' he said, kissing me. 'I'm rushing.'

'Me too,' I said.

He held my face in his hands. I felt sure he could feel my pounding pulse through the skin of my cheeks.

'Henry.' I started to talk without thinking; it was compulsive, the words leaving my body of their own volition, rising up within me and spilling over the edges. 'I have to tell you something.'

'Yeah?'

'Your Uncle Lachlan kind of made a move on me the other night.'

'What?'

'I went down to get some water after I had that dream about Dyl, and he was in the kitchen, and he was being horrible to Dolly. And then he pinned me against the sink and made me feed him water. He said I was a *very sexy girl* or something. It all happened really fast. And when I came back to bed, you were still asleep and I was annoyed with you, for not protecting me. For bringing me here. It wouldn't have happened otherwise.' I said all this at speed.

Henry had gone white.

'But it's fine,' I went on. 'Nothing happened. I got out of there *prontissimo*. Don't worry. I'm definitely glad I came here. Tonight's been really fun.'

All of a sudden, Henry leaned over the parapet and was sick. We were so high up, the splat didn't happen for three whole seconds.

'Hey,' I said, kneeling next to him and rubbing his back, the knots of his spine against my hand.

'You OK?'

He heaved a few drawn-out breaths, then slunk back down, leaning against the wall.

'It's alright,' I said. 'You're OK.'

When he regained his breath, he spoke without looking at me. 'Why are you telling me this?'

'What?'

'Nothing happened. Like you said, you're fine.'

'Yeah, but—'

'My uncle has a bad sense of humour, but he wouldn't hit on you, Joni.'

'Er—'

'Like, just be careful what you say about people.'

'Sorry – do you think I'm making it up?'

'I didn't say that.'

'OK . . .'

'Just, he's like that with everyone. Marla used to say shit

about him, too. Always the victim. Lachlan's crude, but he didn't . . .'

'Wait, did he do something to Marla?'

'No!'

I waited. An angry insect was buzzing around inside me, beating to get out.

'So, what, then?' I eventually piped up. 'I just shouldn't have told you? I should have just let your uncle low-key sexually harass me and—'

'That's what I mean!' Henry interrupted. 'You can't just go around saying someone sexually harassed you if they didn't.'

'I'm not going around, I'm just telling you.'

'Doesn't sound like there's much to tell.'

'Wow. OK. Forget it. I was just feeling weird already after my dream about Dyl, and then Lachlan, doing – whatever you want to call it—'

'Oh my God, would you shut up about your dream? Your psychic connection with Dyl.' Henry was laughing, somewhat cruelly it seemed. 'Like, come on, that's not a thing.'

The separateness, it hit me like a battering ram to the chest. I couldn't make him see. We were speaking different languages. I slumped down the wall beside him, and pulled out a couple of cigarettes.

'Here,' I said, lighting them both and passing him one.

'Thanks.'

We sat and smoked without talking for a little while. A great, dark cloud engulfed the moon like a shark silently swallowing its prey.

'Why don't you go to bed?' I said, eventually. 'I'll go clean up.'

After a brief and unconvincing protestation, he did as I suggested.

Back in the billiards room, the A-side of *Hunky Dory* had started again: 'Oh, You Pretty Things'. I gathered all the clicking balls back into the triangle at the end of the table, cleared our half-empty glasses, and turned off the lights. The next morning, I caught the first train to London.

6

Blue and purple leaves. The poster at Waterloo station informed me that there was a Matisse exhibition on at the National Gallery. The train journey back from Henry's childhood home had been disconcertingly quick, and swimming with images of Uncle Lachlan's bloodshot eyes, Henry's thin body on the green baize, the dream-version of Dyl crying. I made a record of the dream in the notes on my phone, intending to copy it out by hand when I got home.

I decided to walk up from the station to Trafalgar Square to see the exhibit, weaving my way through the half-term crowds. Matisse's paintings had always been worlds into which I longed to jump, like Bert's street drawings in *Mary Poppins*. I skimmed past the shoals of students with their audio guides, the tourists clad as if for arctic winter, and found myself in a perfectly square room, where a sign told me I was among *The Paris Years: 1910–17*. Next to the sign, there was a photograph of the artist: bespectacled and bearded, head bent in concentration over a bronze figure of a woman.

Beside *Interior with a Bowl of Red Fish*, a Gertrude Stein quotation:

> More and more frequently, people began visiting to see the paintings. Matisse brought people, everybody brought somebody, and they came at any time and it began to be a nuisance, and it was in this way that Saturday evenings began.

Yes. This is what I wanted life to be: an endless coming and going of friends and lovers, a buzzing of never-ending conversation, an opera of liveliness. I stood in front of the blue painting for a while, smiling at the poor, tantalised cat, head cocked up at the bowl of fish.

'It's your favourite?' said a French accent next to me. I turned. A tall woman with a large mouth and glasses was regarding me, somewhat amusedly.

'Oh.' I laughed. 'Um, no, actually. I like the one with the violin case, I think. Over there.' I pointed through the double doors at the previous room. 'Basically, I love any of the ones with open windows.'

'Hmm.' She pouted in such a dismissively French way that I smirked. 'You like the open windows? You know what this means, yes?'

'I'm sorry?'

'The open window: always looking out into the world, never looking in. You do not like to be left alone with your own thoughts.'

'Right.'

'It's true?' she said, with an arch smile.

'Maybe,' I said. 'What's yours?'

She shrugged. 'I don't know. I don't really have a favourite.'

'Well, enjoy!' I said, and left the gallery.

There were hundreds of people milling about in the streets, all with places to go and things to do. Headphones in (*Back to Black*), I ploughed my way up the Charing Cross Road to the tube station. Underground, the tunnels were airless and hot. The French woman's face had followed me, her features too large, pleased with herself. *It's true?* What a thing to say to a stranger. It was bullshit, anyway – if I didn't like to be left alone with my thoughts, what did I write for? I had pages and pages of poetry, short stories and other scribblings to prove that being left alone with my thoughts was, in fact, a treasured pastime. More than a pastime: writing was the only way I knew how to express myself.

I had to wait a long time for a train; all the tubes were delayed *due to a person on the tracks*. This was a not-infrequent-enough occurrence in London, and I always found the bureaucratic wording of these announcements at odds with the tragedies they reported.

At the other end, I resurfaced into rain. The hems of my jeans were dip-dyed dark from the wet pavement. Fiona was with a client in the front room. I saw a hand reach for a Kleenex from the coffee table, before retreating back into the armchair positioned at an angle in the bay window.

We caught up in her kitchen together that night. Australia had been lovely. Her daughter, Jenny, was very happy out there. They had visited the vineyards of Tasmania – 'better than France!' – and had Christmas Day on the beach. I told her about my own Christmas, that I'd finally finished *Great Expectations* and was now on *Anna Karenina*. I told her I was back at work, that the kids were well, and I told her about Marla. She stopped chopping garlic.

'Can I give you a hug?' she asked.

'It's alright,' I said. 'I didn't – well, we weren't that close.'

Fiona was making a creamy risotto. She ordered me to open one of the bottles of wine she'd brought back from her trip, which was, indeed, delicious – like an orchard. I nursed my glass at the table while she cooked, nestling into a chair with one leg tucked up under me.

'Can I do anything to help?' I asked, semi-rhetorically.

'No, no you're fine. Make me one of those, would you, hen?'

I was rolling myself a cigarette.

'Let's take them outside,' she said.

The rain had stopped, giving way to a surprisingly mild night.

'How was today?' I asked, taking my seat in the garden.

She grimaced and took a deep suck on her cigarette, making her cough. 'Christ!' she spluttered, reaching for her wine glass.

'You alright?' I asked, standing up. 'Shall I get you some water?'

She gulped some wine and waved me back down, her cough turning into a chuckle. 'Ooph. One of those days,' she said. 'Both my clients this afternoon were pretty heavy going.'

'Oh dear,' I said. 'What sort of thing?'

Fiona smiled. I knew she couldn't answer me to protect her patients' privacy.

I looked down the garden, at the cherry tree beginning to show the first signs of life again.

'It's the ones that hold up an ugly mirror to myself that get me, though of course I learn the most from them, too. Look at me with these, for instance,' she said, with a little laugh, holding her cigarette aloft. 'Something I know is bad for me, but I keep going back to.'

'Sure.'

'You must know what that's like?'

I thought she was simply proving her point, but when I glanced up, she was looking straight at me: the even, steady gaze of a therapist, like she could see right through me. I squirmed a little in my seat.

'Oh, right, of course.' I laughed meaninglessly. 'The fags, for one. Booze. My phone.'

She reached up and pawed the wind chimes, which responded with their tuneless song. I breathed in the sweet mixture of the garden and the wine.

'We all do it,' said Fiona. 'Put our hand in the fire again and again, just checking if it's still hot. Go back to the same relationships, over and over . . .'

'Do you think some people just like the pain?' I asked, out of nowhere. 'In relationships, I mean?'

The briefest raise of her eyebrows.

'Aye, well, there are different theories about that one,' she said. 'Some believe that yes, there is a certain profile of patient who seeks out pain to reinforce an inherited sense of low self-worth – we attract what we think we deserve. Others believe any kind of pain, physical or otherwise, is an addiction like any other: a behaviour employed to avoid uncomfortable thoughts or feelings.'

I noticed I was picking at my thumb. I stopped.

'Personally,' Fiona said, shrugging, 'I subscribe to a different school of thought.'

'Which is?' I asked.

'That some people,' she said, getting up, 'just don't feel whole without another person to complete them.'

'Isn't that what love is?'

'No. Love isn't needing someone else in order to feel whole and to feel that you, as an individual, have an identity and a worth. Love is two already whole people, coming together because they want to. Not because they need to.'

'But that sounds so sad,' I said. *That separateness.*

'I think it's beautiful,' she said. 'There's beauty in the freedom of it.'

I sat very still. I certainly didn't need Henry in order to feel whole – or any other of my previous lovers. None of them had provided me with that satiated sense that all was well. A line from *Anna Karenina* popped into my mind – *There was no other being in the world able to focus for him the whole world and the meaning of life.* Levin on Kitty. There was only one person who did that for me.

'Anyway, duck,' said Fiona. 'Food probably needs a stir.'

*

I arranged supper with Dyl on Monday evening to sweeten the pill of going back to work after half-term.

Our place? Tomorrow at 7?

Yep.

At the school gates, Jem ran squealing into my arms.

'Hey, little one!' I swept him up off the ground. 'How was France?'

He covered his mouth with two chubby little hands joined at the wrists, fingers splaying out over his round cheeks like butterfly wings. 'Good,' he muttered into his hands.

'Yeah? Did you have fun?' I prompted.

'Yeah.'

He'd gone all shy. The kids both had a habit of doing this. They were like fairground goldfish with me: after a brief spell apart, they needed to adjust to me again: to stay in their little bubble bag until they got used to my temperature, before swimming out with confidence into the open water.

Clara arrived, but shunned my open arms, hissing, 'Don't hug me!'

Hugging wasn't very cool.

'OK,' I said, trying to keep a straight face. I took her

bags and Jem's hand as we headed in the direction of their home.

'How was France, Clara?' I asked.

'Yeah,' she said.

'Was it warm?'

Clara shrugged. She was walking a couple of paces ahead, trailing her hand along the railings. Every now and then, she surreptitiously glanced over her shoulder across the street, where the twin brothers from her class were scuffing and chasing each other down the pavement.

'We saw a 'corpion! A, a, scorpion!' said Jem, panting with the melodrama.

'Did you?' I said, suitably horrified. 'Were you scared?'

'Jem was,' said Clara.

'No!' said Jem. 'I wasn't scared.' He paused. 'I was only a little bit scared.'

His inclination for honesty over bravado broke my heart a little.

'I'd be scared,' I said.

Back in their large, overgrown garden, we set up twig goalposts for a football match – me and Jem versus Clara.

Clara kicked the ball hard in the direction of our goal, and I dived dramatically to save it. She was wide by a long way, but clapped her hands to her head in frustration as if she'd only just missed. I let Jem take the goal kick, then dribbled the ball around Clara until she was giggling with excited exertion. I passed back to Jem, who had trotted up to Clara's goal, and he footed it in.

'GOAL!' he cried, executing a victory lap of the garden with his arms in the air. Clara burst into tears and ran into the house.

'Oh, for God's sake,' I said.

Jem failed to suppress his grin.

I left him practising penalties and went inside to find Clara sprawled prostrate across the stairs, her head resting on her arms to conceal her theatrics.

'Come on, Clar! You can still beat us.'

'It's not fair!' she yelled into the seagrass matting. 'It's two against one.'

I sat down on the stair below her and put my hand on her puny back. 'Yes, but,' I said quietly, 'you're better at football than Jem.'

She looked up at me, her face completely dry but red with effort. 'You and me are probably as good as each other, though,' she conceded.

'Yeah, probably,' I said. 'Do you want Jem on your team?'

'No!'

'OK, well, come on. Half-time's over.'

Clara scored twice, and I kicked one in so that we could finish the game at level pegging. Justice really was the dogma of childhood. There was salmon and pak choi for supper. So sophisticated, these urban children; the crispy pancakes and spaghetti hoops of my childhood were nowhere to be seen. The children asked for '*d'lo*' to drink – the Creole word for water, one of a few they'd learned from their dad and liked to whip out from time to time. Raf was second-generation British, but had spent some of his childhood in Trinidad. Clara and Jem had cherry-picked a couple of his Creole-isms as part of their forming identities: occasionally finishing a sentence with 'man', or '*souplé*' (please), and Jem would occasionally introduce himself as 'Jemmarcus' to new children in the playground, if he so fancied.

I put Clara in charge of overseeing teeth-brushing, and was loading the dishwasher when Terry got home, laden with a vast bunch of flowers, heavy bags and the evening newspaper.

'Hiya!' she called down the hallway.

I dried my hands and went to assist her with the shopping.

'How was France?' I asked, lifting the bags on to the counter.

'Oh, all too brief,' she said, massaging her shoulders. 'Raf was holed up in our room stuck on this bloody edit.'

'Oh no,' I said, packing some muesli into a cupboard.

'Yeah. I told him this one better be a box-office smash.'

I laughed. Raf made very niche documentary films, which, while being highly critically acclaimed, no one had ever heard of. I suspected most of the family's income came from Terry, who was the head architect at a boutique London firm.

'How are you, love? How was your week off? Do anything nice?'

A viewfinder clicking on to a new frame, my mind immediately leapt to Henry, standing on the rooftop of his childhood home, arms outstretched and head tilted towards the sky.

'Er, not much. Saw some friends, did some reading.'

'Anything good?'

'*Anna Karenina.*'

'Ah, yes!' She grasped my arm. '"All happy families are alike, but each unhappy family is unhappy in its own way."'

Terry could summon, if not always the first sentence, then any choice line she had savoured from whatever book I happened to be reading. The shelves in this house were teeming with everything from Dante's *Inferno* to *Bridget Jones's Diary*.

'Mummy!'

The kids came hurtling in, Clara in her nightie and Jem completely nude. This didn't reflect all that well on me.

'Jem, pyjamas!' I said.

'Hello, little frogs!' Terry kissed them. Both children were scrambling for a place on their mother's anatomy, their little fingernails clawing into her, desperate to reap as much sensory contact as they could.

'Sorry,' I said. 'I was just about to go up once I'd cleared the plates.'

'Don't be silly,' said Terry, inhaling her young. 'I'm here now. You go home, love.'

*

Breaking my Friday-only tradition, I bought myself my usual Italian chocolate on the way to the tube to meet Dyl, and got one for him, too. At King's Cross, I left the Northern Line for the Piccadilly, and made my way up to Manor House station, where, above ground, I enjoyed the nostalgia of walking through Finsbury Park (which never failed to remind me of my teenage summers, smoking weed on the bandstand), finally arriving at our place in Stroud Green.

'Our place' was Theodore's, a little independent French bistro that did steak frites for a tenner and had served us wine when we were underage. In those days, you were still allowed to smoke inside, and we would get a corner table and pose with our Marlboro Lights and Pinot Noir, swapping our latest short stories and poems. Al, the mercurial Italian manager, had been there forever, and I suspected had a quiet fondness for us. This is where we had come after every break-up, for every celebration. Dyl had once drunk so much he threw up in the toilets; I had once come here by myself after things got weird on a date and I didn't want to be alone. The tables were adorned with gingham linoleum tablecloths and sputtering carmine candles plugged into old wine bottles. The menu had never changed and consisted of just three offerings: steak frites, moules marinière or coq au vin. The one time I brought Mila here, she was going through a vegetarian phase, and Al had thrown us out when she asked if she could just have some chips.

Dyl was already there when I arrived, drowning a piece of bread from a straw basket in olive oil and vinegar.

'How were the little drunk midgets?' he said as I sat down.

'Alright. Have you ordered some wine?'

'Malbec. That OK?'

'As if I would know.'

He chewed his bread. 'Ordered you a steak,' he said.

'Perfect.'

My phone was ringing.

'Fuck, it's my mum. I'll call her later.'

'I'll answer.'

Before I knew it, he had stolen my phone from my hand.

'Mo!' he said magnanimously. 'It's Dylan. How are you?'

The wine arrived and I poured him a glass. He was laughing sycophantically at something my mother was saying. 'Of course I will. I'm sure they send theirs. Yep, I'll pass you to her now . . .'

'Hi, Mum.'

'Hello, love.'

'Ugh,' I said, ending the call a few minutes later and taking a gulp of wine. 'I can't be arsed to go home.'

'Why do you have to go home?'

'Dad's got a new car, they're giving me the old one.'

'You poor lamb.'

'Fuck off.'

'What car is it?'

'Er, a Volvo, I think?'

'Decent car.'

'What the fuck do you know about cars?'

'Enough,' said Dyl, coyly. 'Why don't I come with you?'

'Where?'

'To your parents'.'

'Oh my God, would you?'

'Sure. It'd be nice to see them. I don't get why you're so neg on poor old Mike and Mo.'

I rolled my eyes. 'It's just the same old shit,' I said, refilling our glasses. 'Same meals every week. It'll be casserole on Friday and fish and chips on Saturday. Same shit on TV, then bed. It's depressing.'

'Well, Phil, you've become a snob.'

'They're not like your parents! Jesus, I mean if I tried to talk to them about, I don't know, Simone de Beauvoir, they wouldn't know what I was on about. They'd be mortified if I suggested we watched something other than *Poirot*.'

'Hey,' said Dyl. 'Don't knock *Poirot*.'

I laughed.

'Don't you just feel a bit claustrophobic, when you see your parents? Maybe it's because I'm an only child.'

'So am I,' said Dyl. 'Kind of.'

'Oh, mate, sorry—'

Dyl waved a hand, batting away this line of conversation.

'Plus, you know,' I ploughed on, searching for something to say, 'it'll be all *when are you going to get a real job*, blah blah blah . . .'

94

Dyl had plans for the next three weekends in a row – 'Since when were you so popular?' – so we arranged to go and visit my parents in a month's time.

Our food arrived: my steak, which only came very rare (the way I liked it), and Dyl's mussels. We settled back in our seats, ordered a second bottle of wine, and began to catch up in earnest. I filled Dyl in on my dream, and Uncle Lachlan's salacious antics.

'Shit,' said Dyl, glass frozen in mid-air. 'What a perv.'

'I know.'

'He seemed like a creepy old perv. You can just tell, can't you?'

'Yep.'

'I mean, if someone looks like a pervert, they're probably a pervert, right?'

'Agreed. I just wonder if he did anything to Marla.'

Dyl paled at her name. I had forgotten his proximity to her death. What that ambulance ride must have been like for him.

'Anyway. How was *your* week?'

'Meh,' said Dyl. 'We went dancing. I felt like a bit of a fifth wheel. Paddy was practically fucking some guy on the dance floor, and Mila and Niall left together.'

'It's so weird they're a thing now.'

'Yeah.'

'Slash, it's the least weird thing in the world.'

'Yeah.'

'What about Jess?' I asked.

'Jess doesn't like me that much.'

'What?'

'I don't know. Perhaps it's egotistical of me to even think she gives that much of a shit. I just get that impression from her sometimes. She's always pretty scathing about my writing.'

'She's never read your writing, Dyl.'

'Yeah, well, she's very scathing about it. God, that's good.'

'Is it? Give us a taste.'

*

I walked with Dyl to his bus stop and found myself inexorably waxing lyrical on my favourite subject: Henry.

'The thing is, I think he's essentially a *good person*, do you know what I mean? Like, he does actually have a very strong moral compass.'

Dyl wasn't really listening; his head was bowed over his phone, both thumbs frantically dabbing at the screen. 'You wanna come to a party?' he asked.

'What, right now?'

'Yep.'

My hand found something in my pocket.

'Here,' I said, handing him the chocolate I had bought earlier. 'Whose party is it?'

'Oh, cheers,' he said, unwrapping it and scoffing it in one. 'Cecily Simmons'.'

'Fuck that.'

He gave me a kiss on the forehead, turned on his heel and skipped off. 'See ya!' he called, just making his bus.

On the tube home, I ate my own chocolate in three satisfying bites. I smoothed out the foil wrapper and prised the small wax paper fortune from its film.

> *Being deeply loved by someone gives you strength,*
> *while loving someone deeply gives you courage.*
> – Lao Tzu

7

Fiona, au fait with the language of Freud and Jung, taught me a German word over tiramisu one evening when I was complaining of feeling 'fizzy': *Frühjahrsmüdigkeit*. It roughly translates as 'springtime depression', which was the closest thing I could find to describe my mood over those next few weeks. It happened every year, a perennial tension. It wasn't as simple as a depression. There was a buzz to it, a lonely restlessness that no amount of walks along the river or glasses of wine could abate. This moment of change, this yearly transition – it never failed to rearrange my molecules. Each year, spring made a greater promise than summer could fulfil, and it was as if I was mourning this disappointment before it even came. All I could do was lie on my bed, staring at the ceiling, bearing witness to the cacophony of feelings swirling around my body. I tried to write, siphoning some of this emotional surplus on to a blank page. Smoking helped, or maybe it just made me feel more poetic about it; I don't know. Being with the kids was the best cure, tethering me to something solid and benevolent. Resisting anaesthetising my feelings in the form of Henry became an activity in itself; one which occupied both my time and a surprising amount of mental energy. After our first ever night together last summer, Dyl had advised me to give Henry space. 'Let him come to you,' he had said. 'Men are like animals, they hate to be chased.' Jess had said that this was bullshit, that Dyl was a misogynist who had entirely corrupted my view of the opposite sex. I pointed out the irony of the lesbian among us taking it upon herself to defend the moral capability of young men. In the end, Henry had not 'come to' me, and that was that. I vowed to never again heed Dyl's advice; it was nothing more than juvenile game-playing. Now, however, in the aftershock of his sister's death, I couldn't *not* give Henry space.

'What am I supposed to say?' I asked Mila sadly on the phone. 'I know you're grieving, but can I come over for a shag?'

We had seen each other just once since the weekend in the country, one rainy Sunday – a film followed by sex followed by an emotional outburst from Henry. I cradled him and stroked his hair, let him sob into my breast. He kept saying *sorry* over and over again, and I shushed him. I wanted to tell him that I was the one who should be sorry; sorry that I couldn't make his pain go away, sorry that I was unable to reach in to the weavings of his inner life, during one of the many silences to which he was now prone. I was sorry that I, who had no siblings, had no idea what it was like to lose your only sister, and that, after the initial shock, Marla's death only crossed my mind during selfish ruminations about the impact it might have on Henry's feelings towards me. He made just one request.

'Can I ask you a favour?' he said, wiping his nose on the duvet.

'Always,' I said. 'Anything.'

'The kids you look after.'

'Yeah?' I was thrown by his mention of them. In the haze of his suffering, I barely expected Henry to even remain cognisant of the fact I was a nanny.

'Could I – God, this probably sounds weird . . . it's

just I want to help out more with Marla's' – he cleared his throat – 'with Bear. And I thought well, you do it for a living. So maybe I could, come along, one time. Watch you, help out? Sorry, it does sound weird, now I say it out loud—'

'Of course,' I said. How could I refuse?

On the Friday I was leaving for my parents', he joined me at work. It didn't feel terribly professional, but there it was: Henry asking to spend time with me, handing me the power to be the one person who could remedy his heartache, if only for an afternoon.

Clara was immediately taken with him. I saw through her eyes how his pale skin and haunted features must have appeared slightly vampiric, beguilingly dangerous. Jem was sold as soon as he asked if Henry liked dragons, to which Henry responded by pretending to be one, chasing Jem around the playground, roaring and flapping his arms.

An entirely new side of Henry appeared: a lighter, warmer side. He made it look so easy, I couldn't help wondering where this other persona lived the rest of the time, and I understood, suddenly, why he had craved the company of children. He played with the kids as if he were one himself, rather than an adult doing their best to join in.

Clara was putting on a display of acrobatics for Henry's benefit that was regrettably ineffectual. She was hanging upside down from the climbing frame, assuming an expression of complete indifference, as if being suspended in mid-air was her natural resting pose.

'Wow, Clara, you're really good at that!' I called from the bench, surrounded by schoolbags.

'What?' she shouted, though I knew she'd heard me.

'You're really good at hanging upside down!' I repeated. 'Look, guys. Clara's been hanging upside down for ages!'

Henry, who was holding Jem, swung him round to his hip so he could see.

'Whoa!' Henry said. 'Like a giant bat.'

Capitalising on his gaze, Clara lifted her hands to either side of her knees on the bar, and dismounted in a fairly impressive somersault.

'Nice!' said Henry. 'You could be a gymnast.'

Clara quickly ran over to me and busied herself going through her knapsack, a little flustered.

'What you looking for, love?' I asked her.

'My *d'lo* bottle,' she said, retrieving it and taking a long suck from the nozzle. She dawdled next to me, unsure of her next move.

'Jem,' I called out. 'Why don't you come and have some water as well?'

'I'm OK!' yelled Jem.

'Come on, you've been screeching your lungs out. I bet you're thirsty.'

'Oh, I'm thirsty actually,' said Henry. 'I think I'll have some water.'

'Well I am, actually, just a little bit thirsty,' said Jem. They galloped over to the bench. I handed him his bottle and he took several long pulls on the nozzle, tipping his head all the way back.

'You having fun, Jemmy?' I asked.

'Yeah,' he panted. 'Henry is a really scary dragon!'

A sudden music filled the air; a high melody I recognised but couldn't name. The first ice cream van of the year was pulling up at the side of the playground. The kids looked stretched to breaking point with longing.

'Nanny Jo,' said Clara in her nicest voice. 'Please may Jemmarcus and I get an ice lolly?'

'I don't know,' I said. 'Don't you think it's a bit cold?'

'No, I don't,' said Jem.

'What do you think, Henry?' I asked.

'I think,' he said, 'that a certain dragon needs an ice lolly after blowing fire all afternoon.'

I handed Clara a fiver and let her and Jem go alone to the van, where a queue had already formed. Henry and I sat on the bench, watching them.

'Do you know the Rilke quote about dragons?' I asked, turning to him.

'I can't say that I do.'

'Shall I tell it to you? It's very beautiful.'

'Go on, then.'

'"Perhaps all the dragons in our lives are princesses, who are only waiting to see us act, just once, with beauty and courage. Perhaps everything that frightens us is, in its deepest essence, something helpless that wants our love."'

Henry said nothing.

'Well?' I said.

'Yeah,' he said. 'It's good.'

We walked back to the house; me intermittently calling up ahead to the boys to 'Slow down!' and Clara dragging her feet along the kerb beside me.

'Right, I'd better go,' Henry said, stroking the cast-iron door knocker in the shape of a fox.

'No!' said Jem.

'I'll come play with you again, I promise.' He gently pinched the little boy's dimpled cheek. 'Have a nice time with your parents,' he said to me. 'See you soon.' And he gave me a fleeting kiss on the lips that caused the children to actually scream. Inside, I did too.

*

Two hours later, I met Dyl at King's Cross. He sauntered towards me – the trademark insouciant swagger I could recognise from a mile away – carrying a plastic bag almost tearing with the weight of the cans inside.

'Hey, bumface,' he said, kissing me on the forehead. 'I got tinnies for the train.'

Installed opposite each other at a table, we swapped notebooks.

'This isn't fair,' I said, handing mine over. 'I've not written anything decent for months.'

'*Plus ça change*,' said Dyl, cracking open a can of lager and beginning to leaf through the scribbled pages.

I opened Dyl's ruby Moleskine, forcing myself not to study his face for reactions. That minuscule handwriting. Being able to read Dyl's poems and stories was, as well as a privilege, a technical triumph. His writing was barely legible, and it had taken me years to become fluent.

'Start with this one,' he said, leaning over the table and thumbing his way to a specific page. 'It's not too long. Would like your thoughts. Can't decide if it's too abstract.'

He had landed on a short story titled 'VOID', wherein the narrator becomes fixated with a patch of mould on his ceiling, describing it in visceral, Joyce-esque detail; a sort of extended metaphor for the character's crumbling psyche.

'I think it works,' I said, looking up at him. He had got out a pencil and was making notes on my own work.

'What are you annotating, you bastard?' I asked, opening a pre-mixed tin of mojito.

'This poem,' said Dyl. 'It's really good. I'm just writing in a couple of suggestions.'

'Oh yeah?'

'Instead of "little by little the ache *passes*", I've put

"lifts" – "little by little the ache lifts". It's nicer, don't you think? I know you're allergic to alliteration—'

'No, you're right, that's better,' I said. 'Cheers.'

He threw me a farcical grimace and continued to pore over the notebook. We passed the first half of the journey in this way; him chewing his pencil and making the odd inscription, me both impressed and disturbed by Dyl's ever-darker themes.

'So,' Dyl said, opening a pack of salt and vinegar crisps. 'How are you?'

I sighed. 'Fine,' I said. We smiled at each other. 'No, I mean, I am fine.' I paused, unsure of why I was telling him what came next. 'Henry came to look after the kids with me today.'

'Did he?'

'Yeah.'

'Why?'

'He wanted to. I think he wants to help out with Bear more.'

Dyl was eyeing me appraisingly across the table.

'What?' I said.

'That poem you've called "Spring" is about him, isn't it? The "you" is Henry, right?'

'Those are meant to be song lyrics, actually,' I said. 'Fuck, I miss Edinburgh. It was so nice having a piano in the house.'

'You always go on about Edinburgh like you went there yourself.'

'I practically did,' I said. After dropping out of my miserable English degree at Bristol, crashing at Dyl's student flat became *living* at Dyl's student flat. I'd got a part-time job, and planned a transfer that somehow never happened.

It was a golden time of house-parties, no responsibilities and strong legs (all the walking up and down hills).

'Answer the question, Phil,' Dyl said.

I laughed. 'Of course it's about Henry.'

He raised an eyebrow at me, and I forced myself not to raise one right back.

'I saw Henry last weekend, by the way,' he said.

'Oh yeah?' I said, helping myself to a crisp.

'Aren't you going to ask me?' he said.

'Ask you what?'

'Come on, Phil.'

'What?'

'Don't you want to know what he said about you?'

I turned to face him, smirking at me across the small train table littered with empty drinks. Of course I wanted to know, but I really didn't *want* to want to know.

'Go on, then,' I said, twisting the bottom of my can around on the table, pretending to read the ingredients. *Serve over ice,* said the can; ours were lukewarm.

'He was pretty wasted.'

'Drunk?'

'E, I think. Anyway, he invited us all to Cornwall again this summer.'

'Oh yeah? We should go. We can take the Volvo.'

'Yes, yes. We should get the whole gang down, see if Niall and Mila can get time off work.'

'What about Jess?'

'Jess is in PR: she can always get time off. And Paddy will most likely be unemployed by then.'

'Oh, fuck,' I said, my stomach plummeting. 'I missed Paddy's play, didn't I?'

'Yes, you did.'

'God, is he pissed?'

'No, he's fine. He didn't expect you to come.'

'What do you mean?'

'You're not about to win any prizes for reliability, Phil.'

'What? That's—'

'Yeah, yeah, yeah.' Dyl leaned back in his seat.

'I'm a fucking nanny, Dyl. I'm very reliable.'

'OK.'

I looked out the window at the unfamiliar Cambridge-shire countryside. My parents had sold my childhood home in the suburbs of North London not long after I left for uni. I hadn't really forgiven them for it, not that I went home that much anyway. Once I had tasted freedom, there was no going back. When I was little, I thought the familiarity and safety of home would last forever; that, despite the quiet and ennui, home was home. And then when I left, I discovered the joy of the stark. Of sparsity. Of being skint and spending every penny I had on a cheap bottle of red wine so I could enjoy a Saturday night. Of making a big vat of spaghetti Bolognese to get me through a week. Dwindling became an art form. Learning to ration: if I don't have another drink, I can buy more tobacco; if we split this takeaway pizza, we can buy more beer. I walked everywhere because public transport was too expensive, which meant I *saw* everything. I breathed it. When it rained, I got wet, because an umbrella was an unnecessary expenditure. And it was glorious: the good times were simpler and purer, and the bad times were nothing a hot bath couldn't fix. There was a hive of collectively skint company who would always be there for me. Nights in with a DVD and a spliff. Nights out with sickly shots, dancing till the sun came up. I learned that I felt more at home flopped on a sofa snuggling with friends or lovers than within the stilted conversations and culture-free zone of my parents' house. When they relocated to the provinces, I had even less reason to return.

'We ended up having a pretty deep chat, actually,' said Dyl, leaning back in his chair.

I didn't respond, but continued to watch the ever-changing scenery flash by. Sweat had materialised on both my palms and I wiped them surreptitiously on my jeans.

'The drugs, you know. It all ends up coming out.'

'I guess.'

'Sometimes I wonder whether drugs bring out our truest selves, or just sort of turn up the volume on our id . . .'

'It's probably all just bullshit, isn't it?'

'He asked me about my brother,' said Dyl, evenly.

'What?' I said, turning to face him. 'Fuck, what—'

'I suppose I'm the only other person he knows who's lost a sibling.'

Why hadn't this parallel occurred to me? I could have asked Dyl for advice about how best to comfort Henry. I could have suggested the three of us go for drinks in order to gently nudge him towards this available counsel. Had I been so myopic in my romantic desire for Henry that I had begun to see his grief as an inconvenience? Though it could just be that I hated to bring up Ben in front of Dyl.

'But, I mean, it's not really the same—' I began to say, but Dyl interrupted.

'Not your arena, Phil.'

'No, sorry. Fuck.'

'Oh, and he said he was in love with you.'

I gawked at him. 'Wait, what?'

'I think his exact words were, "I think I'm falling for Joni, mate, I think I might be in love with her."'

It wasn't beyond Dyl for this to be some sort of cruel, weird joke. I was about to ask him what he said in response to Henry's declaration when a warm northern voice came on the tannoy to announce that we had arrived at Ely.

'Fuck!' I said, gathering my notebook and pens. 'This is our stop.'

'What? Jesus—' He sprang up.

We stumbled out on to the platform, arms full of litter and our coats and bags. I found that I was crying.

'Oh, Phil.' Dyl pulled me into a hug, dropping all our things on to the filthy tarmac. I sobbed into his clavicle.

'I'm sorry,' I said, holding on to him. 'I'm sorry I never ask you about Ben. I never know if you want to talk about it, but obviously we can if you want to. You can talk to me about anything, you know that, right? I think I just suck at talking about death. I didn't even make the connection with you and Henry. God, I'm stupid.'

'Shh,' said Dyl, cupping the back of my head with his warm hand. 'It's OK, you're not stupid.' He paused. 'You're just a little bit of a cunt.'

I spluttered, and began to laugh; the hysteria of the tears making the seamless shift into giggles. We were both doubled over on the platform, our belongings strewn all over the ground: cathartic, shoulder-shaking laughter, the kind only Dyl could elicit, taking me the full one-eighty from sorrow to joy.

'Come on, then,' Dyl said eventually, straightening up. 'Where the fuck are we?'

I heaved a big sigh. We picked up our things and began to trudge across the car park in the direction of the main road and, eventually, my parents' home. The sun had set by now; the orange light of the lamp posts glowed drearily over the quiet streets. Ely was a one-storey, leafy place; model-town-esque in a way that made me feel insane, as if the whole place was a soundstage. A few old men stood outside a pub, smoking and exchanging two- or three-word remarks. We passed an Indonesian restaurant. I could see that only one table was occupied, by a middle-aged couple – he large and bespectacled, she tiny and showing all the warning signs of osteoporosis. The Indonesian staff were patiently lined up at the bar, ready to tend to this couple's every want and fancy.

'Crazy Friday night,' said Dyl, exhaling smoke into the damp night air.

'Literally. What do people *do* here?'

'How much further, Phil?'

'Nearly there, I think,' I said. 'Yes, there's the off-licence. Five more minutes.'

'Why couldn't one of them pick you up?'

'Didn't ask. I suspected we could do with a pre-game walk and a smoke.'

'Hull-oh!' came Dad's sing-song greeting, as insistent as a doorbell.

My parents stood at the open threshold, my mother's hand on the doorframe, my father's hand on my mother's frame.

'Hi, Mike, Mo,' said Dyl, stepping forward and hugging Mum, shaking Dad's hand.

'Hey, guys,' I said.

'Ooh!' said Mum, backing out of my outstretched arms, flapping a hand across her face. 'Someone's been smoking.'

This house – a house that had nothing to do with me or my childhood – smelled of cat, though my parents didn't have one. It was a newly developed, end-of-terrace cottage: three-up, three-down. We gathered in the kitchen-diner. I had no familiarity with this space, no friendly armchair or usual seat at the table to which I could attach myself, so I hovered mid-room, freshly self-conscious of my own smoky odour.

'Can I get you a drink, Dylan? Glass of wine? Beer?' asked Dad.

'Red, please, Mike, if you've got any.'

'Jo?'

'Same, please.'

'We're having a casserole,' said Mum. 'Friday tradition!'

Dyl and I caught eyes.

'Smells lovely,' said Dyl. 'The house is great. Can't believe I've not been here before.'

'We'll have to give you the tour,' said Mum.

'How are your parents?' Dad asked Dyl.

'I mean, you've probably spoken to them more recently than I have,' he said. 'But well, I think. All fine.'

'Good, good.'

'What's burning?' I asked.

'Oh bother, can you still smell it?' said Dad, going to open the French windows. 'The pudding went over a little bit.'

'Oh, I am hopeless.' Mum smiled and looked at Dad in a *What am I like?* way.

My mother could not cook. Dad had done most of the cooking when I was growing up, and when he wasn't available, Mum would serve frozen ready-meals. As a child, I loved these high-salt, high-sugar cartons of mush; they were novel and reminded me of the food I saw on American television. I would even say grace, just to more closely imitate the characters on those shows. No one in my house was religious, and once, upon witnessing me clasp my little hands together and mumble something about gifts in a Nickelodeon-inspired voice, my mother called me 'a strange one'. She persisted in calling me 'a strange one' whenever I behaved in a way that she did not understand.

We ate the casserole, Dyl doing most of the conversational heavy lifting, me washing away the strange taste of the tap water with my wine. The water in Ely is 'hard water', which means it either has too low or too high a mineral content – I can't remember which. Either way, it was ineffective for both drinking and washing; never quite quenching the dryness of my throat.

'Here we are!' said Mum, bringing out a slightly blackened tray of sponge.

'Lovely,' said Dyl, sliding his third glass of wine out of the way so she could place the dish on the table.

'What flavour?' I asked, aware that I hadn't spoken in a while.

'Apple,' said Mum. 'With just a little bit of cinnamon – thought I'd push the boat out.'

I tried to catch Dyl's eye again, but he was busy pouring cream for Dad. Mum handed me a large portion. Then my father said the word I had feared was coming all evening.

'So.'

I filled my mouth with sponge, buying myself some time.

'How's the job hunt going?'

'Mm.' I nodded, bringing my hand to my lips, indicating I was just finishing my mouthful. They were all turned towards me, forks suspended in mid-air.

'Have you applied for anything yet?' said Mum.

'Yeah.' I swallowed. 'Yeah, I have.'

'And?'

'Well, I'm just waiting to hear back from a couple.'

'When will you hear back?' asked Mum.

'Where did you apply?' asked Dad.

'Um, an internship, at a publisher's.'

'Internship?' said Dad. 'Presumably that's a non-paid position, then?'

'I'm not sure.'

'Didn't you look when you sent off your application?' asked Mum.

'Yeah, yeah, I think it's paid. Anyway, there's that, and another one, at a bookshop.'

The truth was I had been rejected from both the job and the unpaid internship. It seemed a half-finished degree was employment leprosy.

'Okey dokey,' said Dad. 'Well, fingers crossed!'

'Wait – but you love nannying,' said Dyl to me.

'She can't be a nanny forever!' Mum laughed.

Dyl continued to address me. 'And it means you've got time for your writing?'

'Yeah.'

'And you love those kids?'

I looked up at him: the kindness in his eyes; his curly hair that was scruffy even when it was neat.

'Yeah, I do. And they love me.'

'No one's saying you're not very good at the nannying, love,' said Mum. 'We just want to see you a bit more set up, that's all. Isn't it, Mike?'

'Hm?' said Dad, mouth full. 'What? Yes. Set up.'

'I know it might be tempting to start spending Grandma Helen's money, but that'll come in really handy on a rainy day,' said Mum. 'You haven't touched it, love, have you? It's so easy to fritter away, and before you know it . . .'

'No, of course not,' I said.

'Good.'

There was a pause in which I could feel Dyl studying me across the table.

'Mind if I have a quick ciggy?' he said.

'Oh, if you must,' said Mum. 'I won't tell Sharon this time!'

'Oh, Mum's given up on bribing me to quit,' said Dyl. 'Joni, come keep me company. Thanks so much, Mike, Mo. That was delicious.'

'Yeah, thanks, guys. Yum,' I said, standing. 'We'll clean up.'

I followed Dyl gratefully out to the garden, closing the glass double doors behind us.

Trampling on some pink hellebores, we shimmied up the garden wall, and sat straddling it to smoke our cigarettes.

'Thank you,' I said.

Dyl reached out an arm and gave me a squeeze on the shoulder.

The wall was cold and slightly damp in a pleasing, sobering way. I rolled my vertebrae slowly backwards until I was lying flat along the length of it, looking up. The skin of the sky was pulled tight and wide over the earth like a drum.

'You OK?' said Dyl.

'Yeah.' I blew a couple of smoke rings into the air, a trick I was childishly proud of being able to do.

'Wanna go to the pub?' asked Dyl.

'What?' I craned my neck to look at him; he was gazing blankly out towards the town. 'You serious?'

'Why not? Have you got your wallet on you?'

'No.'

'Well, I do. Come on, let's go get a couple of drinks. It's Friday night.'

'Dyl, no. I've got to go inside and do the washing up.'

He threw his cigarette butt out on to the road. It landed almost perfectly in the centre. 'Do it later.'

'No.'

'Shall we watch a film, then?'

'Meh.'

'Alright then, Pollyanna, what do you want to do?'

I sat up again, and rubbed my hands over my face. 'I want to clean up and go to bed,' I said.

'Alright,' said Dyl, dismounting the wall on the street side.

'What the fuck are you doing?'

'I want another drink or two,' he said.

'You're going to the pub?'

'Yep. You coming?'

'No.'

'Fine.' And he sauntered away.

I looked down at the road, the little red light of his cigarette still glowing on the ground; the fiery butt seeming rebelliously urban in this parochial cul-de-sac.

I could hear my parents exchanging mundane comments about something on the TV. I scraped the plates, loaded the dishwasher, and headed quietly upstairs.

'You off to bed, love?' Mum's senses had always become superhuman in the vicinity of her only child.

'Think so!' I called back. 'Night.'

'Dylan, too?'

'He's just having one last cig.'

'You've got to stop, the pair of you,' called Dad.

'I know,' I said, already halfway up the stairs.

'See you in the morning!' said Mum.

The guest bedroom was almost never utilised. I think my mother had decided to use it as an experiment in interior design. The walls were a muddy purple colour – 'aubergine', she called it – and the lampshades and bedding were all a matching lime. The bedhead was a feature in stitched black leather. A triptych of unframed canvases hung on the wall, depicting crimson hearts on yellow backdrops that were vaguely reminiscent of the McDonald's logo. I got into bed with the intention of achieving unconsciousness as soon as possible, but as I lay there in the dark, my thoughts pressed in upon me with a gravity so insistent I had to sit up and switch on the chartreuse lamp. Inside my handbag were my notebook and a magazine I'd planned to read on the train. It was a shitty glossy aimed at women (while explicitly hating women), but I liked looking at the clothes and celebrity gossip: it switched off my mind. Notebook first. Empty something out.

> *The year is dying*
> *In the night, you said*
> *Your gaze unchanged*
> *Since we were just babies*
> *Playing games we did not understand.*

'Oh, hey there.'

Dyl came in and headed straight for a shower, singing 'Country House' over the hiss of the running water.

I quickly stowed my notebook away and was skimming the back-page interview with some soap star when he came out, a towel wrapped around his head in a feminine way.

How do you relax?

I love Pilates!

'Stimulating read?' he asked.

'Shut up.'

'Is that *Vista*?'

'Yeah.'

'Do the interview on me.'

'How was the pub?'

'Surprisingly jolly.' He suppressed a burp.

'You're rude.'

'Do the interview!'

'Fine. Who do you call for a night out?'

'You,' he said, drying himself.

'What's your party trick?'

'High chemical tolerance. Next.'

'Best place for a first date?'

'Theodore's,' he said, smiling at me.

'Do you take girls there?'

'Obviously.'

'Did you take Cecily there?'

'No, she wouldn't get it. Why are you so obsessed with her, anyway? You jealous?'

He had pulled on some boxers and a T-shirt, and now came and lay on the bed beside me.

'You stink of booze,' I said.

He stuck out his tongue and blew air out on an 'H' into my face.

'Ew, go away,' I said, pushing him off. 'What do you like to cook?'

'I prefer to be cooked for.'

I narrowed my eyes at him.

'What?' he said, innocently.

'Best holiday?'

'Laos. Next.'

'How do you relax?'

'Spliff. Next.'

He wriggled under the covers and lay on his side, facing me, one hand tucked under the side of his face, the other resting on my stomach.

'What is your exercise routine?'

'Ha, ha.'

'Favourite TV show?'

'Anything where you get to look inside people's houses.'

'Animals or babies?'

'Both.'

'Who are you thankful to?'

'The NHS.'

'To whom would you like to say sorry?'

'Ugh. Everyone.'

'Tell us a secret.'

'You look about twelve years old right now.'

'That's not a secret.'

'Kind of is. No one else knows it other than me.'

'No, come on, that's boring. I want juice.'

'I don't really have any secrets. What does' – he leaned over to see the name of the interviewee – 'Sheila Shalcross say?'

'Sheila Shalcross says, "I'm a giant racist."'

'Fuck. I've got nothing on that.'

I dropped the magazine on to the floor and switched off the bedside lamp. We lay there in silence, the darkness giving us permission to play our interior monologues for a while. Henry. Dyl. Ben. Marla.

'Dyl?' I whispered.

'What?'

'Your poetry is getting very dark.'

He laughed and reached for my hand under the covers. We fell asleep that way.

Now Lachlan was stamping on Dolly the dog, eye-balling me, laughing cruelly, Dolly's paws frantically scratching the ground . . . and then I was the dog, Lachlan towering above me, and I couldn't breathe, and he was telling me I liked it . . .

I woke up, heart racing, soaked in cold sweat. I curled into the back of Dyl's warm body. It was pitch black outside. I had been awake alone at this time many, many times before, suspended in the heavy abyss of the limbo between night and day, and was grateful to have company now. I rubbed my cheek against the soft cotton of Dyl's old T-shirt. He stirred, taking a sharp inhale and then shifting round to face me.

'What's up?' he mumbled.

'Sorry,' I whispered. 'Bad dream.'

He pulled me into a tight cuddle, my face nestled into the hot skin in the nook of his collarbone. It was so warm and so silken that I kissed it reflexively. He let out a little hum of pleasure. I kissed it again, for longer this time, enjoying the soothing contact of his flesh with my mouth. And then, in silence, we started to kiss each other. He held me incredibly tight to his body – whether urging me to stop or go on, I didn't know.

*

I woke before Dyl, showered and dressed in the locked bathroom. At breakfast, Mum filled me in on the weight loss and gain of the various women in her Zumba class. When Dyl came down, she said: 'Someone's looking a little worse for wear!' Dad gave me a comprehensive demonstration of the mechanics and apparatus of the Volvo. I thanked them profusely for the car and told them I'd call them soon.

'Keep us posted about the job hunt!' Mum said, holding up crossed fingers on both hands.

'Will do!' I said.

'Unleaded, remember,' said Dad. 'Don't make the same mistake I did!'

Mum and Dad both laughed and rolled their eyes at each other in the *What are you like?* way.

It started to rain just as Dyl and I drove off. He lit a cigarette.

'April showers,' said Dyl, after a silence I realised was my first agonising one in his company. I wondered whether it had been for him, too.

'It's March,' I said.

'It'll be April next week.'

'God, this year is going quickly.'

It took a while to get accustomed to driving again; it had been years since I had enjoyed the reflexes of gears and mirror-checking. Once we got out on to the motorway, I felt comfortable enough to switch on the radio, pushing buttons until I heard the middle eight of 'I Don't Feel Like Dancin'' by the Scissor Sisters, tapping the steering wheel and starting to sing along.

'This is crap,' said Dyl.

'I like it.'

'Is there an aux cable?' he asked, opening the glove compartment and revealing nothing but the car's papers and a couple of CDs.

'Doubt it. It's a really old car.'

'Your dad doesn't want these, then?' he said, examining the small plastic squares of albums.

'Guess not.'

'Yeesh . . . OK, Guns N' Roses or U2?'

'God. Which U2 album is it?'

'*Joshua Tree.*'

'Go on then.'

He slid the disc into the car stereo and skipped a couple of tracks. I watched his hands, so long-fingered and clumsy. How different to the way he'd used them last night.

'Oh yeah,' he said, as 'With or Without You' started up. 'Christ.'

He lifted his feet up on to the dashboard, drumming the tops of his thighs.

'Don't.' I leaned over to push his legs back down. 'You'll leave a mark.'

The chorus came in, nasal and passionate. I reached across and skipped forward to 'Trip Through Your Wires', the bluesy harmonica and arpeggios immediately cheering me up.

'Oi, I was enjoying that.'

'This is much more conducive to driving.'

'I was having a real moment there with Bono.'

'You're a dickhead.'

The drive passed in this way: smoking and disagreeing over what music to listen to and which route to take once we got back into the city. We were short with each other. The previous night was not mentioned, nor did Dyl ask me what I was doing later, which was unusual for him on a Saturday night. He made a rushed and clunky exit in the brief standstill of a red traffic light on Camden Road, a short distance from his house.

'Speak soon!' I yelled as he slammed the door, sounding like someone else.

He kissed the outside of the car window, his full lips pressed up against the glass. It repulsed me a little. They left a faint pout print there. Dyl moseyed off as the traffic began to move again. I wound down my window and lit a roll-up, drinking in the sights and smells of London: old rockers on the Kentish Town Road, jerk chicken sizzling on a market stall, the Mary Poppins street lamps. From my new perspective at the wheel, I felt like the city was mine; I'd forgotten the giddy feeling of freedom that driving gave me.

Fiona had left a note: *Chicken in the fridge needs eating if you want it!* She, too, was visiting her parents this weekend, up in Glasgow. I texted the group:

Roast at mine tonight? Fiona away.

Mila replied privately saying that she and Niall already had plans for dinner. Jess was in. Paddy called, answering the phone singing Joni Mitchell, as was his custom with me. On this occasion, it was 'Both Sides Now', in what was a pretty decent imitation of the 2000 re-recording of the track.

'Hello,' I said as he finished.

'What's all this about tonight then, are we doing something? My stupid date just cancelled so I'm all yours.'

'Oh no.'

'Never mind. Think he was straight anyway, just curious.'

'Not curious enough.'

'Well, quite. The thing is I was counting on the prick to eat tonight, I'm poor as a church mouse.'

'Fiona's left me a full fridge.'

'Bless that woman.'

'And Jess is free, too.'

'Divine. I'll come soon, if that suits?'

'Sooner the better.'

I took a bath, rinsing away the hard water of Ely, washing away last night's sins. Sweeping my bath sponge between my legs, I felt, if not quite a soreness, a tingling. My body holding on to the memory I was trying desperately to banish from my mind. Lying on my bed, I added a few more lines to last night's entry.

> *The year is dying*
> *In the night, you said*
> *Your gaze unchanged*
> *Since we were just babies*
> *Playing games we did not understand.*

Just for Today

Plus ça change
You said on the train
Before handing over what I thought
Were all your secrets.

I don't know
The bigger surprise:
The darkness I found there
Or the astonishing light
you shone
Last night?

I shut my notebook. There. Something on the page; now I could forget about it. Paddy texted to say he was walking from the tube station now, and I took a cigarette on to the street to await him. The sky had turned a murky indigo and the temperature had dropped a couple of degrees. I wandered over to Haverstock Hill to see if I could spot him coming. Red brake lights winked on and off as cars and buses inched their way through the rush-hour traffic. People were going out for Saturday night. The beat was starting up, that buzz of activity and hope: the hope that she would notice you tonight, that he would be there, that the money you spent on that new dress/shirt/gram of coke was worth it. It infected me, and I was flooded with the urge to get wasted and go dancing.

Paddy showed up, cheeks flushed, apologising for having nothing to contribute to the meal. Jess arrived not much later in an Uber, laden with good wine and chocolate. The wood burner lit in the large kitchen, we gathered around with improvised Negronis (there was no vermouth to be found, so we used sherry instead) and indulged in our freedom to discuss the absent members of our group.

'Do you think they'll get married?' said Jess, half an hour into our discussion on the Mila–Niall liaison.

'Steady on,' I said.

'Oh, without question,' said Paddy, supine in front of the hearth.

'Really?' I said.

'I think you're forgetting how conventional he is, our Niall.'

'I think you're forgetting how tricky she is, our Mila.'

'True,' said Jess.

'OK, hang on,' Paddy said, propping himself up on his elbows. 'You two both go on as if Mila turns into some Alex Forrest type—'

'Who's that?' I interrupted.

'*Fatal Attraction*,' they said in unison.

'What I mean to say is that I am yet to see any proof!' Paddy went on. 'Come on, spill the tea. The time has come.'

Jess and I looked at each other; communicating our mutual willingness to entrust Paddy with this information, and our mutual guilt at this willingness. Paddy had a way of coaxing out secrets. He made you feel as if you, the teller, were being invited into *his* small circle of trust in the telling; when, of course, it was the other way around.

'Well,' said Jess, taking a sip of 'Negroni' and grimacing. 'There was the time she made us create a fake Instagram account to catch Daniel cheating.'

'Pardon?' said Paddy, in comic flummox.

'God, I'd forgotten about that,' I said.

'To be fair, he *was* cheating,' said Jess.

Paddy grinned at us wickedly. 'What else?'

'The worst one I remember,' I said, 'is when she kept Tom's passwords after they'd broken up, and didn't stop snooping around on his Facebook for months.'

'Yep,' said Jess. 'I think ultimately she came clean, though.'

'What?' said Paddy.

'She called him and told him to change his password, because she'd got to the point where she couldn't stop herself.'

Paddy cackled. 'There's more, isn't there?' he said, the firelight dancing in his eyes.

Our silence was the confirmation.

'It only happened once,' I said.

'Joni, no. I feel like we shouldn't go there,' said Jess, her tone implying she was only semi-committing to her own statement.

'It won't leave this room,' said Paddy. 'I swear.'

'You say it,' said Jess. 'I'm not saying it.'

Paddy looked at me imploringly, his expression as innocent as a schoolgirl asking her teacher to please explain Pythagoras' theorem.

'Gah,' I said. 'No. I can't, it's not my secret to tell.'

Paddy exploded. 'No, no, no!' He got up from the floor. 'Unacceptable. Unacceptable levels of tantalising. You cannot get away with it.'

I laughed. 'Sorry,' I said, getting up too. 'I should make a start on this food, anyway.'

I began to arrange ingredients on the counter, leaving Paddy in a frenzy of whimpers and petulance. He prodded us to relent several times over the course of the food preparation, but neither Jess nor I surrendered.

The wine was opened. We roasted the chicken, along with potatoes, cavolo nero and carrots, which Jess glazed with orange juice and coriander seeds, outshining all other elements of the meal.

Paddy, weary of his own line of questioning, changed tack. 'I saw a bee today,' he announced.

'Gosh, well done,' said Jess.

'No, but listen.' He held up a finger like a conductor's stick. 'It was really profound. I was walking home this morning and it flew straight past me on the Kingsland Road. I almost cried.' He took a long, brilliant pause. 'Summer is coming,' he said, raising his glass.

'Summer is coming.' We toasted and drank. The wood burner crackled and filled the room with its delicious smoky scent. Paddy soon had us bent double with impressions of older, more 'lovey' actors he had worked with, embodying the physicality of an old dame precisely, and riveting us with gossip about a certain well-known elderly actor's predilection for overweight young men.

'Oh, Paddy my boy,' he purred. 'I veritably swoon at the sight of a juvenile chubster.'

Jess and I creased with hysterics, clutching the side of the table to stay upright.

A few hours later, the dishwasher on, bottles in the recycling bin, Jess ordered herself a cab home.

'Need a lift to the tube, Paddy?' she asked, pulling on her jacket.

'I'm sleeping over,' he said. He hadn't actually asked if he could.

'God, I'm jealous,' said Jess. 'Really can't be bothered for this charity thing tomorrow.'

'We'll have fun soon,' I said, hugging her, 'Thank you for the wine. Love you.'

*

'Is it just me,' Paddy said, upstairs, half an hour later, studying himself in the mirror in his boxers and the old

T-shirt I had given him to sleep in, 'or do I look *in*credible in this top? Like, devastating?'

'You're absolutely right,' I said, from the bed. 'You do. You should have it.'

'Oh, darling, I would never presume.'

'It's yours.'

He jumped into bed with me, and drew an impressive inhale before saying, *'So'*, as if the night had only just begun. 'Tell me everything about you and Henry Taschen.'

'Oh, God.'

'What's the sex like? Do you love him? Does he still cry all the time?'

'Er, it's good. I don't know, and yes.'

'Said the writer.'

I laughed. 'Sorry. No, things are . . . OK? A lot has happened this weekend.'

'Go on.'

Maybe it was the dark; that illusion of anonymity, the stillness of the night setting the stage for confession. Maybe it was because I had teased him earlier, dangling Mila's secret before him and then snatching it away, and I felt I owed him some other pearl of confidence. Maybe I just had to tell someone. Whatever the reason, out it came. I told him that all I wanted was to be Henry's girlfriend, that I had done since we were sixteen years old, that Dyl had said Henry loved me, and it was all too good to be true, and then – last night.

'Stop,' Paddy said, finally, when I arrived at this reveal. 'You and Dyl?'

'I know. What the fuck.'

'Well it was bound to happen sometime, I suppose. At least you've got it out of the way.'

'What?'

'Oh, come on, darling. Jess and I were *convinced* you were going to hook up after Pride last year. Not forgetting that infamous Halloween when he punched that guy who groped you. We've had bets on and off for years.'

'Sorry, what?'

'Babe, did you think you were the only one who enjoyed a good verbal dissection about our friends when they're not around?'

'Don't tell anyone,' I said.

'I won't.'

'Seriously. No one can know. Things finally might be going somewhere with Henry, I don't want to ruin everything.'

'I'll take it to the grave,' he said, finding my hand beneath the covers and giving it a squeeze. 'So out of character for you, though. To self-sabotage,' he added, dripping sarcasm.

'Ha, ha,' I said.

Not much later, Paddy fell asleep. I lay awake listening to him breathing for what felt like a very, very long time.

8

The city was heating up. It was T-shirt weather. The windows were open on the London buses. Drinks then dinner then more drinks, followed by coffee and vanilla cream cannoli at Bar Italia, the neon lights illuminating our sweaty sheen. Walking all the way home because it felt so good to be outside. Teenagers, not yet off school for the summer, stalking the streets and waiting for their lives to appear around the next corner. The inviting mystery of a private square: negotiating the spiked black railings and climbing in. Tumbling down beneath the rhododendrons and sharing a spliff, the giant flower heads translucent in the glow of a lamp post. Mila's laugh. Jess's new tattoo smiling at me in flashes: the whiskery face of a leopard, eyes as reproachful and knowing as her own.

I was like a junkie for contact from Henry, which, though increasing in frequency, was still as unpredictable as the roll of a dice. One week, we would meet on a Monday night, and then he would text me the next day at work asking if I was free to reconvene again that evening; then another week would go by where I didn't hear from him at all. Far from being distressed by this emotional turbulence, I was hooked. I felt certain that he would tell me he loved me any day now. I needed to hear him say it. When he did, I would know for sure the depth of my own feelings, which presently blew so tempestuously through me it was impossible to pin them down.

Painfully cinematic moments would pass between us: caught under a plane tree in the rain, an electric catch of the other's eye over some exquisitely mundane task, holding hands in the back of a taxi; and I would stare at him, my eyes boring into the beautiful bones of his face, thinking *say it, say it, say it.*

My mornings before work, previously dedicated to writing (or at least some form of productivity, whether creative or domestic), became neglected and then abandoned altogether; replaced by lie-ins, hangovers and brunches in the nearest greasy spoon, last night's make-up still glittering around my eyes.

One morning in Jess's bed: ironed sheets, the smell of lavender. I stirred, half-awake, just enough to register that I had evaded a headache, but that nausea snaked threateningly through my innards. Nothing another couple of hours of sleep wouldn't sort out. Jess had got up already, as she always did. Mila was probably still asleep next door. The sudden and importunate sound of hoovering. Maybe just some spilled coffee grounds; it would end soon. It didn't.

'Morning, babe,' I shouted, barefoot in the hallway.

Jess was fully dressed, on all fours, scraping the nozzle of the hoover along the crease where the carpet met the wall. She glanced up at me.

'Fuck. Sorry. My mum's coming round,' she said, squinting at the skirting board.

'Oh, shit.'

'I know. Completely forgot it was today.'

'Shit. Shall I go?'

'No, no, stay. She'd love to see you.'

'OK. Can I borrow something to wear? I've only got my dress.'

'Of course, babe. Help yourself.'

'Right. I'd better get showered then. Have you told Mila?'

Mila appeared in the doorway of her own room, her headscarf slipped halfway back over her hair, her face puffy and pissed off.

'It's a Saturday,' she said, deadpan.

'Lin's coming over,' I told her. Jess continued to vanquish every molecule of dust from the apartment.

'Are you kidding?' said Mila.

'Nope,' I said. 'Bagsy the shower first.'

Mila groaned and retreated back into her bedroom. I disrobed, showered and dressed up as a pseudo-Jess: Katherine Hepburn slacks that were too long for me, and a black turtleneck. Lin, Jess's mother, arrived twenty minutes later.

Lin scared us. I think she scared everyone. Dyl once saw her walk into a room and whispered to me, 'Yeesh. It's like the Kriat Yam Suph.' To which I had obviously asked what the hell he was talking about, and he explained he meant the parting of the Red Sea. He had a point. Her presence seemed to ripple the atmosphere around her; the vulnerable sensing a need to flee for cover. The girls and I still giggled, with a disbelief that had ripened with memory, about the parents' evening at which Lin had made our maths teacher, Mr McIntosh, cry.

In all the years Jess and I had been friends, I had still not graduated to hugging terms with her mum. Jess's own maternal hug was so perfunctory I felt sad to see it: my friend's willowy arms reaching around her mother, lingering there long enough for Lin to clear her throat, Jess craving some kind of intimate connection despite being raised on a diet of polite propriety that never, not even for a moment, forgot itself.

'I made fresh jasmine tea,' said Jess, tucking a non-existent strand of hair back into place.

'Water is fine, thank you, honey.'

The table between us was spotless. God knows how early Jess had risen to clean up.

I envied the girls' apartment. The marriage of Jess's perfectionism and Mila's vibrancy; the whole place so unmistakably feminine. Shelves were lined with Jess's oud-scented candles and thick history books from Mila's time at Edinburgh. A well-stocked fridge of nut milks and fresh fish. Pleasingly clashing throws on the sofa: an old batik that had belonged to Mila's grandmother, and a luxury herringbone cashmere of Jess's. Nights in at the girls' place never felt like you were missing out on whatever other fun the city had to offer, a syndrome I often experienced up in my annexe, leaning out of the window with a wistful cigarette. And yet, nestled in their living room of an evening – the window thrown all the way up, waxy magnolias bowing in, sharing a second bottle of wine, the easy conversation – I felt fourteen again: demoted to a different maths set, losing my grasp on the three-way handshake that sealed the deal of our friendship. I pictured them sharing meals in front of the TV after long days at work, swapping myriad micro-data on the prosaic intricacies of their lives. Discussing real, adult things, like company meetings and which end of the tube station platform is best for securing an empty seat on the train. My chipped-in anecdotes about something funny Clara or Jem had done, the cute videos I showed them on my phone – these felt so professionally spurious compared with their daily routines of commutes and offices. The girls always laughed at my stories, always cooed at my videos, but with the air of a family member swapping casual, unimportant gossip.

'How are things with you, Joni?' asked Lin, boredom dashed so thinly within the politeness it was almost untraceable.

'Fine, thank you,' I said, with what was almost a bow of the head. Jess spotted me and smirked behind her mother's back.

'Are you still a nanny?'

A perfectly reasonable question – why did it feel like an insult?

'Yeah, yes I am,' I said. 'I love it. The children are really wonderful, so fascinating. You can learn so much from young children, I think.'

Lin said nothing, as if expecting me to not only elaborate but empirically prove this statement to be true. Jess joined us at the table, with tea for herself and me, and water with ice and a slice of lime for Lin.

'How are you, Mum?' she said, sitting next to me.

Lin took a few healthy gulps of water and allowed an ice cube to fall on to her tongue before answering, her mouth full. 'I'm great,' she said, before biting down onto the ice, the crunch making me wince. 'I ran a 10k this morning in under an hour.'

'Wow,' I said.

'Not by much, but I'm getting there. I'd really like to shave it down to fifty minutes.'

'How's work?' said Jess.

'Work is work,' said Lin, eviscerating the ice cube and swallowing its remains. 'So, what's new with you girls? What's the latest?'

Jess and I looked at each other.

'Er . . .' I began.

'How's that Jewish friend of yours, Joni? What's his name? I liked him.'

'Mum, you can't say that.'

'What?'

'Jewish.'

'Why not? Isn't he Jewish?'

'No, he is, but—'

'Well then, what's the problem?'

'It's just problematic to refer to someone solely by their race,' said Jess, before adding, 'I think.'

'What do you think, Joni?'

'Um. I don't think Dyl would mind that much, but—'

'Dylan!' said Lin. 'That's his name. What's he up to?'

'Second year of his PhD,' I told her.

'In what?'

'English. Creative writing and journalism.'

'Is he any good?'

'Yes. Yes, he's brilliant.'

'Yes. I liked him. I have a good eye for that sort of thing.'

'I'm seeing him tonight, actually,' I said, and made to get up, as if 'tonight' were imminent. 'I'll tell him you said, um, hello.'

Jess eyeballed me; I knew she didn't want me to leave, but the tea had awoken a rabid hunger in me and I had a sudden and urgent craving for ramen. I said goodbye to Lin, and ran into Mila's room as I was leaving. She was back in bed.

'Go in there and help her,' I whispered.

'I feel like death.'

'Same.'

'She'll smell it on me. I still stink of booze.'

'Go!'

The day was gorgeous; the sun, sights and sounds all a little too loud in my fragile state. I wove my way down to the good ramen place in Peckham, and slurped my noodles at the counter in the window.

Shall we meet for a drink beforehand? I texted Dyl. The plan was for us to have dinner with his parents at a semi-fancy place in the West End. He replied with a thumbs-up emoji, as well as a tricolour and a house, letting me know which pub to convene at on Dean Street.

At Fiona's, I showered before changing back into the clothes Jess had lent me that morning, with the addition of some dangly earrings and red lipstick. In the mirror was another girl. Jess's sophisticated clothing appeared to have the opposite effect on me: I looked like a teenager playing dress-up in her older sister's, or possibly even mother's, garb. The androgynous shapes, which looked so elegant on my friend, seemed blocky on my short torso. I stepped into some high heels, which helped, and rolled myself a cigarette for a little added *je ne sais quoi*.

Dyl was ten minutes late, and when he arrived, he stood back from me and declared loudly, 'Those aren't your clothes.'

He was not sober.

'Happy birthday!' I said.

We necked a pint and a half each, me filling the air with superfluous detail of my previous night out with the girls, before wandering out through Soho and down Piccadilly to meet his parents. We were passing the front of the Albany on our right. I said nothing to Dyl, but stole a glance up at the grand edifice, my heart constricting with an emotion clean in the middle between hope and dread.

The evening was balmy and golden; men in suits trickled down from Mayfair, their ties removed and top buttons undone. We fought our way upstream through the dolled-up trios on their way towards Old Compton Street.

'Hang on, I want one more cig,' said Dyl, grabbing my arm and swinging me into the recess of a doorway.

'We're already late,' I said.

'They'll be later.'

Our bodies were incredibly close to each other in the arch of the single door, and it struck me that before Ely, before that night we had still not discussed, I wouldn't even have noticed. In this moment, my senses seemed to sharpen to his every bodily output: I could smell the spirits that had preceded our beers, on his breath; I winced at the sight of his massacred nail beds. I stole the cigarette from him and took a drag. Here, too, the moistness repulsed me in an entirely novel way. The strange thing was, I wanted to tell him. The most unnatural part of it all was not being able to say, *Hey, it's so weird: I'm incredibly physically aware of you all of a sudden!* Censorship was not an explored feature of our friendship. Since neither of us had been able to say, *So, we had sex,* it appeared more and more things were remaining at the threshold between thought and speech. If we carried on like this, would our friendship eventually stagnate? Would we ultimately become amiable but formal with one another? I made a vow to discuss it with him tonight: after supper, once we had said goodbye to his parents, I would expose it to the air.

*

David and Sharon were, as Dyl had prophesied, late.

'Let's order a bottle of something,' said Dyl, at our table.

'Shouldn't we wait?'

And then there they were, taking up the whole room somehow: his parents. We could hear them across the entire restaurant: David's warm and booming 'Good evening!' as if addressing a packed theatre, and Sharon announcing, 'We have a reservation, it's my son's birthday!'

Hugs and exclamations, both of Sharon's bejewelled hands on my face, a long and thoroughly debated perusal of the wine list, before at length we settled into salty focaccia dipped in oil and balsamic, and large, delicious glasses of burgundy. Dyl also ordered a double gin and tonic. Everyone's mouth was full of either bread or wine for the first garrulous thirty minutes of catching up, which was how long it took for Sharon and David to settle on what they wanted to order (Sharon couldn't decide whether she wanted Wiener schnitzel or *choucroute d'Alsace*, so she ordered the schnitzel for herself and the *choucroute* for David, on condition that he swap with her if she so bade).

'Joni!' Sharon finally rounded on me. 'What are you writing? Poetry, still? Tell me everything.'

I hesitated. David's eyes, which were Dyl's, peered kindly across the table at me; his face expressing all the compassion of a man who is both apologising for his wife's intensity and madly in love with it.

'Yeah, some poetry, still. Some of which I'm experimenting with turning into songs. It's just difficult because I don't have access to a piano at Fiona's place.'

'The shrink doesn't have a piano?' cut in Sharon.

'No.'

She barked a little laugh as if a point had been proven.

'And then a couple of short stories,' I went on. 'I don't know. I was feeling very creative at the beginning of summer and now . . . It's hard trying to write every morning knowing I've got to go and pick the kids up from school any minute.'

'*Plus ça change*!' said Sharon. 'Welcome to every female

artist's life! Wait until you have your own. *Then* try and find time to create. No, you must be disciplined, Joni – now, while you're young. How extraordinary that you've *shackled* yourself to the regime of childcare – what does your shrink have to say about *that*? You think you're *busy*? You have all the time in the world! All this time stretched out before you. You both do.' She turned to Dyl. 'And yet this one claims he can't find time to jump on a bus to come see me.'

'I'm doing a PhD, what more do you want?' said Dyl, smiling at her.

'When I did my undergraduate year in California,' Sharon began, and launched into a long story that at first was about her annoying roommate Diana, but ended up revealing how one of her college professors at UCLA had once lunged at her while they shared a joint outside the AV building, describing in detail the scratchy feel of his thick beard around her lips.

'And I *kicked* him!' she declared. 'I kicked him right in the shin and I said "Shame on you."' She looked quite irate. Sharon's stories always seemed to transport her right back into the scene.

'But Mum,' said Dyl, who had been watching her, a little exasperated. 'What's that got to do with us?'

Outside, I thanked David for the meal. He waved a genial hand and said, 'Please, please.' Dyl's trajectory from the restaurant door to the kerb, where we installed his parents safely into their cab, was not quite linear. He was flushed and slurring a little; not that I was much better by now.

'Come and see us!' they both said from the back of the taxi. 'We'll invite your parents, too, Joni, it's been too long!'

'That'd be great,' I said. 'Thank you!'

'Happy birthday, my Dylan,' said Sharon, a little teary. '*Haim sheli.*'

'Happy birthday, darling,' said David.

'Where shall we go now?' said Dyl, once the car had pulled away.

We ended up in the basement of the St Moritz Club, a cavern-like little dive bar where you could reliably go for a dance. I texted the others and invited them out.

Still hungover, mate, sorry from Mila.

On a date. Maybe see you later, I rather hope not – this guy is Adonis from Paddy.

Just finishing food – see you in twenty from Niall. Jess arrived not long after.

Staking our claim on a little booth, we hid our bags under our jackets and took to the dance floor. The DJ was playing mostly ska records, which had the effect of making me feel drunker than I was, or possibly informing me (accurately) that I was very drunk. Niall was an extremely pleasing dancing companion, partly because it was such a delightful surprise that he enjoyed it so much. Niall looked, to the untrained eye, like a square, but he came to life on the dance floor. He let loose. It was also useful for me and Jess to be accompanied by two men, staving off any unwanted advances.

The crowd in the club made me feel old. Newly legal boys and girls, probably born post-Millennium, boogied self-consciously around us. One kid with a bucket hat was trying to get the girls' attention by performing distinct rave dance moves, throwing his hands in the air on a pulsating beat, completely out of time with the funky reggae that was playing. He kept accidentally knocking into Niall, who politely ignored him. The boys of his age apparently couldn't be seen to dance without affecting some kind of irony, while the girls danced pouting and holding each other's hands. I felt a wave of affection towards them and smiled at the nearest duo. They looked at me like I was insane and then giggled to each other. One of them had braces.

Jess and I grabbed a couple of overpriced Red Stripes and took a breather.

'How was it with your mum?' I yelled into her ear.

She rolled her eyes and downed half the tin of beer. I laughed.

'It just seems that no matter how much I avoid the subject,' she said, 'it always comes up.'

I nodded sympathetically. I knew she was referring to the subject of her own sexuality, a topic on which Lin possessed an endless trove of barbed commentary.

'Maybe she went through a bisexual phase at uni and has repressed that part of herself,' I pondered. 'That's why she's so angry about it.'

Jess looked at me like I'd just denied climate change.

'Sorry.' I clasped her wrist. 'Was that rude?'

She shrugged. 'I don't know. Not unless I've internalised her homophobia. I guess' – she lifted her beer to her mouth, freeing herself from my grasp – 'I guess maybe you just don't have to analyse everything so much.'

'Fuck, sorry, babe. Fiona's rubbed off on me.'

There was a scream, and sudden shouting: the animalistic bass notes of male aggression. We scrambled out of our booth to find the dance floor parted, a heavy bouncer dragging a bloody-nosed Dyl towards the stairs. Bucket Hat was being held up by one of his mates, his lip bleeding, a few of the boys baiting Dyl with provocative yells. Niall was trying to calm things down, one hand on Bucket Hat's shoulder in full rational-dad mode.

'Shit.' I turned to Jess, who was looking on, similarly horrified.

We grabbed our things and Niall and left, finding Dyl on the street in a stand-off with the bouncer.

'Are you fucking serious?' he shouted. 'That jumped-up little twat punches me and you're throwing *me* out?'

The bouncer was looking disconcertingly pleased with himself. 'What you gonna do about it?' he said. He was three times the size of Dyl.

'Come on, mate,' said Niall, coming between them.

'Fuck you. You fucking *bouncer*,' Dyl spat.

'Dyl!' I said, despairingly.

'What's that supposed to mean, then?' said the bouncer, heating up.

'You know exactly what it means,' said Dyl, being edged away slowly by Niall. 'You're rock hard for the tiny little smidgen of power you wield over others.' His voice was thick. Scarlet blood was gushing down his face.

'Sort out your friend,' the bouncer said to Jess and me.

'We will,' I said. 'We're taking him home now.'

'Fuck's sake,' said Jess, nearly laughing as we traipsed our way up Wardour Street.

'Little shit,' said Dyl, wiping his face on his sleeve.

'What exactly happened?' I asked.

Niall answered. 'The boy in the hat kept knocking into us. And then there was a sort of domino effect, and I fell into Dyl, and Dyl crashed into one of the girls. And she made a bit of a fuss about the whole thing, which was ridiculous because she was ostensibly fine.'

'Attention seeking,' Dyl chipped in.

'Yes. A real overreaction.' Niall went on: 'Anyway, I think the one in the hat thought he'd get all macho and defend her entirely untarnished honour, and he just bloody swung at Dyl. No warning. Little coward.'

'I just felt this fucking *smack* and tasted blood. Is it bad, by the way? God, it hurts. I haven't been punched in the face for years, I forgot how much it hurts.'

Soho Square stank of piss. It was still warm, the air velvety and humid. We sat Dyl on an empty park bench and tried to clean him up a bit. Jess soon made her excuses and headed off for the last tube home. After a while, Niall, too, seemed to lose his conversational momentum and, after making us promise we'd take care of each other, left.

'Shall we go to Milroy's?' said Dyl, the two of us side by side on the bench.

'I don't know if they'll let you in, mate.'

'I'm not that drunk anymore. That dickhead sobered me right up.'

'You're covered in blood, you moron.'

'Oh.'

'Ugh,' Dyl groaned. 'Mate. I'm twenty-six! It's not even my birthday anymore. I'm just a twenty-six-year-old with blood all over me. In fucking *Soho*.'

I looked at the statue of Charles II and tried to conjure up some witticism comparing him to Dyl, but couldn't think of one.

'Mila was telling me about the Saturn Return,' I ventured.

'The what?'

'The Saturn Return. So, when you're born, Saturn is in a certain position of its orbit, in relation to Earth, and then, because Saturn is so much further away from the sun than us, its orbit is way bigger, and it takes around twenty-seven years for it to reach that same position again.'

'So?'

'So I think it means that we all go through a change every twenty-seven-ish years. Because like, Saturn, it's really powerful.'

'Bullshit,' said Dyl. 'Why not Jupiter Return, in that case? Or Mercury? The orbital period just fits with societal expectations and pressures imposed on us in our late twenties.'

'Maybe,' I said.

'I just need to get out of the city,' he said. 'That's all.'

'Soon,' I said. 'I've almost got everyone pinned down for Cornwall.'

'"Where the slate falls sheer into the tide."'

'What's that?'

'Betjeman.'

For a moment, I let myself picture the rocky cliffs and gorse-covered fields.

Then Dyl's tone changed. 'Phil?' he said, scratching one of his trainers over a drop of dried blood on the other.

'Yeah?'

'Is it weird that I keep thinking about Marla?'

'About Marla?' I said.

'Yeah. No one's deleted any of her social media; it's still there, like a weird shrine. I keep looking at it.'

'Shit. That is weird.'

'Fuck, I'm perverted, aren't I?' he said.

'No,' I said, hastily. 'No, I mean it's weird that no one has taken it down.'

'Oh, right. Yeah,' he said, sounding relieved. 'I guess it's all we have left.'

'Christ,' I said.

'Yeah.'

I should have talked to him. If I had just acknowledged that things had got a little weird between us it would have smashed the tension. He might have even opened up to me about what the hell was going on with him. I should have said *'So'*, and he would have turned to me on the bench and said *'So'* back, and we would have been in hysterics at the relief of it all. But instead, I said, 'Come on then, we're still technically celebrating. Let's go get a nightcap. I reckon they'll let you in at Trisha's.'

9

Lighter days. I began to feel increasingly claustrophobic in my attic and yearned more and more for the countryside and the sea. I spent hours wandering London aimlessly until the time came to pick the kids up from school. I would meander through residential streets to the Heath, tracing elaborate loops with my footsteps, trying to picture my routes from a bird's-eye view and create interesting patterns across the fields. Sometimes I'd bounce down Malden Road into Camden, notebook and biro in hand, and find a cheap coffee and a seat by the canal, scribbling the odd paragraph of nonsense.

It was one of those days, a bright and hazy Friday.

Fiona's voice came calling up the stairs. 'Joni?' she cried, her tone agitated.

I leaned half my body through the door. 'Yeah?'

'Could you come and give me a hand? It's the computer.'

Moments later, I found Fiona at the kitchen table, regarding her laptop as though it was a prelinguistic child crying out for some unknown need.

'Ah,' she said, seeing me. 'Thank you, hen. I'm going mad.'

'I don't know what good I'll be,' I said, leaning over to view the screen. 'I'm utterly hopeless with technology.'

'It's just bloody Skype again. It's logged me out, and I can't for the life of me remember my user name.'

'Oh, OK. That's fine. We can find it in your emails.'

Fiona allowed me to lean down and amend the problem, at last sighing when the application made its happy little trill to welcome her back in.

'Superstar,' she said. 'I'm having a big catch-up with Jenny tonight.'

She insisted on making me a frothy coffee in return.

'You're glowing,' she said, out of nowhere, as if seeing me for the first time.

'No,' I said. 'Probably just still red from the shower.'

She smiled her knowing smile at me.

'You up to much this weekend?' I asked.

'Yes,' she said. 'I'll be working on the talk I'm giving in Amsterdam.'

'Oh yeah, at the conference?'

'Indeed.'

'Do you get nervous? Talking in front of that many people?'

'No. Public speaking I can do. It's writing the thing that's the challenge. Trying to remain phlegmatic on a subject about which I care so passionately.'

'Which is . . .?' I winced apologetically.

'Addiction.'

'Of course.'

'And you?'

'This weekend? Seeing Henry tonight—'

'No,' she interrupted. 'Are you writing?'

'Oh,' I said. 'A bit.'

'Wait!' she declared suddenly, standing up. 'I saw they're holding a competition in the paper – I cut it out for you. Let me find it.'

'Oh, that's so kind of you, Fiona, but—'

'You should enter, Joni,' she said, opening one of the

kitchen drawers and squinting down at it. 'Where've I put the bloody thing?'

'Don't worry,' I said. 'Honestly, I'm sure I wouldn't be right for it anyway.'

'There's a monetary prize.' She flicked through some cut-out recipes. 'Few thousand quid.'

'Oh, shit.'

She smiled. 'Oh, shit, indeed. I'll find it later. I'll leave it on the stairs and you can have a look.'

*

Later, I was sagging out of my window, smoking. The plan was to meet Henry that night after work; he was taking me to see the Philharmonic perform *Tristan und Isolde* at the Royal Albert Hall. Surely tonight was the night – the epitome of romance, not to mention the expense. It was still only half past twelve, the sun warming the roof tiles from its apex. On a whim, I decided to head over to Terry and Raf's house early to set up some sort of after-school activity for the kids: maybe a quiz or a treasure hunt in the garden. *Yes.* This would keep them – and me – outdoors for at least an hour. I could write little cryptic clues and hide chocolates and pick-n-mix in flowerpots and branches. It was exactly the sort of thing I would have loved as a child, but no one had ever done for me.

Sunny schooldays called for Belle and Sebastian, and I skipped along with *If You're Feeling Sinister* in my ears, open to the minutiae of gifts my habitual walk had to offer this afternoon: a waterfall of hair as a girl tied her shoelace; the light through crinkled horse chestnut leaves; the whiff of cinnamon and bacon as I walked past a café. In Tesco, I filled my basket with penny sweets and a multipack of mini chocolate bars. I even picked up some neon-coloured stationery, in which I knew the kids would be far less interested than the sucrose-based prizes, but which would look more virtuous to their parents once they got home and all the edible treasures had been devoured.

At the little fox knocker of the front door, I paused my music just as 'New York Catcher' came on, and wound my headphones into a little spool from which they would undoubtedly stray in my pocket. I had already planned to set up at the kitchen table, from where, through the large French window, I could spot appropriate outdoor features (the bird bath, the bed of tulips) and pen rhyming riddles to accompany each treasure:

> *Your next clue shall be found, if you can think*
> *Of the place where Wren or Robin would take a drink*

It was the sort of mild brain exercise I enjoyed, writing without self-consciousness or effort. I dumped my bag in the hallway and headed straight for the kitchen to get to work. The door was closed, which was unusual – the door from the hallway to the kitchen was one of those vestigial features of the house that no one used. I opened it without thinking, without hearing the noises coming from the other side.

'Oh fuck!' I blurted out, and immediately slammed the door shut again. I fumbled for my bag and left the house as quickly as possible, fox bouncing on his hinge, marching back down the street to – where? The school? It was still only two o'clock. Clara and Jem wouldn't be out for an hour. Just away, away. I ducked into a café and bought a bottle of water, sinking into a corner armchair. *Fuck.* The two pairs of eyes that had spun to meet mine seemed to have followed me here; I felt exposed, ashamed. I lifted a hand to my brow and let hot tears break behind it. My phone was ringing in my pocket. *Terry Mobile.* I flicked it on to silent and placed it with unnecessary force onto the table in front of me, waiting for the ringing to stop. The two women at the next table turned and shot me an unfriendly glance, before continuing their conversation. They were having exactly the kind of discussion you would expect of two women in this part of London, in this café, on a Friday afternoon.

'I mean, I haven't even had time to have a massage this week,' said one, her voice creaking: slack with privilege, as if she was used to having someone else say her words for her.

'Oh my God,' said the other.

I hated them. A text flashed up on my phone. I read it from the table top.

Joni, many apologies, wasn't expecting you so early. Please call back. It's not—

I would have to open the message to read on. Without lifting the phone from the table, I slid one tentative index finger across the screen and read:

Joni, many apologies, wasn't expecting you so early. Please call back. It's not what you think. Pyotr is an old friend I haven't seen since I was a child and is visiting from New York for just a few days. Things are complicated. I'd appreciate it if you didn't mention anything to Raf. I will deal with. T x

'Ha,' I said aloud. The women looked at me like I was a dangerous lunatic. *It's not what you think.* What did she think I thought? Not ten minutes ago, when I had opened that stupid door, Terry had been standing against the kitchen counter, her arms stretched upwards over the cupboards, as if she had been reaching for some canned good at the back of a shelf. Her designer jeans were around her ankles, and attached to the back of her, like an enormous parasite, was a man, monstrously rutting away. He had one hand out of sight and the other pulling Terry's hair, so that her head was yanked back and her neck looked painfully bent. He was short, and pinkish, and had fair hair turned a shade darker by sweat. When they had both turned to look at me, startled as animals at gunfire, I saw that he had pale blue eyes and a wispy goatee that threatened to be ginger. But the main, glaring fact about this man, this frantically grinding imp, was that he was not Terry's husband, Raf. The father of her children. Raf, for whom I felt a surge of fondness in this moment. Sweet, kind Raf, with his old Converse and his big laugh. Raf, who was responsible for giving Clara and Jem their dimples, their long, dark eyelashes, their dainty feet. I let the pathos of their innocence flood me with emotion, leaning forward so that my hair was covering most of my face, and cried quietly into the back of my sleeve.

Fuck you, Terry. 'It's not what you think.' Oh, sorry, you weren't just fucking another man? Or you mean it's not a full-blown affair, just some casual sex in your family home? In the room where your children eat their meals and do colouring and homework? I didn't reply to her message.

I took Clara and Jem to the playground. Though I was sure Terry would have left the house by now, I couldn't bring myself to make orange squash and crumpets in the space where I had seen what I had seen. I presented the bag of treats to them as presents – so much for the treasure hunt – and they were suitably thrilled. I watched proudly as they shared their hoard with other children.

Worst day ever, I texted Henry. *Can't wait for a drink.*

The sky was nectarine in the west and cobalt in the east when I took the kids home, just in time to feed them some supper before their dad got in. He came home earlier on Fridays, meaning playtime and food were my responsibility, but he would take over for the bath/bed/story section of the evening. The ghost of my memory hung by the kitchen counter, and I gave the area a wide berth – grabbing forks from the drying rack for the kids' salmon and peas in order to avoid the cutlery drawer.

'Nanny Jo?' said Jem, leaning solemnly into the steeple of his tiny hands. 'I'm full.'

'Finish your peas.'

'I can't!' he said, clutching his stomach.

'Come on, three more mouthfuls and you're done.'

'I've finished mine,' said Clara.

'Well done, love.'

Jem heaved and sighed the last mounds of peas into his mouth, before sitting up straight and asking, 'What's for pudding?'

There were three fruit yoghurts left in the fridge. Clara went for the strawberry and Jem the raspberry, leaving me the apricot. I heard the scrape of Raf's key in the lock, and steeled myself. On a whim, I started tickling Jem on the bench next to me, stirring up a cloud of giggles on the back of which I hoped I could float through the next five minutes of pleasantries.

'Hey, guys!' called Raf, wheeling his bike into the hallway, his glasses slightly askew.

'Hi, Papa,' said Clara into her yoghurt.

'Hi, Papa!' Jem echoed.

They didn't get up. They loved their father – you could tell by the pride they took in using the Antillean word he had taught them for *Daddy*; you could see it in their eyes when enraptured by some goofy stunt performed for their amusement, and hear it in their peals of laughter when he would grab one of them by a wrist and an ankle and twirl them around as weightlessly as a doll. However, whether it was simply their ages or some fundamental difference between male and female parents, bearing witness to their respective welcome-homes for Raf and Terry was a bit pitiful. From even the furthest corner of the house, they would bound to the front door to greet their mother, descending upon her like carrion, desperate to ingest her. On the evenings their father came home first, they seldom stopped whatever they were doing, and occasionally even expressed disappointment that he wasn't Terry. I had seen him deal with this, sometimes semi-mockingly – *Gee, thanks, guys, what a warm welcome!* – and sometimes sincerely – *Hey, how do you think it makes me feel when you don't get up to say hello?*

I never knew how to respond as the third party in this scenario. As time passed and our intimacy solidified, I felt more justified in trying to play my own small part in their emotional education. I had taken to standing up for him, both in secret – *Daddy's had a long day, he'll probably need a big cuddle when he gets in!* – and in person – *Guys! Dad's here! Go say hi!*

Today, I could barely look at him. I stood up from the table, slightly embarrassed to be eating the small 'no-bits!' yoghurt that he had bought for his children.

'Hi, Raf!' I threw in his direction before occupying myself with the dishwasher.

He came through to the kitchen. It was a hot day, and he had generous dark ovals of sweat under his arms.

'Hey, pickles.' He kissed Clara and Jem. 'How was today?' he asked me, his smiling face glistening.

I looked up from the dials of the machine – he was standing centimetres from the scene of the crime.

'Yeah! Great! It was so lovely and warm, we had a nice long time at the playground, didn't we?'

'Nanny Jo gave us loads of sweets!' said Jem.

'Aw, well, it is Friday.' I laughed nervously. 'But we shared them all, didn't we?'

'Still ate all your supper, I hope?' said Raf, cupping a hand around Jem's cheek.

'We had salmon and peas,' said Clara.

'Yum!' said Raf. 'Oh, Joni – did you manage to hand in the permissions slip for swimming?'

'Yep, we gave it to Miss Kelly, didn't we?' I said brightly to Clara, realising I was directing all conversation through the children. I forced myself to look Raf in the eye.

'Got anything nice planned for the weekend?' I asked.

'We do, actually! It's our anniversary, so we're going to the theatre and then for a late dinner at some eye-wateringly expensive place Terry's found.'

'Oh nice,' I said. 'I didn't realise. Happy anniversary!'

'Thank you. Twelve years. Makes me feel old.'

'Congrats. I didn't – um, do you need me to watch these two?'

'Oh no, they'll be at my mum's, don't worry.'

I laughed again, possibly too much. Raf looked at me, a little confused.

'Well, have a lovely time!' I said. 'Be good, you two.'

I left with moist kisses from both of the kids fresh on my cheeks.

*

Henry and I sat opposite each other in the underbelly of the Royal Albert Hall. A bottle of deliciously cool Laurent-Perrier lay tilted in an ice bucket between us.

'It's not funny,' I said, wiping champagne from the

corner of my mouth, which was curling traitorously upwards the more Henry laughed. He had gone from open-mouthed shock at my discovery, to chuckling at my description of the gremlin Pyotr, to full-on cackling into his cupped hands.

'What's so hilarious about it?' I said. 'She's having an affair, and it's their anniversary this weekend! Those poor kids . . .'

He righted himself. 'It's not her, it's you,' he said.

'Me?'

'The way you're narrating it. Don't take this the wrong way, but you sound like you're doing bad soap acting.'

He laughed even more.

'What?!'

'Sorry. You're just getting very worked up.' He took my hand. 'Look, why do you care so much? Don't you think you're overreacting, just a little bit? I mean, people have affairs. My parents sure fucking did. And, you know, it's not like they're your kids.'

'That's not—' I began, but I didn't know how to respond. It had suddenly struck me how good it was to see Henry laughing. Properly laughing. As he wiped his eyes, sitting across from me in this candlelit mahogany bar, his cheeks flushed as the last convulsions of mirth left his body, I realised: I hadn't seen him laugh like this all year. Smile, yes. A grin, the odd polite phonetic *ha ha*, a joyless chuckle, yes – but nothing real. It was a huge relief: finally, after all my strained efforts, I had accidentally made him happy.

We nestled into our velvet box, the lights in the concert hall lowering before the music struck up. Just a minute and a half into the prelude, there was a crescendo of spectacular intensity, which then released into the saddest sound I'd ever heard. I snatched up Henry's hand with such urgency that he turned to me in surprise, and proceeded to wipe away the tears which were running freely down my cheeks.

Afterwards, back at the Albany, we lay facing each other on the bed.

'That moment when you grabbed my hand,' he said, stroking my hair down my back.

'Yes?'

'It's very famous. It's one of the most notoriously heart-wrenching moments in all of classical music.'

'Oh,' I said, disappointed. 'So I only like the really obvious parts? Are you trying to tell me that I'm a philistine?'

He smiled. 'No. No, the opposite. It's famous because Wagner invented a new type of harmony.'

'How can you invent a new type of harmony?'

'Well . . . you know how chords tend to be tertian – a chord is three notes? In intervals of a third?'

'Yes, Henry, I have a basic grasp of chords, thank you.'

'Sorry, I was just—'

'Being patronising.'

'Yes, sorry.'

'Go on.'

'Up until then, no one – in European music, anyway – had really thought to make chords that weren't in thirds. It wasn't done. Chords were meant to sound, well, nice.'

'Right.'

'*Non*-tertian harmony was becoming more fashionable, but Wagner was the first one to really employ it, so they named the structure of the chord after his opera. It's called the Tristan Chord.'

'So, he invented a chord? No one had ever played those exact notes together before?'

'Well, I'm sure they had. I suppose you could say he got dibs on it.'

'Finders, keepers.' I rolled on to my back, looking up at the glass chandelier, Henry's hand falling on to my hip. 'So what is it exactly, notation-wise?'

'Help. I *think* the Tristan chord is F . . . B . . .' He squinted his eyes and spread his fingers across my stomach as if along an imaginary keyboard, tapping the place where each note would be as he named them. '. . . D sharp and G sharp? But it can be any chord made up of those intervals: augmented fourth, augmented sixth and augmented ninth above a bass note.'

'You're clever,' I said, and kissed him.

*

'I think I'm in love with Henry,' I said over my full English the next morning, Mila and Jess looking back at me. It was truly brimming over my edges, this feeling. Love. *Shit.* I was in love with Henry. Saying it aloud had released some tiny, neglected valve inside me, and I began to cry.

'Sorry,' I said, cupping my hands over my face.

'Steady on.' Jess was laughing. 'Hey. Hey, you're alright.' She jumped up and shuffled into my side of our booth, squeezing me.

'I'm in love, too,' said Mila.

'Don't make this about you,' said Jess.

Mila ignored her. 'I haven't told you guys yet. Me and Niall, we've said the L-word.'

'You and Niall have been dancing around this since Edinburgh,' said Jess.

'That's great, babe,' I offered, dabbing my face.

'Thank you, Joni. Correct response. It happened last

week. We went to the funfair on Blackheath and he told me at the top of the Ferris wheel.'

'How saccharine,' said Jess.

'It was so cute. He's not a big fan of heights. Did you know that about him? He was squeezing my hand so tight it hurt. And then we were at the top, you can see right over into the city from there, it was amazing. The whole skyline kind of melting into the haze. I was like, "I love London." And he was like, "I love *you*."'

'Barf,' said Jess.

Mila threw her one of her most formidable looks – a look that had saved our skins when we were teenagers being picked on by scary kids from other schools. Seldom did she turn it on us.

'Babe.' Jess reached over and took her hand. 'I'm happy for you. Really.'

'Thank you,' said Mila, reaching her other hand across the table for mine, so we were all joined together. 'I told him I love him too. It's crazy. All this time we've known each other.'

'About fucking time,' said Jess.

'Can I tell you something weird?' said Mila.

Jess and I nodded avidly.

'I feel like I've always loved him.'

'Oh, babe.' I said. 'Since uni? I mean, we all thought you liked him.'

'No,' said Mila. 'Before then. Retroactively. I feel like I've loved him throughout his childhood and adolescence, right up until we first clapped eyes on each other in the bloody student union bar. I just hadn't met him yet. It doesn't make sense, I know.'

'Deep,' I said.

Jess cleared her throat; we had trespassed beyond the comfortable limits of her arena of sentimentality. 'So. When are you going to tell Henry, Jo?' she said.

'God,' I said. 'I've no idea.'

*

On the stairs was the newspaper cutting Fiona had promised to leave for me:

THE CHRONICLE ANNUAL
SHORT STORY COMPETITION
First Prize: £3,000
Second Prize: £2,000
Third Prize: £1,000
Admissions judged by our expert team
of authors and critics.
Deadline: 1st October.

I tucked it into the back pages of my notebook. It was time to call Dyl.

'Yo.' He answered after just half a ring.

'Expecting someone?' I asked.

'Maybe.'

'So, I need to talk to you. That night at my parents' house—'

'Oh. Good. I was wondering when we were gonna talk about it.'

'What?'

'What?'

'Do we need to talk about it?' I said.

'You just brought it up.'

'Fuck, no. Listen,' I said. Deep breath.

'What? Oh, God, what, Phil? I hate *Listen*.'

'It's good. It's good news, I think.'

'Out with it.'

'I'm – I do, in fact, am, in fact, in love. With Henry.' There.

'Oh.' He sounded relieved, possibly disappointed. 'I thought it was something more dramatic.'

'Well, that's it.'

'Congratulations. It's great for the complexion, I've heard.'

'So you can't tell anyone, Dyl. About what happened at my parents', OK? It's serious now.'

He made a noise, like a sigh, but without opening his mouth. 'My lips are sealed,' he said, and I had a sudden vision of his mouth pressed against my car window.

'Thank you,' I said.

'That all? I've got to go, I'm expecting another call.'

10

The plan was finalised. After pages and pages in our WhatsApp group (Dyl barely responding, Jess throwing in a lot of 'Will let you know ASAP's and Mila losing it in all caps and liberal exclamation marks), everything was arranged. The weekend after next, I would be driving myself, Dyl, Paddy and Jess down to Cornwall, to the Taschens' family cottage by the sea. Henry would already be there, looking after Dolly while his mother *summered* in the south of France. Mila and Niall would catch the train together, as they kept repeatedly informing us. Love had truly made them a smug couple.

As for Henry and me, things were still uneven. Since realising I was in love with him, I'd grown awkward and affected in his company. A new shyness gripped me whenever called upon to offer an opinion on anything from the tiny ('What do you want for supper?') to the significant ('I'm not sure if my father is handling looking after Bear'). Until now, I had always offered Henry advice unsolicited, freely stabbing at ideas like pasta in a bowl, but something had moved in me. Everything I said now needed to be *right,* to chime with what Henry would say, what he would think; autonomous thoughts of my own had no place. Creatively, I was deluged, filling my notebook with pages and pages of short stories and love poems I wondered if I would ever be bold enough to let him see.

*

The kids broke up for the summer at the end of the week. The atmosphere at the school gates was palpably jubilant.

'It's summer!' Jem ran out and declared the news.

Clara took her time, showing up a good fifteen minutes later with pen all over her face.

'Clara!' I gasped. 'Did you get a tattoo?'

'They're not real,' she said. 'Duh. Our teacher said we could.'

They were both laden with an academic year's worth of crap: bags of dirty gym kit, forgotten lunchboxes, folders of drawings, some cress growing in a plastic tray. I loaded myself up like a mule, letting the kids run around and say goodbye to friends, free for the next six whole weeks.

The unauthorised after-party was at the park. Just about every kid in the school was there, parents and nannies in tow. I pitched up on a vacant patch of grass, kicking off my espadrilles and creating a little hill out of the pile of bags, sinking down and reclining against them.

'I'll be right here, OK?' I told the kids.

They were normally allotted thirty minutes of park time after school, but today there would be no cap. I pulled out *Anna Karenina* – I had only sixty or so pages left. The crumpled copy had been knocking redundantly around in my bag for weeks. On occasion, as I did now, I would retrieve it, in coffee shops or on public transport: simply holding it, inching closer to the possibility of diving back in for the last leg. Once again, I let it lie untouched in my lap and sank back in the sun, closing my eyes and listening to the chorus of children. It was a dry heat that day, beads of sweat materialising in the creases of my elbows and along my hairline. I thought of Cornwall, and the sea into which I would soon be plunging.

Jem returned with a little girl I hadn't seen before.

'Nanny Jo?' He gave me a little shake, as if he thought I'd be sleeping.

'Hello, love,' I said, one hand held up to the sun in order to make out his earnest little face.

'I'm hungry.'

I located a couple of lukewarm squeezy tubes of yoghurt, and gave one each to him and his new friend.

'What's your name?' I asked her.

She sucked her yoghurt.

'This is my friend Olivia,' said Jem, debonair.

'Hi, Olivia.'

The girl rested her chin on Jem's shoulder, and stood that way, humming a little. The sun was behind them where they stood, picking out wisps of their dishevelled hair. A sense of déjà vu came over me. Was this a memory of my own or just a photograph I'd seen? Dyl and I, not much bigger than them, my head on his shoulder, golden light on smooth skin.

'Sorry!' A man appeared next to the kids, arriving in a sort of faux jog. 'Is she stealing all your snacks?' He nodded at the little girl.

'Oh, hi. Are you Olivia's dad?'

'Yeah, hi. I'm Rich,' he said. 'Did you say thank you to the nice girl, Livvie?'

Olivia ignored him.

'Don't worry, we've got loads,' I said. 'They were getting warm, anyway.'

'Yum.'

I squinted up at him. He was attractive, for a dad: lean build and stubbly black beard flecked with grey across his cheekbones.

'You must be Jem and Clara's au pair?'

'Yeah. I mean, well, I'm their nanny. I don't live with the family.'

'We should get a play date in,' he said. 'Lot of time to fill now.'

'Yay!' said Jem. 'Nanny Jo, can we?'

'Yeah, sure. I'll have to check with their parents, but sounds good.'

'Cool,' said Rich. 'Shall I give you my number and we can set something up?'

'Er, yeah, OK.'

I got out my phone and saved his number as *Rich Olivia*.

'Great. Jo, is it?' he said.

'Joni.'

'No way – your parents Joni Mitchell fans?'

'No, actually.'

'Ah, shame. I love her.' He smiled. 'Come on then, Liv. See you soon!'

Back at the house, the kids took off their shoes and socks, and we ate mango lying in the garden. Bees hummed in the overgrown honeysuckle. Clara attempted cartwheels, which I marked out of ten (generously); Jem made a daisy chain and hung it around my neck.

'Do I look nice?' I asked.

'You look beautiful, Nanny Jo!'

Raf arrived and came outside to say hello. 'Happy summer holidays!' He pulled Clara up on to his hip and planted a kiss on her cheek. 'All well, I take it?'

'Wonderful,' I said.

'Good, good.'

'Papa, look, I maded Nanny Jo a daisy chain!'

'Made,' said Raf.

'I made Nanny Jo a daisy chain!'

'Well done, darling.'

'I love it,' I said.

Raf seemed more tired than usual. 'Can we have a quick word, please, Joni?' he asked.

'Sure.' I got up from the lawn and dusted myself down. It wasn't uncommon for Raf to take me aside, duly requesting a briefing on the kids' behaviour that week, but I hadn't been alone with him since catching Terry mid-coitus with Pyotr, and I felt a little sick at the prospect.

Jem followed us into the house.

'Give Papa and Joni a minute, please, Jemmy,' said Raf.

'I want to stay.'

'We won't be long. Go outside, please.'

'But I want to stay.' Jem clutched on to my leg.

'Hey,' I said. 'Can you make me another one of these?' I touched the flowers around my neck. 'I'd really love a bracelet to go with the necklace.'

Jem nodded solemnly and trotted his way back out to the garden. Raf scratched his head.

'How are you, Joni, you well?'

'Yep, fine, thanks. Lovely weather.'

'Yes, isn't it? Do you want a tea or anything?'

'No, no, I'm fine.'

'I might just make one myself.' Raf flicked the kettle on and pulled a mug down from the shelf. He leaned against the kitchen counter, waiting for it to boil. I perched on the end of the bench at the table.

'You're going away soon, aren't you?' he said.

'Oh, yeah. I'm going down to Cornwall with some friends while you guys are in Trinidad.'

'Ah, yes, that's right. Sorry, Terry did say.'

I smiled. 'You looking forward to it?' I asked, as Raf poured his tea.

'God, I don't know if I'd go that far.' He laughed. 'Got to get through a nine-hour flight with those two first.'

'Oh, yeah.'

'There we go.' He had stirred his tea and now threw the bag in the bin. He came and sat at the table with me. 'So, I wanted to have a bit of a talk with you.'

'OK,' I said, my heart rate quickening.

'Basically – I won't keep you in suspense – Terry and I have been talking, and we feel that it might be time for us to take the mantle now, with the kids.'

'Oh.'

'Yeah, we've had a talk about it, and er, Terry really feels that she should be spending more time with them, while they're at this critical age.'

'That's great.'

'It is great, it is. And listen, you've done such a fantastic job. Jem and Clara just adore you.'

A lump formed in my throat.

'We honestly can't thank you enough for everything. Seriously, you've been a life saver,' Raf went on. 'And, of course, we'll give you some severance pay, you know, a bit of a bonus.'

'A bonus?'

'Of course. And, look, it's up to you whether you want to see out the next week – we're happy for you to do that – or just draw a line in the sand today, you know, it being the end of term and everything.'

'OK.'

'OK, you want to stay another week, or . . .?'

I looked out at the children. They had found a caterpillar and were squatting side by side, transfixed as it crawled up Clara's arm.

'Was this decision both of yours?' I asked. 'Or just Terry's?'

Raf looked taken aback.

'Did Terry suggest it?' I demanded.

'She may have suggested it, yes. It's so she can spend more time with the kids, as I say.'

'Of course.'

'Yes. And Terry and I, we've discussed it, and come to the decision together that we feel is best for everyone.'

'Including the kids?'

'Nothing is better for children than more direct contact time with their mum.'

'Of course.'

'Like I say, Joni, we're so grateful for everything you've done, and if you want to stay another week—'

'I'm fine, thanks.'

'No?'

'I'll just call it a day today.'

'If that's what you want.'

'I guess I should go and say goodbye to the kids,' I said.

'Right, yeah. So this is the other thing.' Raf wrinkled his nose to shift his glasses back into place. 'Terry and I think it's best if we tell them ourselves, privately.'

It had been almost two years since I first arrived at this house: this colourful house, brimming with life behind the fox door knocker. The children had emerged like spirits from the walls, as nervous of me as I was of them. Of course, curiosity had quickly taken over, and within minutes, Jem was on my lap and Clara demanding to know what my favourite animal was. Small, tender moments over those first few weeks. On a walk back from nursery, Jem had reached for my hand before I had his. Clara let me hold her as she cried over her first taste of humiliation on the rounders pitch. They had each celebrated a birthday with me – on both occasions, I had filled the house with balloons, so that when we got back from school, their home would seem full even if their parents couldn't be there. There had been blood, pee, spit, teeth, vomit and even, once, faeces. There had been a lot of tears, some my own; the children were highly empathic and the kindest of carers, gently placing small round hands directly on my cheek. There had been fights, bruises, homework, disappointments, secrets, play dates, laughter, victories, cuddles, treats, movies, days out.

The hardest part was telling them I'd see them on Monday.

Raf walked me to the door and handed me an envelope, thick with cash. *So he'd already got the severance money, then.* He continued to thank me, told me to keep in touch and wished me luck with everything.

I stood still on the street outside. The world remained the same: pigeons on the lamp post, London humming, people in cars going home. I riffled through the notes in the envelope Raf had given me. Five hundred pounds: the ransom for my silence. I craned my neck back to look at the sky. It was still light.

*

With Fiona away at her conference, I had invited the gang – plus Henry – over for dinner that night for a pre-Cornwall bonding session: Mexican food and gallons of homemade margaritas.

'Chin up, darling. Unemployment's wonderful,' said Paddy, lighting a cigarette off the gas stove.

I was stirring chorizo into the *frijoles*.

'You get to lie in every day, see friends all the time, focus on your own creativity . . .' he went on. 'And it's summer. My God, darling, there couldn't be a more perfect time for it.'

'Perfect time for what?' Mila had drifted over, margarita in hand.

'To be jobless,' said Paddy. 'It's ideal.'

'It sucks,' I groaned into the saucepan. 'It's fine. You know what? It's fine. I've got a whack of cash out of it, I'll find something else. It's ideal.'

'Atta girl,' said Paddy.

'I can get another job. Maybe it's the kick up the arse I needed to do something more, you know, creative.'

Mila put an arm around me and gave me a squeeze. 'So, do you think he knows Terry's cheating?' she asked.

'God knows.'

'I just can't believe how obvious she's being. You catch her at it and then next thing you know, boom, you're fired.'

I burst into tears.

Three drinks down, and a little vitriolic, I messaged Rich – the dad from the park – on a trip to the loo: *Hi, Rich, it's Joni from the playground. Just to let you know I won't be looking after Jem and Clara anymore, so if you want to arrange a play date best to contact their parents directly. I can give you phone number if you need it. Cheers.*

He replied straight away: *That's a shame. I was hoping to see you again.*

Together, we carried the kitchen table outside, and ate our meal by candlelight, the balmy Friday night filled with laughter and tequila. Niall had made a fruit crumble, Mila contributing some cherries from the garden in a display of wholesome foraging skills I knew was entirely for his benefit.

Later, Dyl slid into the kitchen behind me. 'Phil.'

'Oh, hi there.'

'Are you OK?'

'Yeah. You?' I began to load the dishwasher.

'No, but, are you OK? I know your job was—'

'I'm fine,' I said, not looking up.

'You're not, though.'

'I don't want to think about it, OK? Go back outside. Have fun.'

Dyl didn't say anything.

My martyrdom swelled within me with each dirty utensil I packed. 'I just, I gave them a lot, of myself. And maybe it's egocentric of me to even think this, but when I think about Clara and Jem hearing that I'm gone—' I looked up. Dyl had already gone back out to the garden, as I had asked.

The smug couple were the first to leave, Niall's arm around Mila's waist. Dyl – blind drunk – went next, in search of more fun. Paddy and Jess helped clear up and crashed in Fiona's guest room. Henry came to bed with me.

'You know, there is another silver lining about you losing your job,' he said on our pillows, his hand on my chin.

'What?'

'Well, you can stay longer with me in Cornwall – if you want to. I was planning on pitching down till the end of August, or thereabouts.'

'Henry, no one says "thereabouts".'

'Sorry. But what do you think? I know Dyl wants to stick around to get his essay done, so you'd have him for company, too. And Dolly.'

'Oh, Dolly.'

'And you could try and write? It's very beautiful there.

I'm sure you'd find it, you know, *inspirational*.' He said the word as if borrowing a foreign term.

'Hey, your daisy chain's broken,' he said.

'Fuck.' I got up and carefully laid the dried-out flowers along my bookshelf. They were already limp and disintegrating. 'I'd love to stay in Cornwall with you,' I said.

The next morning, Paddy offered to go and get brunchy things.

'Let me give you some cash, hang on,' I said. Might as well use some of the guilt money Raf had given me.

The envelope was distinctly thinner: several of the notes were missing. I rifled through my bag to make sure the cash hadn't fallen out, but I knew it was gone. And I knew exactly who had taken it.

11

Many hours outside London, the sunlight was beginning to fade, and the trees arched over either side of the road to form a green tunnel. The old house waited for us, alone at the end of a single-lane track.

Dripping in pink clematis, the cottage faced south-west, towards the sea. Out front, on weed-ridden flagstones, a long wooden table stood surrounded by spindly metal chairs, white paint peeling off in flakes. Beyond the terrace, a lawn curved downward towards the cliffs, surrounded on three sides by hedges filled with meadowsweet and red campion, croquet hoops poking out of the turf. In the walled kitchen garden to the west grew tomatoes, root vegetables and more herbs than I had ever heard of. To walk through it was an aromatic feast. The main garden, behind the house, seemed to go on and on forever, inviting you further and further away. Mature trees – oak, willow, ash and elder – were positioned like guardians around its perimeter. Lavender bordered the gravel pathways and, at the far end, a freshwater stream bubbled clear over smooth, flat stones.

We stretched, blinking in the last glare of shining sea, before filing into the house to dump our bags in bedrooms. Despite Henry referring to it as a 'cottage', the house was really quite substantial. The gumboot-lined hallway led on to a large kitchen, a living room, a study, a dining room and a cellar. Upstairs, creaky floorboards took you between the five bedrooms. In the airy central bathroom, a cast-iron tub stood on a raised plinth by the window, allowing the bather to see the sea from where they lay. Two smaller en suites hid at opposite corners. Henry and I were in the 'blue room': a neat, square bedroom that overlooked the garden. I laid my suitcase on its side on the floor and sat on the edge of the bed. So this was to be my home for the next few weeks. Muted evening light kissed my knees. The smell of frying garlic wafted up from downstairs. I could hear Paddy making Jess laugh through the wall, the quiet murmur of Dyl and Niall talking in the garden. My very bones seemed to relax. I unpacked a little, hanging my nicest dresses up in the armoire and putting my book on the bedside table, before wandering downstairs for a cold beer and a squeeze from Henry.

'There she is,' he said, as I entered the kitchen. He was darting between a Le Creuset on the Aga and the table, on which small piles of ingredients were methodically laid out, as well as a can of lager that I helped myself to.

'Oi, get your own.'

'What you making?' I asked, sniffing the contents of the pan.

'Just a sort of summer minestrone. Might add some pasta; thought you'd all be starving after that drive.'

'Yum.'

'How was it?' he asked.

'Fine. We took it in turns to be quizmaster.'

'Oh yeah? Who won?'

'Dyl, obviously. Where's Mila?'

'I sent her to the shop to get something for pudding.'

'Divine.'

I took my beer out to the garden to see the boys. Niall leapt up to greet me, and Dolly ran over.

'Hi, dog,' I said, bending down to scratch her head.

'You look very summery,' said Niall.

'Is that a euphemism for something?' I laughed.

'No, of course not. For what could it be?'

'Slutty,' said Dyl.

'Thanks,' I said, kicking him where he lay on the lawn. 'Give us a cig, Dyl.'

He emptied his pockets on to the grass and I stooped down to pick up the smoking paraphernalia.

'Oh, hello,' I said.

Nestled inside the bag of tobacco was a little ball of powder wrapped in cling film.

'This for us?'

Dyl scrambled up and grabbed it from me.

'Alright, don't share,' I said.

I lit my cigarette and sat down next to Dolly, who rolled over for her pink belly to be rubbed. 'Did you manage to get the whole week off, Niall?' I asked.

'Almost. Got a meeting on Thursday I have to go to, but other than that, I'm all yours.'

'You're going to London?' said Dyl.

'That is where my meeting is, yes.'

'Could you pick some stuff up for me?'

'Like what?'

'Just some things I forgot,' said Dyl. 'Don't worry, we'll talk about it later.'

Piano music struck up from inside the house, shortly followed by Paddy's voice, singing a jazzy show tune. We smiled and lay back, listening. The sun had sunk just below the horizon now, its rays still colouring the sky. The ground was soft beneath me, the smell of grass sweet and nourishing. A female voice joined in the melody: Jess. Swallows raced over us. Dolly heard the car before we did and started to bark – Mila back from the shop. Henry came out to tell us supper was ready.

We all went to bed early that night, tired from our long journeys and bellies full of soup. Henry opened the window in our bedroom, and with each rhythmic crash of the waves below, I thought *say it, say it, say it*.

*

On Saturday, I woke early to a quiet house. I went downstairs to sit in the garden for a while before the others woke up, lifting my chin to soak my face in the morning sun. It was already warm, and very still. The sky was that hazy shade of white particular to summer mornings. Dew across the lawn caught the light in beads. From the cliffs on the far side of the house, I heard the wretched caw of seagulls, their voices tuned to the wildness of the landscape.

'Morning,' a voice behind me said.

'Jesus.' I turned and saw Dyl, in dressing gown and trainers. 'What are you doing?' I asked.

'I woke up around six, so I thought I'd walk the dog.'

'Thought I was the only one up.'

'Nope,' he said. 'Niall and Mila are too. They've gone on a run. I bumped into them on the coast path.'

'As if they're on a run.'

'Don't worry, I told them they make me sick.'

'Good.'

'How'd you sleep, Phil?'

'So well. Better than I have for ages. You?'

'Meh. It's very fucking quiet, isn't it?'

We went in and brewed some coffee. Jess, in silk pyjamas and flushed from sleep, came and joined us, followed by Henry, and finally Paddy.

'Why are none of you hungover?' Paddy demanded.

'Sorry, mate,' said Jess.

'Ugh, I think I got too excited. First night on holiday, you know.'

'Where can I set up my laptop?' Dyl asked Henry. 'Study best bet?'

'Yes, I should think so.'

'For God's sake, Dyl. Can you at least wait until Monday to start being an insufferable swot?' said Paddy. 'Let's enjoy the weekend.'

'Once I hand this essay in, I'll be free to play, I promise,' Dyl said. 'Besides, you're unemployed. It's always the weekend for you.'

'I'll drink to that! Oi oi, Joni.'

Paddy and I clinked coffee cups and I stuck two fingers up at Dyl.

Niall and Mila came in, their hair wet and skin glowing, he with a newspaper tucked under his arm. 'Morning.' They both greeted us chirpily.

'Did you go for a run?' said Jess.

'Yes,' Dyl and I chorused.

'Wake me up next time, will you?' said Jess. 'Or is it a couple thing?'

'No, come, that'd be great,' said Niall.

'Such a gorgeous day,' said Mila. 'We went all along the coast path and down to the beach, and the sea looked so tempting that we jumped in, had a quick dip.'

'You're all cunts, the lot of you,' said Paddy. 'Henry, I must have some food. Where will I find bread?'

'Larder,' said Henry, nodding at a little door in the corner of the kitchen.

Paddy heaved himself up and trudged over, groaning aloud as he moved. 'Anyone else want toast?'

We all did.

'Henry?' Paddy called from inside the larder. 'I don't want to alarm you, but you appear to have a family of immigrants living in here.'

'What?'

Henry went over.

'Oh, bollocks,' I heard him say.

I got up myself, curious to see what Paddy was talking about. The larder was bigger than I expected, hollowed out beneath the stairs along the back wall of the house. Wooden shelves were filled with cans, boxes of cereal, dozens of small glass jars of spices. Henry and Paddy were standing by the small window, looking not out of it, but at the frame itself.

'Ants,' said Paddy.

A winding loop of black specks threaded its way right from the window, down the wall, and on to the nearby shelf, where a seething mass of them had discovered an open bag of muscovado sugar.

'"Good yeoman, whose limbs were made in England, show us here the mettle of your pasture",' said Paddy to the ants.

'Well, they don't seem to be doing any harm,' I said, watching the tiny beasts transport sugar on their backs: some with heavy, stuck-together lumps and others with one single grain. All just as earnest.

'We'll have to get some poison,' said Henry.

'No!' Paddy and I both protested.

'We can't have them crawling all over the food.'

'They're not all over the food,' I said. 'They're sticking to the sugar, which I think is perfectly fair.'

'Oh please, Pop, can we keep 'em?' said Paddy in an American accent.

'Honestly,' said Henry.

'What the fuck are you doing in there?' called Jess from the kitchen.

We trooped out of the larder.

'Some ants have got into the sugar,' I informed the others.

'Ew,' said Mila.

'Someone google whether ants can spread disease,' said Paddy.

'For God's sake,' said Henry.

'They're very intelligent, you know,' said Niall. 'In rising waters, some species of ant are known to gather together as a colony and form rafts with their bodies.'

Mila gazed lovingly at him.

'Here we go . . .' said Dyl, holding up his phone. 'Are they garden ants or pharaoh ants?'

'Garden, I should think,' said Niall.

'You haven't even seen them.' Mila smiled.

'Yes, but pharaoh ants tend to require artificial heat. You find them by radiators and things, which, I'm assuming, is not the case?'

'No,' said Henry.

'"Garden ants do not spread or carry disease, but are more of a nuisance due to their foraging habits",' read Dyl aloud.

'That's that, then,' I said. 'The ants can stay.'

'Let them eat sugar!' declared Paddy.

We spent the rest of the weekend getting our bearings and establishing roles within the house. Over the next couple of weeks, we were mostly outdoors: attempting lazy games of croquet or badminton, smoking on the grass reading books, ambling in groups down the dusty path to the beach. Drinking became acceptable at any hour of the day, from Bloody Marys at breakfast to daytime beers to cocktail hour, and finally minesweeping whatever was left by the end of the night, usually cheap wine. Mealtimes were invariably spontaneous; whoever was the least sun-drunk (or actually drunk) rousing themselves into the role of chef. Niall was everyone's preferred cook. He and Mila would come back with all kinds of things from the town, then he'd leaf through one of the Taschens' dog-eared cookbooks and experiment with great success. Against all odds, only Dyl managed to establish any kind of routine: rising at dawn and walking Dolly along the coast path, before settling down in the study to work, getting through copious amounts of coffee. He insisted that he could only operate in the morning when his brain was still 'bibulous'. Henry and Niall both put in the odd shift of laptop time, despite being on annual leave. Niall had a couple of meetings in London – he would appear in the kitchen early, dressed in full suit and tie, completely uncanny amid the clutter. To break up the long train journeys, he would often spend the night in the city, too. Mila grew palpably twitchy in his absence. Paddy was also called away once or twice for auditions, often with very little notice. Jess would help him with lines in the garden, and we'd all be treated to a performance the night before he left.

As for me, I found the peace and symmetry of the 'blue room' an ideal environment in which to write: sitting cross-legged at the table by the window, scribbling some lines of poetry into an exercise book.

> *High in the clean blue air –*
> *A heron; inviting me away*
> *And you, with one*
> *mischievous smile*
> *Forcing me to stay.*

12

Wherever I was in the house or its grounds, I felt aware of Henry's location at all times, as if there was some sort of orbital pull. I felt aggrieved if I wasn't sitting next to him at meals, longed for him to come and visit me up in our room while I was writing (*if I fill this page, he'll come*), ached for him to touch me spontaneously. Poetry was often abandoned as I filled my exercise book with pornographic short stories starring Henry as a soldier, Henry as a teacher, Henry as a fisherman . . .

Quite simply, I was starving for him. It was bliss.

After an especially good supper of Niall's (sea bass and samphire), we slumped back in our seats; Jess opened another bottle of wine and Mila passed round one of her dainty spliffs. In the candlelight, our faces glowed in that dark cavern of a room. Tucked into the north-east corner of the house, it was the first to lose the light, and its mahogany panels and low-beamed ceiling became tapestries of shadows.

The windows were open, letting in that tonic of damp, salty air, fluttering the candles in the draught. My shoulder lay against Henry's, the bare skin of our arms pressed along each other. Dyl was sitting at the head of the table, monologuing about *Mrs Dalloway*, pausing only to tilt his chair back on its hind legs and tap ash from his burning cigarette out of the window.

'I wonder,' he said, exhaling a long plume of smoke, 'if Woolf wrote Septimus's suicide as a sort of practice run for herself.'

'Jesus,' said Mila. 'Bit macabre, Dyl.'

'Do you think?' I said. 'She wrote *Dalloway* in the twenties, no? And she didn't take her own life till much later . . . the forties, I think. Can the two really be connected? Lots of writers write about suicide. It's great dramatic fodder.'

'True,' said Dyl. 'But I think, in this case, they have to be connected. And Clarissa's own admiration of Septimus's decision is Woolf meditating on the idea. In fact' – he sat upright – 'you could argue that Clarissa represents the part of the author that is constrained by societal pressures, familial life, and Septimus represents her inner self, her id: tormented and tragic, yet free.'

'Well, you'd better put that in your essay,' said Henry. Dyl laughed.

'He already did,' I said, guessing, and Dyl threw me an annoyed look which proved I was correct.

'Would you posit, then, young scholar,' said Paddy, affecting a pompous, lecturing tone, 'that every character within a novel is a manifestation of the author themselves, or at least some facet of them?'

'Yes!' added Jess. 'Like Freud says about dreams – everyone we dream about is, essentially, a creation of our own subconscious. Meaning everyone in our dreams is just us. Perhaps unexplored or unrepresented parts of us, but us.'

'No,' said Dyl. 'I think, in fiction, characters can also be created based on people from the author's own life.'

'Agreed,' said Niall.

'Thank you, Niall,' said Dyl.

Mila gave Niall a kiss. We all seemed to sag a little, off on individual thought-paths.

Dyl poured himself another glass of wine. 'What did you make of *Anna* then, Phil?' he said. 'You finally finish it?'

'Yes,' I lied. I both had and hadn't finished the book. I had technically got to the last page, and read it, and closed the tome for the last time, but I may have skipped certain sections.

'You're honestly the slowest reader,' he said.

'Fuck off.'

'So. What did you think of it?' he asked, sitting back, eyeing me sportingly over his drink.

'Well, obviously it's brilliant,' I said. 'The sheer fucking epic-ness of it.'

He was smiling sardonically at me.

'I just couldn't stand all the stuff about God and workers' rights and land.'

Henry laughed.

'No?' said Dyl.

'I mean I'm sure it was really cool at the time. But I get the sense a lot of Levin's long stream-of-consciousness passages are Tolstoy trying to work out his own feelings. It's like watching him have therapy. It's too esoteric.'

'Haven't you heard of the egotistical sublime?' said Dyl. 'Levin's my favourite character of fiction,' he added, with conscious brilliance.

'Oh, shut up,' I said.

'What's wrong with Levin?' said Henry.

'He's so . . . I don't know. So worthy.'

'I think he's a beautiful character,' Dyl persevered, entirely straight-faced. I wanted to get up and slap him. 'The part where he asks Kitty to read his diary, so she can fully comprehend the man he is – incredible. That, to me, is the most selfless form of love: presenting the darkest and most vulnerable parts of yourself to another person. It's breath-taking.'

'Oh, please,' I said. 'Getting her to read his diary? You're joking, right? Selfless? He wants her to read his diary so she can see all the women he's been with before her. That's not revealing the most intimate part of yourself, that's just a pseudo-Catholic desire for her to absolve him of his previous misdeeds. Not to mention a weirdly machismo act of pride. It's like that scene in *Four Weddings and a Funeral*—'

Mila laughed. 'Finally,' she said. 'Something I can relate to.'

'You know, the scene where Andie MacDowell lists every man she's ever slept with, and Hugh Grant's meant to find it outrageous and yet utterly charming. It's crap.'

'Amen,' said Mila.

'Sorry,' I ploughed on. 'But isn't that what Levin's doing when he shows, in fact forces Kitty to read the diary?'

'It's profound,' said Dyl. 'He's baring his soul, trying to get her to understand him.'

'If that was true, why doesn't he share his spiritual revelation with her at the end? In fact, he actively decides not to.'

Dyl muttered something about faith.

'Look,' I said. 'Maybe – again – at the time, it was really revelatory. I suppose people were much more private in those days, and it was more of a radical act.'

'What did you think of Anna?' interjected Henry.

'I loved Anna,' I said.

'So, basically,' said Dyl, 'you can only relate to the female perspective.'

'I don't—'

'Bet you didn't like Stiva either?' he said, flicking ash on the windowsill.

'Are we supposed to like Stiva?' I said. 'He's a philandering wimp.'

Dyl scoffed. 'That's so reductive.'

'OK, kids,' said Paddy. 'Stop bickering.'

'Agreed,' said Jess, sparking up a cigarette. 'This lovers' tiff is getting old.'

I stared at Paddy. *Lovers' tiff?* Had he blabbed about me and Dyl? He didn't return my gaze.

'Sorry,' I said, and reached for Henry's hand under the table, squeezing it.

Dyl said nothing, but got up and went to inspect the shelf of spirits by the mantelpiece.

'Right,' said Henry. 'Shall we?'

An unwritten rota had formed: if one set of us did the cooking, another did the cleaning, and another made the round of coffees people inevitably wanted after each meal. Tonight, Henry and I took on the cleaning. I set to work rinsing plates and loading the dishwasher while he taxied cutlery and glasses through from the dining room. I had begun to find that any activity, no matter how mundane, took on a pleasant and soothing quality with Henry by my side. We often had some of our most natural, intimate chats while changing our bedsheets or chopping herbs.

Paddy drifted in, passing Henry as he left to collect the last of the plates from the dining room. 'Did we finish all the white?' Paddy said, opening the fridge.

I switched off the taps and darted over to him. 'Paddy,' I hissed. 'Did you tell Jess?'

He crouched down to inspect the vegetable drawer. 'Tell Jess what?' he said.

'There's nothing there,' I said, shutting the fridge. 'About me and Dyl,' I mouthed, barely releasing sound; as if decibels would make the thing truer than it already was.

'What?' said Paddy. 'No. God, no. Don't be silly.'

'Do you swear?'

Henry came up suddenly behind me, drawing a line with his nose from the nape of my neck to my ear. 'Hi,' he said, and I could smell sweet spirits on his breath.

'Hi,' I said.

Paddy made his exit.

'Once this is all done,' Henry said, nodding at the stacked plates, 'd'you fancy a swim?'

'Tonight? In the sea?'

'Yes.'

'With the others?'

'No. Just us.'

We waited for everyone to go to bed before creeping down to the beach. *Just us.* It was very late by then. There had been an impromptu sing-along session at the piano, led by Paddy, and afterwards we'd all lain about drinking peaty whisky, Dyl endlessly filling up everyone's glasses until we were well into the wee hours. Henry ran upstairs and grabbed us a couple of towels, and I pulled a wax jacket from the hall around my summer dress. Dolly looked up hopefully as we left, half-expecting her morning walk, albeit a few hours too early.

'Not yet, my love,' I said, patting her head goodbye.

Treading our way down the dusty path to the bay, it felt as though we two were the only souls awake in the world. I could barely see where I was going in the dark, the vague shape of Henry a few steps ahead guiding my way. The air was warm and the salty dampness of the sea crept into our lungs and mingled with our hair. The high cliffs around the cove held us in a sealed embrace; the wind seemed to disappear completely on the stage of the beach. On the smooth, flat sand, we kicked off our shoes and began to undress wordlessly, just a little out of breath from our descent. Henry stood there, naked. He seemed to me the most beautiful thing in the universe: utterly solid and real, and as fragile and open as a flower.

'Ready?' he said.

And we ran in, laughing and gasping at the shock of it. I kept my limbs moving in a vigorous breaststroke, the moon dragging me further and further away from the shore. Silky trails of seawater rushed through my outstretched fingers and swirled all around my naked body, my bare feet paddling out and in like a frog. The unknown worlds of the deep expanded below me the further I swam, daring me to contemplate what they might contain. Henry grasped my ankle from behind me and I squealed, twisting around to face him in the water. I saw now how far out we were, the murky outlines of rocks just visible on the shadowy beach. Henry kissed me, bashing his mouth against mine awkwardly as we both trod water, our lips already salty and wet. We held hands and floated on our backs, looking up at the stars.

'I wish I knew more constellations,' I said.

'How many do you know?'

'Just Orion and the Plough.'

'That's two more than me,' he said.

'Seriously?' I laughed, surprised. Henry seemed to know everything. There had not yet been a conversational topic on which he could not contribute; whether it was equality in European legislature or what type of stone they used to build Machu Picchu.

I pointed the relevant stars out to him. 'See?' I said. 'Those three in a row are Orion's Belt. You must have seen them before?'

'Well, obviously I must physically have seen them before, but, no,' he said. 'I've never really been one for astronomy. Even less so astrology.'

'Me neither,' I said. 'Though I do have a really dumb superstition about the only two constellations I know.'

'Go on.'

'Well, whenever I see Orion first, it's a bad omen. And if I spot the Plough first, it's good.'

'I see,' said Henry. I could hear him keeping the amusement from his tone. 'And have you any examples of this coming to fruition?'

'Well, I know something bad happened when I was little, and it was around the time I learned how to find Orion, so I've always associated the two.'

'But you can't remember what it was?'

'No,' I said. 'And then later, when I learned the Plough, I guess I just decided that it would be a sign of good things to come, to counteract the Orion rule. It's a real gamble every time I look at the night sky.'

'Which did you spot first tonight?' asked Henry.

'I'm not sure,' I said, truthfully.

A raw and alarming noise made us both snap out of our reverie. It came from somewhere nearby in the water: a deep, aggressive bark.

'What the fuck was that?' I said, my heart racing.

'I don't know.'

We listened, breathing as quietly as we could, the only sound the constant lapping of water. Then it happened again, closer this time, just a few feet away: the unmistakable grunt of animal. The closest thing my mind could place it to was a dog, and I thought wildly that Dolly had somehow followed us here.

'Henry?' I said.

'Look!'

I followed his gaze and saw two glowing eyes bobbing nearby in the darkness, staring at us. I screamed. I
screamed and swam as fast as I could, frantically splashing
my way back to the shore; my mind empty of thought, my
entire being flooded with only one impulse – to get out. My
limbs felt leaden and useless, dragging me painstakingly
inch by inch to the shallows, where I staggered, moaning,
clinging to Henry, reaching for him to pull me onwards,
until I was finally on dry land.

We were both gasping for air, completely nude and
holding on to each other for dear life.

'Oh my God,' I said, and then kept saying it; looking
out to sea for the creature we'd just escaped. We stood
there for a while, shaking, goose-fleshed and clutching each
other. And there it was, close by, smiling at us in the waves:
a seal, its whiskery face as benign as a Labrador.

I collapsed with laughter. 'I thought it was a fucking sea
monster,' I choked.

'What?'

'I don't know. Just that sound it made, it was so scary
– and then all I could see were its eyes, and I thought, holy
fuck, we're gonna die.'

Henry, too, was bent double with laughter.

'It's the *sea*!' I cried. 'It could have been a shark or
something!'

'Christ.' Henry wiped a tear from his eye.

'I've honestly never been so mortally afraid in my entire
life. I felt like we were running from a lion or something.'

'Oh, and you thought you'd throw me to the beast?'
said Henry.

'What?'

'You practically climbed over me to get to freedom.'

'No, I was just—'

'Literally, you were shoving me behind you to get out faster.'

I was laughing so much I couldn't answer.

'It's fine,' he said. 'I mean, now I know where I stand. I'm just fodder for the lion. Don't mind me. I'm the sacrifice.'

'Henry—'

'It's fine, now I know your true colours.' He was smiling widely at me, all of his teeth showing. 'If that's how you really feel.'

'I love you,' I said.

There it was. I looked at my bare feet, pale and ghostly, sand between my toes. A ribbon of seaweed had attached itself to my ankle. It looked quite ornate.

'I love you too,' said Henry.

He gently tucked a wet strand of hair over my shoulder, and kissed me, both of our noses running a little.

'Sorry,' I said, wiping mine. 'Gross.'

'I've been meaning to tell you for ages,' he said.

'Really?'

'Yeah, it's just difficult. We're constantly around people; I never seem to get you to myself.'

'I've been wanting to tell you for ages, too,' I said.

He hugged me, his body firm and slick. We were both shivering a little.

'Come on,' I said. 'Let's get dressed.'

It had grown almost imperceptibly lighter, the structure of the cove around us now visible.

'Is that because our eyes have adjusted?' I asked Henry.

'It's nautical twilight,' he said.

'What?' I said. 'What's that?'

'Nautical twilight. Just before dawn, when the brighter

stars and the horizon are both visible. It means you can navigate at sea. It's when the fishermen go out to catch their load for the day.'

We climbed our way back up to the house, the colours of the fields and hedgerows revealing their splendour as the sun appeared.

'Hang on,' I said, giving Henry's arm a tug. 'If you knew it was a seal all along, why did you make a run for it, too?'

'Oh,' he said. 'Your scream was so loud. I think I just got caught up in the drama of it all.'

The house seemed to radiate the warmth of the sleeping bodies it contained; its outline fuzzy in the dawn. Dyl came out with Dolly just as we approached the front gate. In his threadbare T-shirt and shorts, I noticed how gaunt he looked: even more so than usual. His perpetually unkempt hair seemed thinner, the shadows under his eyes more pronounced.

'Morning,' he said, allowing Dolly to drag him over. 'Where've you two lovers been?'

'The beach,' I said. 'Henry, I'll meet you inside.'

'Alright,' Henry said, heading in. 'Thanks for taking such good care of the dog, Dyl.'

'Oh, it's entirely selfish,' said Dyl. 'Helps my mind.'

Henry laughed and shut the door behind him, leaving us alone on the garden path.

'You're looking very well,' said Dyl.

'You're not.'

'I'm fine.'

'Are you?' I said.

'Yes. Why wouldn't I be?'

'I don't know.'

Dolly wheezed, pulling at her lead to go.

'Couldn't you have given yourself a break for once?' I said, gesturing at the dog. 'You haven't slept.'

'I can't,' said Dyl, kicking at a tuft of grass. 'I'm on my second extension.'

'You're what?'

'I missed my deadline. Twice. Can only play the stress card so many times.'

'Stress?'

'I'm fine. I just have to finish this fucking essay.' He squinted at me, the dawn light exposing the shadows of his face.

'Do you want me to walk Dolly with you?' I said.

'No. Thank you. I get my ideas walking.'

'OK.' I smiled at him, unable to keep the magic of my night at bay. 'We saw a seal,' I said, the image of its bobbing face already catalogued in my heart. 'Swimming a few feet away from us.'

'A seal swam with you?'

I nodded.

'What a privilege,' he said, and set off in the direction of the cliff path, the dog straining to explore the smells of the land.

13

Paddy had an audition to play Hamlet at a small but well-respected theatre in South London. Mila and I teased him relentlessly about *playing the Dane*, watching him strut around Jess – a surprisingly good Ophelia – on the lawn, while Henry and Niall became quite transfixed by their rehearsals.

Dyl and I dropped Paddy and Niall off at the station on the evening before my birthday, before driving over to the local town for a pint.

'Reckon if I put in the odd morning at the office, it should prevent tongues wagging too much,' said Niall, from the back seat of the Volvo.

'As long as you're back for my birthday supper,' I said.

We told Paddy to break a leg and drove to the Albion, smoking out of the car windows and blasting Marvin Gaye at top volume in the syrupy evening light.

'Shall we just pick up a bag of pasta?' said Dyl, as I parked. In an unspoken bid for some alone time, we had told the others we were buying supper.

'Sure. We're having fancy food tomorrow, anyway.'

We settled at a corner table by the hearth, currently barren for the hot summer. Locals with thick Cornish accents shouted cheerfully at each other around the bar. The rest of the clientele couldn't disguise their incongruity: long-haired boys – some not yet old enough to drink – here to surf, families with their two or three grubby children.

A little girl was dragging a toy horse across the stone floor. I thought of Clara and Jem. They would love it here: Jem lapping up all the mythology around pirates hiding their treasure in the deep caves, Clara showing off how far she could swim to terrify her parents.

'You're sad,' said Dyl.

'Yeah.'

'Birthday?'

'The kids. What's your excuse?'

Normally, this would have made him laugh. Dyl didn't say anything; he knew there was nothing to do but let me observe the little girl playing with her horse, and sip my drink till my own tristesse passed and I could focus on his.

'So,' I said, setting down our second round of the local beer. 'Talk to me about your essay.'

'God,' said Dyl, responding by folding forward on to the table, head buried in his arms.

'Come on,' I said. 'I can help.'

'Would you read it?' he asked.

'Of course.'

'I fear I've spent so bloody long on the thing, it no longer makes sense.'

'In what way?' I asked.

'I don't know. There have been such long gaps of neglect that it feels disjointed. Each time I come back to write, it's like I'm starting again with a different agenda, with a different voice, even.'

'It's non-fiction, Dyl. Your voice can only be your voice. I'm sure it's fine.'

'Do you think?' he asked in earnest.

I took his hand across the sticky table. 'I'm fully expecting to be reeling with envy about how brilliant it is,' I said. 'You neurotic bastard.'

'I could just do a you and drop out altogether,' he said, smirking at me.

I laughed, but didn't meet his eye. My being in the blissful flush of new love left us tilted, and I felt guilty and responsible. His chips were down, and he wanted to drag me down with him. Dyl was the one with effortless straight As, who could always get the girl, who had partied harder than any of us, yet still pulled off a first-class degree, and had charmed his way into tutoring jobs that paid four times what I earned doing bar work. I was the one who had cyclical crises: getting dumped, dropping out of university, struggling to make rent. Now the balance was off, the dynamic askew, and though I was the one on the higher end of the seesaw, all I felt was vertigo. I had been planning to talk to him about the money he had stolen from me; to tell him it was OK, he had been drunk at the time, but he needed to pay me back. But this new-found guilt – along with the cruelty that had just danced over his countenance – left me dumbstruck once more in the presence of my oldest friend. There was a membrane between us, and it was calcifying by the day.

He drained his glass. 'I'm starting to think quite seriously about an ayahuasca holiday.'

'Oh, fuck off.'

'Seriously, Phil. Don't you ever just want to, you know, like, restart your brain?'

'Maybe? But an uncontrolled psychedelic trip punctuated by heavy vomiting doesn't sound like the way to do it.'

'People say it's life-changing.'

'People suck.'

'Did you bring your notebook?' Dyl asked, perking up.

'Yes, I did.'

'Hand it over, then.'

He retrieved his Moleskine from the back pocket of his jeans. Swapping the odd note, we read for a while; the little girl on the floor occasionally catching me looking.

'What's this?' Dyl had discovered the newspaper cutting.

'Oh, shit,' I said. 'Nothing. Fiona gave it to me, bless her. As if I'd bother.'

'Three grand?' he said, waving it in the air as if it were Charlie's golden ticket. 'Maybe I'll enter.'

'You should,' I said.

He got out his phone and took a picture of the clipping. I drained my pint, and suggested we get back to the others.

*

Back to the house with linguine and garlic. Dyl – I hoped rather than knew – was a little bit lighter. He fetched some basil and a little thyme from the vegetable garden, and we made fresh pesto to serve with the pasta. The others joined us in the kitchen and we ate at the wooden table, abandoning our usual ritual of supper in the garden or dining room. Everyone appeared rather sun-fatigued, slumping back in their chairs after the carbohydrate-heavy meal and heading up to bed just before midnight – which, by the precedent we had set for ourselves, was an early night.

Henry and I had run out of toothpaste. I crept along the landing to steal some from the main bathroom and found the door was shut. I knocked.

'Yeah?' called Jess's voice from inside.

'Only me, babe. Can I nick some toothpaste?'

She was lying in the bath, her dark hair spun into a bun at the top of her head; a few wisps falling down around her face and shoulders.

'You look so pretty,' I said.

'Thanks, babe.'

Mila poked her head around the door. 'Oh, I see,' she said. 'Party without me.' She came in and began wrapping her own hair in a scarf, fingers twisting the silk into a knot at the front.

'Fuck,' she said, pulling the scarf abruptly from her head. 'I hate this.'

'Hate what?' I said.

'Niall being away.'

'It's one night,' said Jess. 'Come on, you can't miss him that much.'

'I don't miss him,' she snapped.

Jess and I caught eyes, understanding where this was going.

'My love,' I said. 'You have nothing to worry about. Niall is literally the most honest person I know.'

'Legit,' said Jess.

'There's a girl at his work,' began Mila.

'Wait, what?' said Jess. 'OK, I take it all back. A female in his place of work? How could he?'

I smiled, but Mila wasn't having it.

'She's hot,' she went on, now winding her scarf round the opposite wrist with increasing firmness. 'She does kick boxing.'

'Oh my God, stop going on Instagram,' said Jess. 'Seriously, babe, it's like self-harm.'

'Come here,' I said, hugging Mila. 'He loves you. Don't worry.'

'Ugh.' She groaned into my hair. 'They're all liars.'

'This one isn't. I really don't think this one is.'

'It's even harder this time. I've never felt this way about anyone before.'

'We know, we know,' said Jess. 'You've loved him since he was a child. You paedo.'

At this, Mila finally laughed. 'Sorry,' she said. 'Shit, mate. It's your birthday in, like, less than twenty minutes!'

'Yep!' I said, going to brush my teeth. I perched on the edge of the bath, enjoying the citrusy vapour wafting up at me.

'So,' Mila continued. 'How has twenty-five been for you?'

I considered this. 'Well,' I said. 'I've had three hundred and sixty-five goes at it. And I would say . . . about three hundred of those were successful.'

'I call that a good ratio,' said Jess.

'Hell, yeah,' said Mila.

'Does this mean I'll be in my late twenties now?'

'No,' they both said.

'Mid-twenties?' I asked.

'For sure.'

*

The day of my birthday was even more sweltering than the previous one. Even the ants, trafficking back and forth across the larder wall, expanding their empire, seemed lethargic. Dyl returned from his morning walk ruddy and shining with sweat. The stone path was already warm under my bare feet as I went out to drink my coffee on the front lawn. I blinked in the bright glare shimmering off the sea, and wondered if this beautiful day meant that my twenty-seventh year on earth would be wonderful or terrible.

After croissants and strawberry jam, we all set off for the long public beach, a short drive away. The girls and I had clearly been struck by the same impulse for wholesomeness today: I'd put on a gingham dress, Jess had packed a picnic basket (beer, French loaf, cheese and apples), and Mila was wearing a straw hat she'd nabbed from the hallway. On the pebbly beach, Henry laughed and took a picture of us on our towels – wicker basket open, sunglasses and smiles, Dyl lying on his front looking scornfully back at the camera, Dolly tongue-out in the sun. We took it in turns to swim, one or two of us keeping the base camp safe, the dog running loops around us. With paperbacks propped open, we dipped idly in and out of conversation. I'd pulled down a dog-eared copy of *The Awakening* by Kate Chopin from the shelf in our bedroom.

'Have you read this?' I'd said to Henry, in bed last night.

He shook his head.

'It might have been my mother's,' he said. 'Or Marla's.'

It was difficult to imagine either of Henry's female relatives having such a romantic inkling, much less enjoying early-feminist American literature. I had reached out and held his hand, anticipating one of the sudden outbursts of emotion to which Henry was prone when his sister's name was mentioned, but he'd smiled.

'Can I tell you something weird?' he'd said then.

'Always.'

'It sounds so stupid.' He dug the heels of his hands into his eye sockets. 'Argh, no, it's too mad, I can't.'

'Hey,' I said, sitting up straighter in bed next to him. 'You can't back out now.'

'You'll think I'm insane,' he said.

'Me? Never.'

'Promise not to judge?'

'I swear.' I kissed him on the shoulder. 'Henry, it's me. I have silly superstitions about knowing two sodding constellations, I think I'm capable of having telepathic dreams about Dyl, I once saw a swan, and it made me—'

'Shall I tell you or not?' he interrupted.

I made a zipping motion across my lips.

'Well,' he said, addressing the foot of the bed. 'You know the seal we saw the other night?'

'I mean, she didn't give me her name, but yeah, we're acquaintances.'

I looked up, and could see something was churning within him.

'Sorry, sorry,' I said. 'Tell me.'

'I've been thinking,' he continued. 'It's quite rare for a seal to come so close to humans. They're very playful and curious animals, but it was only a yard or so away from us, wasn't it? Extremely close, for a wild animal.'

He didn't seem to want to make eye contact, so I watched his hands as he spoke. He had lovely hands. He was pushing hard on his fingertips, one by one, pressing the pad into the nail: a self-soothing tick I'd noticed before.

'I just thought, maybe . . . God, I am insane. The way it looked at me, the eye contact, it felt so familiar. It took my breath away. And in that moment, I felt so sure. I just knew it. It was her – visiting me, letting me know she was OK. It was Marla.'

His hands were still now, clutched together tightly. I said nothing.

'Do you think I'm crazy?' he asked. 'I feel less certain now, but in that instant it was so obvious, so unquestionable. I almost said hello to her. It was like, *Oh, there you are.*'

He finally looked at me, his eyes pleading for reassurance.

'If you saw her, you saw her,' I'd said.

I regarded Henry now on his beach towel: lying on his front, leaning on his elbows, brow furrowed over his book. He was reading a three-inch-thick copy of a Richard Dawkins. I smiled to myself in the sunshine.

Mila planted herself down next to me, sand caked up her slender calves.

'Niall texted,' she said, unable to hide her relief. 'They just got on the train; they get in at quarter to five.'

'Great.'

'And,' she said, squeezing sun cream on to her shoulder, 'they've got a surprise for you.'

Jess bought us all ice creams from the beach café (I had mint choc chip, two scoops in a wafer cone) and we loaded back into the car, sandy and windswept.

Niall nobly set straight to work cooking the minute he got back; shirt sleeves rolled up, tie loosened. A single roast quail for each of us, hasselback potatoes, the bluest purple sprouting I'd ever seen, chargrilled cauliflower and a huge salad sprinkled with toasted hazelnuts. As 'birthday girl', I was forbidden from helping, so I sat in Dyl's dressing gown sipping an Aperol spritz and watched as he, Mila and Paddy chopped and peeled in the hot kitchen.

'Think you got the part?' I asked Paddy, topping up his drink.

'We shall see,' he said. 'But it did go unusually well, I must say.'

'You were absolutely buzzing when I met you at Paddington,' said Niall.

'Bravo,' I said. 'How exciting. Well, for entirely selfish reasons, I really hope you get it. I've never seen *Hamlet*.'

Paddy froze midway through peeling a carrot. 'Never seen *Hamlet*?' he said, laying on camp mortification. 'It's the second-most-performed Shakespeare in the world.'

'Is it?' said Niall. 'What's the first?'

'*Midsummer Night's* fucking *Dream*,' said Paddy.

'What's wrong with that?' said Mila.

Paddy let out a harassed sigh. 'Just the comedies,' he said. 'All that laboured mistaken identity bollocks. Such a bore to act. Absolutely nothing to sink your teeth into.'

'Puck's a decent part,' said Niall.

'If I get Hamlet,' Paddy announced, changing tack, 'I think I'll play him gay.'

'Because you are?' said Mila.

'Ha, ha,' said Paddy. 'As a matter of fact, I've always thought Hamlet was gay. He's obsessed with his mother and her sex life, he rejects Ophelia, and he's clearly in love with Horatio.'

'Has that interpretation been explored before?' said Niall.

'Probably in endless theses. But not in a production I've ever seen.'

'Will you do one of the speeches later?' I asked. 'I love that one about the unweeded garden.'

'Maybe. As a birthday treat.'

Mila returned from the larder with a tub of bouillon. 'Those ants,' she said, 'do not stop.'

'Got to admire them, really,' said Niall.

'Agreed,' I said. 'I've grown quite fond of them. It's nice to see them trucking on every morning, still at it.'

'They're everywhere, man,' said Mila. 'It's getting gross.'

Jess appeared at the doorway in shorts and an oversized plaid shirt.

'OK, birthday girl,' she said. 'Clear off. Need to get the garden ready. And no peeking.'

*

'Isn't that Dyl's dressing gown?' Henry said, joining me in the bathroom.

'What?' I said. 'This? Er, yeah. Why?'

He shrugged.

He sat with me while I bathed; his back against the sill of the open windows, the warm evening breeze playing over his hair.

'I made you something,' he said. 'Here.'

He produced a small white parcel of muslin cloth.

'It's some things from the garden – rose petals, lavender, geranium leaves, a little rosemary. If you put them in the bath, you'll smell like flowers all night.'

With one arm dangling over the rim, he swirled the bag around in the water. The heavenly, almost medicinal scent began to waft up and fill the room. I sank back in the tub and imagined the botanicals infusing themselves into my pores, performing some kind of magic.

'It's looking pretty good out there,' he said, head twisting over his shoulder to see the garden. 'You're very spoilt.'

'Yep,' I said. 'I am.'

*

Everyone made a special effort to dress up that night. None of us knew how much longer we would stay here. At some point, we'd all have to return to the city – to our routines and jobs (or, in my case, job hunt), to early starts and laundry – and the evening had a sort of last-supper melancholia about it that I decided to combat with alcohol.

The garden really did look spectacular: Jess had hung

lanterns on the plum trees, lit candles, arranged wild flowers on the table, and chalked our names on to pebbles from the beach as place settings.

Endless wine was drunk. The vast platters and bowls of food left no inch of the table unoccupied. I attempted a speech, thanking everyone for being there and telling them how much I loved them, their smiling faces glowing back at me in the golden dusk. The plates cleared, it was time for my surprise: Mila and Niall emerged from the house with a white-frosted cake, besieged with burning candles, gardenias surrounding it on the plate. 'Happy Birthday' was sung, followed by much applause and toasting.

'To Joni!'

'To summer!'

'To Cornwall!'

'To friendship!'

'To us!'

The sun had taken her final bow, and the candles on the cake gifted light upon the scene. I hated to blow them out.

'Make a wish,' said Mila. And I did.

The cake was delicious: vanilla sponge with thick, American-style buttercream icing. I forked up a glorious mouthful and poured myself more wine, wanting to maintain the precise merry stage of inebriation I had reached.

'Come on then, Paddy,' I called over the table to him. 'Time for your show.'

'Oh, for fuck's sake,' he said. 'I can't, I'm too drunk. I won't remember the lines.'

'What's this?' said Dyl.

'Paddy's going to give us his Hamlet,' I said, licking icing from my finger.

'No,' Paddy said.

'Yes!' said everyone else.

It didn't take too much begging to get him on his feet. We arranged the chairs in a semicircle facing the house, wine glasses in hand. The paved terrace beyond the kitchen door became the stage.

'Right,' said Paddy, swaying on the spot. 'What level of depressing do you want?'

'The more depressing, the better,' called out Dyl.

'It's all quite depressing, isn't it?' said Jess.

'Encore!' called Mila.

'I haven't started yet,' said Paddy. He inhaled loudly through his nose, steadying himself, his body becoming so still that we were all pulled into an awed silence. He fixed his gaze beyond us, out into the dark garden. A look of horror came over his face, so disquieting that I checked behind me to see what he was looking at.

> *Angels and ministers of grace defend us!*
> *Be thou a spirit of health or a goblin damn'd,*
> *Bring with thee airs from heaven or blasts from hell,*
> *Be thy intents wicked or charitable*
> *Thou com'st in such a questionable shape*
> *That I will speak to thee. I'll call thee Hamlet,*
> *King, father, royal Dane. O, answer me?*

None of us moved. We were rapt, held in Paddy's palm, glued to our seats.

> *Let me not burst in ignorance, but tell*
> *Why thy canonised bones, hearsed in death,*
> *Have burst their cerements; why the sepulchre*
> *Wherein we saw thee quietly inurn'd*
> *Hath op'd his ponderous and marble jaws*
> *To cast thee up again. What may this mean*
> *That thou, dead corse, again in complete steel,*

Revisits thus the glimpses of the moon,
Making night hideous, and we fools of nature
So horridly to shake our disposition
With thoughts beyond the reaches of our souls?
Say, why is this? Wherefore? What should we do?

Mila let out a scream. My breath felt trapped in my chest. I seized Henry's hand. A man had appeared in the kitchen door behind Paddy: tall, looming, a sinister smile across his lips.

'Don't mind me. Didn't know I'd be interrupting a performance. Please, please, carry on,' said Uncle Lachlan.

14

Nobody knew when he would leave. Though he was out most days, spending his afternoons and evenings in the Albion, in his absence there was the chronic dread of his drunken reappearance. There he was: hunched over like a great spider, the *Telegraph* spread across the kitchen table; napping along the length of the living room sofa, mouth agape; leaning back in one of the garden chairs at the front of the house, ready to intercept any one of us coming back from the beach like a bellicose gatekeeper. Mealtimes were strained and short-lived: Niall asking Uncle Lachlan polite questions about the history of the house; Lachlan draining the wine supply. One Saturday, Lachlan took it upon himself to do some gardening, and we all stayed trapped in the house like prisoners. Dyl's morning walks became longer and more ambitious, tracing the thread of the treacherous coastline all the way to the next town and back. Niall was spending more and more time in London, Mila often going with him, and Jess, who had been semi-keeping-up with work from her laptop in the kitchen, was making noises about getting back. Henry, whose private equity firm had taken a lenient attitude to his timetable since Marla's death, was also beginning to feel the pressure of an expiry date to our idleness. I myself was finding it impossible to write anything with Lachlan in the house, instead meandering up to the woods and killing a couple of hours on a rug among the enchanter's nightshade, pen and notebook in hand. Here, I carefully took out the newspaper clipping and looked at it. *First Prize: £3,000.* Enough to replace the hole I had made in my inheritance; enough to afford me a happy amnesia of Dyl's betrayal. I leafed through my crowded pages. Was anything I'd written worth that amount of money? Of course not. The prize would go to a real writer, someone with qualifications and published work. I was just another girl with a notebook and far-fetched dreams.

Paddy was called back for a second audition for *Hamlet,* and since the meeting was on a Friday, he declared he'd be staying in the city for the whole weekend to catch up with his housemates and a boy he wanted to see again 'for some cardio'. Jess immediately volunteered to go with him, and Mila and Niall leapt at the opportunity as soon as they heard the plan.

'Should we go, too?' I asked Dyl, sharing a cigarette as we walked with Dolly down to the sea.

'I'm not ready,' he said. 'I can't quite face the idea of life just yet.'

'Me neither,' I said, 'but I'd almost rather deal with life than with Creepy McPervert up there.'

'I know,' said Dyl. 'Maybe you should talk to Henry about it.'

The beach smelled almost pungent with salt, the sun having boiled each rock pool to arid weeds.

'Henry wasn't exactly understanding when I tried talking to him about Lachlan before,' I said, pulling my hair up into a bun.

'What do you mean?'

A vision of Henry being sick over the side of his castellated roof.

'He just got quite defensive. I mean, it is his uncle.'

'What a prick. He should have been unequivocally on your side about that shit.'

'Don't call him a prick.'

'Fine,' said Dyl, unbuttoning his shirt. 'Well if you need back-up, I'm here.'

'Thanks,' I said. 'Jesus, Dylan. I can see your ribs. Like, each individual rib.'

'Ew, don't call me Dylan.'

'Have a bloody sandwich, then.'

He ran into the sea, Dolly bounding into the surf behind him.

In the end, I did speak to Henry about the possibility of leaving.

'It's your family's place,' I said. 'Maybe we should just leave your uncle to it.'

Henry said that Lachlan was unlikely to stick around much longer: he was meant to be joining Henry's mother in the south of France for the final weeks of August.

'We might as well see it out,' he said. 'I have to get back to work soon, anyway. Let's make the most of it while we can.'

*

Mila and Niall appeared in the hallway the next morning, their suitcases packed. Paddy and Jess had already loaded theirs into the car.

'You are coming back, aren't you?' I said.

'Of course,' said Paddy. 'Frankly, I doubt the London stage is ready for an openly gay Prince of Denmark.'

'I'm sure we'll find a way,' said Niall, less optimistic.

I could see from the girls' faces that the next time I saw them would be in the city.

Alone in the car, I cried on the way back from the station. I rolled down all the windows. The air smelled different – sweeter, but almost rotten. On the turn. The house felt astonishingly empty without them there. I stood for a moment in the hallway, praying for signs of life, but heard none. Only the distant sound of the sea: permanent and agitated.

*

When clouds appeared on the horizon on Saturday morning, it was as if I had forgotten they existed, so spoiled had we been by the last few weeks of ceaseless bright blue skies. I had slept terribly, woken by Lachlan stumbling in at the witching hour, and unable to fall back into any kind of satisfying slumber. At least he wouldn't be up for a few hours, shut up all day to sleep off his hangover. Leaving Henry snoozing peacefully, I crept out of bed to see if I could join Dyl and Dolly for their morning walk.

'Dyl?' I whispered, peeping my head around his bedroom door. He was gone. His bed was unmade. Several empty tumblers sat along the windowsill and atop the side table, books and print-outs lay strewn across the floor, and his suitcase was a maelstrom of dirty clothes. I realised I hadn't been in this room for weeks. There was a faint smell of something I suspected I had encountered once before but couldn't identify – vinegary and sour.

My head throbbed from lack of sleep, and my whole body felt stiff and sore as I descended the stairs to the kitchen. One of the chairs had been knocked over. An empty bottle of gin lay on its side by the sink, the counter sticky with its remnants. A greasy frying pan and spatula sat abandoned on the Aga, and on a plate on the table, a knife and fork lay half-sunk into a rind of animal fat. Lachlan must have made himself a midnight snack – his shoes and coat were in a pile on the floor. Weak and achy, I went to the larder to fetch some cereal, needing some sustenance before clearing up this mess.

They were dead, all across the windowsill and along the shelves: the ants. Those diligent little warriors I had come to call our friends for the summer, their minute black bodies as unmoving as the grains of sugar they had been bearing. So many of them. I could smell the poison. Lachlan had obviously taken his gin-fuelled vengeance last night. Without thinking, I made a bowl with the front of my nightie and scooped them all in, every single one of them, as gently as I could. Even in their great number, they weighed nothing in my skirt. I carried them down to the bottom of the garden and shook them all out into the brook, half-hoping they would come back to life as they hit the clear water. It carried them downstream, as quick and weightless as tiny leaves.

The clouds had rolled their way in from the sea, the daylight strange and glaring. My nightie whipped around me. I stood for a while watching the stream run over the grey stones; rivulets of sand filtering their way through the weeds. A door was slammed in the house. I turned, the wind beating my ears. It must have been Lachlan, finding one reason or another to release a deluge of hungover aggression at Henry. I headed back, ready to defend him if I had to. Coming through the lavender along the garden path, I heard voices. It wasn't Lachlan and Henry. It was *Dyl* and Henry.

I found them in the hallway: Dyl pacing around the small space like a caged animal, Henry standing, one hand on a hip and the other held loosely around his own throat.

'Calm down,' said Henry. 'For God's sake, please.'

'Hi,' I said.

'Oh, Phil.' Dyl covered his face when he saw me. 'Oh, God.'

'Hey,' I said, going to him, taking his wrists. 'What's wrong?'

It was Henry who spoke. 'He lost Dolly,' he said, causing Dyl to yell an expletive into his cupped hands.

'What?' I said.

'On their walk this morning,' Henry went on, 'Dolly ran off and didn't come back.'

'Oh, God, I called and called for her,' said Dyl, pacing again. 'But she didn't come.'

'Shit,' I said, then instantly regretted it.

Dyl's eyes were wide and frightened. 'I'm sorry,' he said, fists pulling at his hair. 'I'm so, so sorry, Henry. I don't understand it. She always comes back when I call.'

'Yes, she does,' said Henry, his agreement ominous.

'We'll find her,' I said, resolute. 'We'll go looking for her. She probably got lost chasing a rabbit or something.'

I looked at Henry, whose stare was fixed on the ground.

'I'm sure she's fine,' I pressed on. 'She's a clever old girl.'

'She *is*,' whimpered Dyl. 'Fuck. I'm such an idiot. I'll leave. I'll get the train back to London.'

'Shut up,' I said. 'Go have a coffee. Or a whisky. Henry and I will go out looking for her now. She knows his voice, I'm sure she'll come back.'

Henry said nothing.

'Right, Henry?'

'Yeah,' he said.

'Tell us where you were?'

'Oh, God,' said Dyl. 'Miles away. It was over by Porthcurno, on the coastal path.'

'For fuck's sake,' Henry muttered under his breath.

'I'm so sorry,' Dyl said again. 'I'm so, so sorry, Henry. I'm a twat, I should just go.'

'What the fuck is all this?'

Lachlan had appeared at the top of the stairs, still in yesterday's crumpled clothes, one hand holding him steady on the banister.

'Dolly's run off,' said Henry. 'We're going to find her.'

'Stupid fucking beast. I always told Christiane she was a wrong'un. Useless gun dog.'

'Let's go,' said Henry, walking out the front door before I had a chance to answer him.

'Dyl,' I said, squeezing his bony shoulder. 'Stay here. It'll be alright. I promise.'

We drove some of the way at a crawl, calling Dolly's name out of the windows and scanning the landscape for signs of her. At the next cove, we parked the car and walked the public footpath along the coast. A strong wind came up off the sea, buffeting and swallowing our cries. Coconut-scented gorse carpeted the land. Every time I bellowed the dog's name, I waited to see her head pop up from the golden flowers, for her to come bounding over to us – tongue lolling, ears flapping as she ran. Henry walked in front of me, ploughing onwards and onwards, communicating nothing to me. When we'd set off, the sun had warmed my back even through the clouds; now it broke through ahead of us in the west. When we passed a beach café, I looked longingly at the customers in the booths enjoying cream teas. The physical symptoms of my insomnia, which had disappeared in the initial panic, sank back over my body. If this had been the path that Dyl had taken this morning, where was there for the poor dog to disappear to – if not over the high cliff's edge, into the crashing foam of the waves?

'Dolly!' we yelled until we were hoarse. The landscape remained still. It was like waiting for a painting to start talking to you.

At long last, Henry marched into an old seaside tavern and I gratefully hurried in after him.

'Go and sit down,' he told me, heading to the bar. He returned moments later with a pint of stout, which he placed on the table in front of me.

'Drink this,' he said, not joining me. 'You'll feel better. I'll pay for it when I get back. Didn't bring my wallet in all the commotion.'

'Where are you going?'

'I'll go back the same way and keep trying, then I'll come and pick you up. Give me the car keys.'

I handed them over.

'Henry,' I said. 'It'll be alright. You'll come back with her in the passenger seat, I can feel it.'

He nodded. 'I've told the barmaid here to keep an eye out, and I'll tell the owners of that café we passed to do the same.'

He left. I sipped the thick, dark beer. It was extremely bitter, but it filled me up, and I felt my muscles relax under its influence. The kindly barmaid served me two more pints of it by the time Henry returned, alone.

'Let's go,' he said.

In the car, his silence was so oppressive I could barely face him.

'I still think she'll show up,' I said, not believing myself. 'Fiona's old cat went missing for a whole week once.'

Henry said nothing, but continued to glare ahead, his jaw set.

'I know you're upset, but don't get mad at Dyl, OK? He's not in a great place. Underneath all that bravado, he's actually incredibly sensitive. He's too proud to say anything, but he's fucked up his deadline, and it looks like—'

Henry suddenly thwacked his palm down hard on the steering wheel. 'Fucking hell,' he shouted.

'What?' I said, almost trembling with shock.

'His *deadline*? Big fucking deal. He needs to grow up.'

'I don't—'

'Oh just shut the fuck up, would you?'

I swallowed. 'Don't speak to me like that,' I said.

A few moments passed in silence, then Henry said, 'I buried my sister this year, Joni.'

I looked at him for the first time since we'd got in the car. His knuckles white, tears in his beautiful green eyes.

'I know you did, Henry. I know.'

'And Dolly.' He cleared his throat. 'We've had her since I was at school.'

Finally, I found the courage to reach out to him, placing my hand on his leg.

*

Dyl became more and more remote over the next few days. I never saw him eat. The evenings were especially difficult. He hated the thought of darkness coming in and Dolly being out there alone, lost and afraid in the gorse. When Henry and I had returned in the empty car, Dyl was standing by the front door waiting for us, an exhausted cigarette butt in his hand. We hadn't been able to stop him tearing down the garden path, refusing to give up the quest. Since then, he had spent hours out of the house, searching the paths all along the Cornish coast for Dolly, arriving back in the afternoons windswept and silent, only to go out again as the sun set. For my part, I was grappling to hold on to any hope of ever seeing poor Dolly again, the notion slipping away like water down a drain. Henry and Dyl were tense and strained around each other, with me hopelessly caught somewhere in the middle. I tried to keep up a semblance of the happiness we had enjoyed here all summer, suggesting picnics and sea swims to no avail. In the end, I kept myself engrossed in domesticity: cleaning the bathrooms, doing laundry, taking sole responsibility for the preparation of meals. The house, which had felt like a safe haven, a wild and beautiful sanctum far away from reality, seemed to have lost its magic spell. I could no longer keep away thoughts of my own imminent departure for the city.

I fell asleep reading one day, and woke to find the light in our bedroom paling. The window was wide open – I don't think we'd closed it once since arriving here, weeks ago – and for the first time, I felt a chill in the air; a premature hint of autumn coming in. I pulled on Henry's woollen fisherman's jumper and crept down the upstairs landing. There were voices coming from the bathroom. Henry's voice, adopting the matter-of-fact, soothing tone I had only heard him use with Clara and Jem. I stopped and listened at the door.

'Don't worry. Just try not to talk for a minute, OK? I won't tell Joni.'

'Tell me what?'

Dyl was sitting in the bath, the knuckles of his spine visible in his curved back, muttering nonsensically. Henry was crouched down next to him, pouring a jug of steaming water over his shoulders.

'Tell me what?' I said again, crossing the room to look Dyl in the eye.

'Nothing,' said Henry, standing and gently attempting to usher me away. 'He's fine, just stayed in the sea a bit too long.'

'What?' I said, batting Henry's arms off me. 'Dyl, what happened?'

'I'll tell you later,' Henry whispered.

'What's happened? You went for a swim?'

'Yeah, just a swim,' Dyl said quietly.

Henry was eyeballing me, the set of his features odd and pregnant with an emotion I couldn't name.

'Henry?'

He said nothing. I left.

Further and further away from the house; right down to the bottom of the garden, to the brook. I waded in, the water so cold it burned my feet, so cold it ached, so cold it was nearly unbearable. It took all my strength just to stay there, the stream rushing past my ankles, the pain pushing out thought and feeling until numbness came.

I was lying on the bank in the darkness when Henry came and found me. He joined me among the meadowsweet, tumbler of whisky in hand.

'There's Orion,' he said, waving his glass up at the sky.

We lay there for a while, bodies sinking into the earth.

'Is he OK?'

'He's asleep.'

The brook kept up its melodic trickling over the stones. I caught a whiff of Henry's Scotch and sat up, taking it from his hand and swallowing the rest of it in one gulp.

'So,' I said. 'What happened?'

'He's an idiot. He stayed in for too long and was borderline hypothermic. He'll be fine.'

'Right.' I tucked my legs up and pulled Henry's jumper over my knees.

'Don't do that, you'll stretch it,' said Henry.

'I'm cold.'

'You should've put a coat on.'

'What didn't Dyl want you to tell me?' I asked.

'What?'

'That's what you said – "Don't worry, I won't tell Joni."'

'Oh. Nothing. He didn't want you to worry, I suppose. Just embarrassed.'

'Dyl doesn't get embarrassed around me.'

'OK, fine,' Henry snapped. 'Since you know him better than anyone else, why don't you go inside and wake him up? Ask him yourself.'

'Why are you being weird?'

'You go on as if you're the ultimate authority on him. He does it, too, about you. It's fucking annoying.' Henry went into an impression of Dyl's North London accent, lazier than Henry's own. '*The thing you have to understand about Joni is . . . Oh yeah, typical Joni . . . Well, Joni would never admit this to you, but . . .*'

'Stop it.'

'Sorry, but it's maddening. Do you have any idea how difficult it is falling in love with someone who comes with a tour guide?'

I laughed. 'Dyl is many things to me, but I don't need a fucking tour guide. He knows me well – yes, probably better than you, we've been friends our whole lives. That doesn't mean, you know, that we—'

'*We*!? You're a "we" with someone else. This is what I'm talking about. You come with a side order of each other. You're totally fucking *enmeshed* or something.'

I swallowed. The sea crashed beneath the sound of

the wind. In the moonlight, the old willow tree appeared ghostly and apathetic.

'I was going to say that doesn't mean we, as in *you and I*, Henry, need to let that get in the way of our relationship.'

He let out something between a laugh and a sigh. 'I suppose we should go back to London tomorrow,' he said.

'Yes,' I said. 'I think we should.'

*

Lachlan was out at the Albion when we drove away from the house, Henry next to me in the front and Dyl lying over his rucksack in the back. It rained a little when we got to the motorway. Henry inserted one of the CDs I'd added to the glovebox, and we let first the Arctic Monkeys, then various *Now That's What I Call Music!*s, then finally Leonard Cohen take us all the way back to the city.

'See you soon,' I said to Dyl, pulling up across the street from his flat.

'Yeah. Thank you, Henry. For everything.'

'Bye,' said Henry.

I didn't get out and hug him, but watched as he made his way up the steps to his front door, turned his key in the lock, and disappeared inside without looking back.

'Am I coming back to yours, or . . .?' I asked Henry, without looking at him.

'If you like,' he said.

It had been a long drive.

The sun came out again as I opened the windows inside the stale Albany apartment, its sepia, late-summer light spilling over the dusty carpet.

Henry began kissing me in bed that night. It was a shock; we'd barely spoken all day.

I went with it, searching for something at the bottom

of his kisses. There was an urgency to his movements that impressed on me the sense that he, too, was searching for something. What, I don't know; but I suspect he didn't find it either.

15

One night when we were sixteen, I told my parents I was staying at Mila's house, and Dyl told his parents nothing. It seemed that, because he was a boy, he could get away with staying out all night, no questions asked. There was no real plan other than to get away, even if it was just for one night. Both of us were living in the apotheosis of teen-age disillusionment, using words like apotheosis a lot. We weaned ourselves on to Marlboro Lights, on the threshold of filling out UCAS forms – apparently responsible enough to decide what single occupation we were ready to devote the rest of our lives to.

It was a Friday, about halfway through our first term of sixth form, the euphoric post-GCSE summer now behind us. The stress and regimens of those exams now seemed risible: all that highlighting and extra tutoring for tests that looked like a walk in the park compared to those we were now studying for. We thought we'd reached the top of the hill, only to find it was merely a plateau on the way up a mountain. Dyl and I both felt it was time for a blowout.

The night began at Theodore's, sharing the cheapest bottle of red wine on the menu. I remember Dyl was sporting a beret, which made him look both handsome and ridiculous. In my bag was a four-pack of lager I had taken from my parents' fridge. Al, the manager, swept over, his black hair slicked back with grease.

'Will you be having anything to eat with your Shiraz?' he said, one hand leaning on our table.

We smiled sheepishly back at him.

'Sorry, Al,' I said. 'On a budget.'

'Yeah, yeah, yeah. You can afford to drink my wine, though.'

'How are you, Al?' asked Dyl.

'Me? How am I? Terrible. Dreadful. Not good.'

'Oh no,' I said, accustomed to his hyperbolic pessimism. 'Why?'

Al let out a long, exasperated sigh. 'My wife,' he said, 'she is wanting a bigger house. I tell her, you go to work, we can have a bigger house.'

'What did she say?'

'She said she does not want to take tube train every day, every morning. People packed in like small fish.'

'Fair enough.'

'She's very spoilt, my wife. I buy her nice things every week: a new bag, new shoes. You know, she loves shoes. Very spoilt woman.'

'Lucky her.'

'It's never enough! She wants to live in a big palace. I tell her, you have to go get a job for this.'

'Couldn't she work here, with you?' asked Dyl.

Al looked completely affronted, as if we'd just suggested he employ a team of terminally ill children. 'And see her all day, every day? No, no, no. It's bad for marriage.'

'Yes,' I said, sympathetically.

'You know, life,' Al said, gaze fixed on some faraway mental image, 'is not for the faint-hearted.'

'Cheers to that,' said, Dyl, raising his glass.

'Where is the nice girl you were here with the other day?' Al asked.

'We broke up,' said Dyl, mournfully.

I scoffed; Dyl had dumped his latest fling because he said she was 'too nice'.

'It's too bad,' said Al. 'I bring you something to eat, no charge.'

'Aw, thanks, Al,' I said. 'You're the best.'

He ignored this, and returned a few minutes later with a couple of bowls of French onion soup.

'Delicious,' said Dyl. 'Thank you.'

Al walked off, waving a laconic hand behind him.

We were tipsy and full by the time we left, lips and teeth stained burgundy.

'What now?' I said.

'Texted my dealer,' said Dyl, 'but he's not answering. Do you know anyone?'

'I don't. But Paddy will have someone. Hang on.'

'He the one you met at Pride?'

'That's the one.'

Paddy sent an address for one John Johnson in Kensal Green, with instructions to say we were 'friends of Caroline'. Forty minutes later, we nervously rang the doorbell of a basement flat on a posh street of imposing Victorian four-storeys, with bars across their windows and security cameras over their front doors. I told Dyl to take off his stupid hat.

'Yeah?' said a voice over the intercom, thrumming music audible in the background.

'Hi,' I said. 'We're friends of Caroline?'

'Hang on,' said the voice.

A couple of minutes went by and we wondered whether to ring again, but eventually the door opened, and there stood a man of about fifty, his thinning hair styled into a spiky quiff at the front, a Metallica T-shirt straining over his belly.

'Come in, come in,' he said, and we followed him down a narrow hallway to a boxy room towards the back of the building. He took a seat at a desk and gestured for us to sit down. A faded Indian throw covered in dog hairs was strewn over a low futon on one side of the room, and we perched here cautiously, side by side. Across a small table covered in old cups of coffee was another sofa, on which sat a skinny man and a fat bulldog.

'Alright,' said the skinny man, dozily.

'Hey,' said Dyl.

Repetitive house music blared from a pair of pink and silver speakers in the corner. The air hung thick and dank.

'What you after, then?' said John Johnson, spinning around in his office chair.

'Just an eighth, please,' said Dyl.

'Weed?' said John Johnson.

'Yeah.'

The skinny man was toking on what I had assumed was a spliff but didn't smell like any weed I'd ever come across before – it smelled like vinegar. He offered it to us with a start, as if remembering his manners. We declined as politely as we could. The dog looked sadly up at us.

John Johnson had produced the largest bag of marijuana I'd ever seen in my life, and was extracting a swollen bud from it, which he now placed on some digital scales on his desk.

'There you go, three point six: little bit extra for you there,' he said.

'Oh, cheers,' I said.

He licked his finger and pinched out a small plastic baggy from a dispenser, into which he carefully laid the bud, then looked up at us, expectantly. Dyl got out a twenty-pound note and handed it over. John Johnson gave us the weed and turned back to his desk, engaged with some other dubious paraphernalia. I gave Dyl a pointed look. *Can we go now?* Dyl shrugged and relaxed into the futon.

'Alright if we sample the goods?' he asked.

John Johnson remained hunched over his work. 'Be my guest,' he said.

Dyl got out some king skins and tobacco and started rolling us a joint, grating some of the bud up in his Jimi Hendrix grinder. I watched as he created an elaborate L-shaped formation, showing off for the benefit of the skinny man, who laughed a high-pitched giggle and said, 'Someone's done that before.'

I dug the heel of my Doc Marten into Dyl's foot. *Let's go.* He shifted his leg out of the firing zone and sparked up. I noticed a collage of newspaper cuttings tacked up above John Johnson's desk: photographs, scraps of handwritten notes and articles assembled forensically from floor to ceiling. The word 'Stonehenge' jumped out at me, as well as what looked like maths homework in red crayon on the back of an envelope.

Dyl blew a long plume of smoke past my face. 'Aw, mate.' He coughed. 'That's nice.' He held the joint out to the skinny man. In leaning over to take it, the skinny man knocked over a half-empty mug of black coffee, brown liquid spilling on to Dyl's jeans.

'Fuck,' said Dyl, leaping up.

'Whoa, sorry, brother,' the skinny man said, chuckling.

'That's gonna stain.' Dyl was rubbing at a patch on his leg. 'Can I use your loo, please?'

'Second door on the left,' said John Johnson.

'I'll come with you,' I said, not wanting to be left alone with the men.

Locking the door behind us, I hissed at Dyl, 'Can we leave, please?'

'Give me a second. I finally found vintage jeans that fit me perfectly. They're irreplaceable.'

'You're a dick.'

Dyl was splashing water from the sink in the general direction of his stained trouser leg.

'For fuck's sake,' I said, desperate to speed things up. 'Take them off a second, I'll do it.'

Dyl swore and kicked off his shoes, before removing his jeans and handing them over. 'There,' he said.

'You mean, thank you,' I said, taking them and holding the stain under a tap.

With the aid of some dog shampoo, any trace of coffee was removed, albeit leaving the jeans pretty wet.

'Christ,' I said, handing them back to him. 'You're literally so vain you'd rather look like you've pissed yourself than wait till you get home to wash them.'

'Couldn't risk it, mate.'

As Dyl hopped to get dressed again, I noticed his bare thigh for the first time, and the lines of white and red across it.

'Dylan, what the fuck?' I said.

There was a loud knock on the door and I yelped.

'Alright, kids,' shouted John Johnson. 'This isn't a hotel.'

I was staring at Dyl, but he wouldn't catch my eye. He straightened himself up and headed back to the living room. I followed helplessly behind, dropping onto the sofa again, speechless.

'Hey, man,' said Dyl in John Johnson's direction. 'You got any brown?'

I couldn't speak, the shock from the bathroom crashing into this one, my brain struggling to catch up.

John Johnson spun hastily round to face us. He stared, unreadable, his eyes boring into us and yet not seeing us at all. I thought he was going to yell at us when, out of nowhere, he burst out laughing. The skinny man started to laugh, too, a little behind him, as if there were a delay in his brain. I looked, panic-stricken, at Dyl.

'Ah,' sighed John Johnson, righting himself. 'The kid wants some H. Alright. You got cash?'

'Dyl,' I said, finding my voice, looking on in disbelief as he got out his wallet once more.

The skinny man was still shaking with his high-pitched giggle.

'Let's see it,' said Dyl.

John Johnson opened a drawer in his desk and produced a metal safe box. He took two steps over to the sofa and petted the bulldog.

'Good girl,' he said, stroking her wrinkly head. 'Good girl.'

He put his hands around her neck. I gasped in panic, thinking he might hurt her, but he twisted her collar around to reveal a flap in the buckle, from which he removed a small key.

'Abracadabra,' he said, unlocking the safe box. 'High-grade, from Morocco.'

Dyl bounced over to inspect the heroin. As if he would have any idea what he was looking at. I pulled my bag over my shoulder and gripped the strap tightly, like it was a seatbelt holding me into a particularly fast car.

'How much?' said Dyl.

'Forty,' said John Johnson. 'First-time buyer discount.'

I could feel the skinny man watching me.

'Dyl,' I said. 'Let's go.'

'Alright,' he said, not to me.

'Dyl,' I said, louder this time. 'Stop it. For fuck's sake.'

'She's nervous,' said the skinny man.

I stood up, John Johnson suddenly taking me in. 'Where are you going?' he said.

'Calm down, Phil,' said Dyl. 'It's not a big deal.'

'Yeah, it is. I want to go. I'm leaving, are you coming or not?'

Dyl laughed. 'Just wait two minutes.'

I was halfway out of the room when the doorbell rang.

'Oi!' John Johnson yapped. 'Sit down.'

I froze.

'Wait here,' he said, and went out to the hallway to answer the intercom. We waited, silently, listening. 'Yeah?' he barked, and then we heard his voice change. 'Oh, hello, darling. Hang on.'

He returned moments later with a girl: tall, dark hair, just a few years older than Dyl and me. It was Marla Taschen.

'Hi,' I said, recognising her from the warehouse rave where we'd met in the summer.

'Hi!' she said, friendly enough, but definitely not remembering me.

John Johnson simpered around her like a fawning aunt. 'Can I get you anything, darling? Beer? Mushroom tea?'

'I'm good, thanks, Johnny,' she said, kicking off her ballet pumps and going over to the dog. 'Hey, Maudie, girl.' She gave the animal a big kiss. 'Y'alright, Lee?'

'Alright,' said the skinny man.

'How've you been, Johnny?' asked Marla.

'Not too bad, darling, yeah, not too bad. Business is a little quiet since the raid.'

'Oh no,' said Marla, condolingly.

'You still want this, or what?' said John Johnson to Dyl, one meaty hand over the lockbox.

'We're fine,' I said. 'We'll get going now.'

'Suit yourself,' he said, snapping it shut. 'See yourselves out.'

I didn't need telling twice. Dyl was not far behind as I marched out of the basement flat and back out on to the street. It was dark now.

'Literally, Dylan, what the hell?' I continued to walk, marching blindly onward, wanting to create more and more distance between us and that flat, the awful house music still pulsing in my bloodstream.

'What?' he said, chasing me. 'I didn't get any!'

'You would have if Henry's sister hadn't shown up.'

'Is that who that was? I thought I recognised her.'

'Fucking hell,' I said, still going.

I didn't stop until we got to the cemetery, ducking in through the iron railings; an impulse to hide drawing me away from the streets. Ploughing deeper and deeper, taking spontaneous turns down the avenues of tombstones, I finally stopped at a wooden bench, where I plonked myself down and took a can of lager from my bag. Dyl caught up, a little out of breath.

'I think we lost 'em, Captain,' he said, sitting down beside me.

We smoked a joint in silence until Dyl began to invent stories about the names on the graves.

'Enid Wyndham,' he said. '1811 to 1863. Beloved mother and part-time dominatrix.'

'Hugh Stanley,' I joined in. '1890 to 1915, stamp collector and cat-person.'

'James Moore: taxidermist.'

'Susan Presley: distant cousin of Elvis.'

Mellowed and a little buzzy, we left by way of the Dissenters' Chapel, and walked out into the night. A lazy mist obscured the houses, the lights inside seeming brighter and more glorious. The invincible teenage freedom of walking through the city at night had me giddy. I felt we could go on and on forever, out of London and into the fields, all the way to the sea, catching a boat to the continent, making a pilgrimage to the equator. Why not? We followed the canal, the countryside smell of coal fires coming off the boats, the damp gently stealing down and coating every surface with a sheen that glistened in the light of the windows. At Regent's Park, we climbed back out of the waterway and headed north, through the Rose Garden and past the zoo, slowly ascending the winding path up Primrose Hill.

'I might be quite stoned,' said Dyl, 'but damn, it looks good tonight.'

The skyline of London rose, majestic and twinkling, out of the trees. There wasn't another soul to be seen. The empty park, the whole city, felt entirely ours. It was faintly apocalyptic.

'What would scare you more . . .' I said, opening another beer.

'Don't,' said Dyl. 'You'll get me pranging.'

I laughed. 'What would scare you more: if we saw a woman in white, just walking through the trees—'

'Stop it.'

'Or creepy Victorian children, right behind us.'

'Dude,' said Dyl. 'You're killing my buzz.'

'You have to answer,' I said.

'Ugh. I think the children would be worse. The woman in white could just be a girl on her way back from Camden on a Friday night.'

'OK,' I said, thinking. I had no idea why I was trying to freak us out; perhaps the ghostly atmosphere of the murky night was just too palpable not to vocalise.

'I've got it,' I said.

'Here we go.'

'What would be scarier: if we saw creepy Victorian children hanging from that lamp post, or if we saw us.'

'Huh?'

'If we saw ourselves. Our doppelgängers. You and me. Like, twenty feet in front of us. Wearing the exact same clothes, having the exact same conversation, with our faces and our voices.'

'Shit,' said Dyl, and shuddered. 'That'd be grim.'

'I know!' I said, rushing at the thought.

There was a moment as we both pictured it, our THC-addled brains painting the scene before our eyes.

'We'd have to kill them,' said Dyl, which gave me the giggles.

Red eyes from the tops of distant cranes winked at us. It grew colder and the wind more lively. We huddled together.

'Dyl,' I said, as we shared our final drink. 'You weren't really serious earlier, were you? About buying smack?'

He smirked out at the horizon. 'I don't know,' he said, and laughed. 'It seems like a terrible idea now, doesn't it?'

'No shit.'

'Nah. Just being stupid, I guess.'

I snuggled deeper into the warmth of his body; he smelled of fags and cheap aftershave.

'Your leg,' I said.

'Don't,' he said.

And I didn't.

16

'I won't mince my words, Joni,' said Fiona. We were sitting on a tartan rug underneath the ash tree in her garden. 'Jenny's visa expires in a month, and I've said she can have the annexe when she gets back, until she finds work.'

'Oh,' I said. 'So, I need to move out?'

'I'm afraid so, hen. I think it's time, anyway. Jenny has found it difficult how close you and I have become, what with you two being a similar age. I think she feels displaced, or to put it bluntly, *re*placed. I didn't point out to her that she's the one who moved to bloody Australia.'

I laughed.

'But there we go,' she said, smoothing out her corner of the rug. 'Perhaps she needed to miss me.'

'I'll miss you,' I said.

'I'll miss you too.'

I sipped my ginger tea and watched as a robin hopped from the rim to the centre of the stone bird bath, ruffling its whole body happily in the water.

'I might as well pack today, while I'm here,' I said.

'Oh,' she said. 'Jenny won't be here for weeks. Take your time, hen.'

The leaves were turning brown, and the sun, though bright in the clear sky, cast long shadows from its lower axis.

'It's alright, Fi,' I said. 'I think it's time, as you say.'

'I didn't mean today!' Fiona said, laughing even as tears

welled in her eyes. 'I've barely seen you lately – you're almost never here. I hoped we could have a proper good-bye, cook you a farewell supper.'

She was right: I hadn't really been living here since we got back from Cornwall. At some point, it had become a given that I spent every night at the Albany. There weren't even that many of my belongings left up in the studio. I had unpacked my summer suitcase at Henry's, only return-ing a couple of times to retrieve books and warmer clothes. It was a relief in a way, her asking me to go. I certainly could no longer afford the rent, generous as the rate was.

I went up to the top of the house, to the rooms I'd been living in for the last two and a half years. Packing away my remaining belongings didn't take long, and I didn't afford myself time to pause and contemplate the history of each possession. Once it was cleared, I stood in the empty bedroom and smoked a final cigarette out of the window, as I'd done hundreds of times before. I thought about the notable cigarettes of my time here: the ones that had slowed my tears, the ones that had punctuated celebration, the ones I had smoked post-sex. The sex I'd had in that bed – the number of orgasms I'd faked; the much smaller number I hadn't. The late-night giggles with friends, the quiet days when these rooms had simply held me. I thought about how much had happened in the time since I'd been here. Twenty-three years old. It seemed so young now. I saw myself arriving for the first time: her cheap jeans and bad make-up; her irreverence, her hope.

Everything I owned fitted into two large suitcases and one laundry bag. I considered throwing it all away.

Fiona held me and told me to come over any time. She promised to cook me my favourite meal, which wasn't really my favourite anymore, but I didn't have the heart to tell her. I drove away from that house and that chapter of my life. I no longer worked for Terry and Raf, I no longer lived in that particular corner of North London. The entire evidence of my life was in this car, sinking down into a tunnel at Hyde Park.

*

Paddy had got the part, and Henry and I came with Mila and Niall to see him perform on his opening night. It was our first attempt at a double date, and it felt peculiar and adult to be hanging out in this new formation. We hadn't seen each other much since Cornwall. Everyone seemed infected by the back-to-school atmosphere of the autumn – my attempts to organise gatherings had been met with various versions of 'Got too much work on, sorry'. Henry came home tired, too, and our nights in at the Albany were culminating in arguments more and more frequently. I was glad to be out at last with friends.

The play was spectacular; Paddy was spectacular. The production was modest and unpretentious: the simplicity of the sets and costumes allowing space for the language and performances to shine. Sitting there in the dark, the collective consciousness of a hundred strangers fine-tuned to every syllable, I was struck by how much of it I already knew. Not just the plot, but whole lines and turns of phrase, written by Shakespeare centuries ago, that had found their way into my frame of reference. It gave me the sense of being told a story I had perhaps heard as a child. Paddy was utterly transformed. I saw nothing of my friend before me. I saw Hamlet – anguished, intelligent, desperate. Unrecognisable as he was, the experience of hearing these words spoken, as if directly and solely to me, by someone I knew so well, was mesmerising.

Afterwards, we took our starlet to a little bar above Borough Market and drank to him.

'Bravo,' said Niall, clinking all of our glasses.

'Congratulations,' said Henry.

'You were so good!' said Mila.

'Seriously,' I said. 'Incredible.'

'Oh, please,' said Paddy, dragging one hand roughly over his face as if removing the mask. 'Don't stop.'

I was more than happy to indulge him. Paddy and I got through several rounds discussing the play.

'I'm in awe,' I said. 'You transformed.'

'Thank you, darling, really, I'm very touched,' he said. 'Frankly, it's just a wonderful excuse for me to work out some of my daddy issues.'

I laughed.

'Shall I tell you something?' he said, still smiling despite the noticeable gear change.

'Always.'

'Sometimes I look out to the audience, during O, *what a rogue*, and I think I see him. My father.'

'I didn't know you knew what he looked like,' I said.

'I don't. Not really. I just see some random middle-aged man, and my heart skips a beat, and I think, *What if it's him?* I sound crackers, don't I?'

'No,' I said. 'I think I understand.'

'You know, I sometimes think it's why I became an actor,' said Paddy, transitioning back into jest on the turn of a penny. 'So I'd become horrifically rich and famous, and my father would inevitably come looking for me, after a bit of my fortune to buy Strongbow and women.'

'What would you say?' I asked.

'I'd tell him to go fuck himself.'

'You should put that in your bio in the programme,' I said.

'Ha!' he laughed. 'Paddy Mears trained at the Royal Acting Academy. His credits include *All My Sons* at the Queen's Theatre, and he's doing all of this for revenge.'

We drank to that.

'What was that line,' I said, gripping his arm, 'about a straw, in your final soliloquy—'

'"To be great is not to stir without great argument, but greatly to find quarrel in a straw, when honour's at the stake",' Paddy quoted instantly.

'What does that mean?'

'It means that to be truly great isn't about only fighting for great causes; it's about fighting over nothing if your honour is at stake.'

'Yeesh.'

'Quite.'

'Honour. What does that *mean*? We don't really have honour anymore, do we?'

Paddy laughed. 'Is honour dead?' he said.

'It just seems so anachronistic now, doesn't it? The very notion of honour. Of that being something so sacred and autonomous, something worth fighting for.'

'Don't worry,' said Paddy. 'No one's about to ask you to fight for your honour any time soon.'

'But I don't think I *have* any!' I said, waving my hand wildly in the air, spilling the last of my vodka and Coke. 'Oh, shit.'

'Henry,' I said. 'Henry, can you get me another drink?'

Henry looked me over as if I were a broken piece of furniture. 'Er . . .'

'Come to the bar with me, Joni,' said Niall, jumping up.

'Thank you, Niall,' I said, turning away from Henry.

Niall wrapped a strong arm around my waist as we walked. I felt flooded with warmth for him.

'You're so generous,' I said. 'Always getting the rounds in.'

He laughed.

When we got to the bar, he poured me a large glass of water from the jug on the counter.

'Drink that quickly,' he said. 'Before you have another.'

'I don't want it.'

'Come on, or you'll feel horrible tomorrow.'

I gulped it down and stuck my tongue out at him.

*

Henry barely spoke as the taxi wormed its way through the dark city streets. I felt like a child in the back seat, my head lolling on the window frame, sleepily watching the buildings pass by. We got out on the corner of Savile Row, and walked silently through the courtyard and up the stairs.

'I'm just getting in the shower,' Henry said. My head hit the pillow, wondering how to fill my time tomorrow. There was only so much walking around – notebook and pen poised – I could do. My habitual rule of no drinks before 5 p.m. was slackening each day. I had taken to retrieving the newspaper cutting from my notebook and simply staring at it, as if a genie might appear. It was almost October and the deadline loomed ever closer.

I needed a job, and was utterly unqualified to do anything. I could nanny again – Terry would no doubt give me a glowing reference out of guilt – but the thought of looking after children who weren't Clara and Jem held no appeal, and something in my gut told me that a change was the best way forward.

233

Henry came to bed, and we proceeded with our new routine of wordless and mechanical sex. He fell asleep, as always, before I did; leaving me lying there wondering what I could do to make things normal between us again. Wondering why Dyl wasn't replying to my messages. Wondering how the hell I would become even remotely solvent again. Wondering what the hell I was doing.

*

T. C. Recruitment Agency was in the City, where the gothic and glass buildings seem shipwrecked along the riverbank. The pavement was wet. My tights kept slipping down as I walked, and every time I stopped to hoist them up, the strap of my bag fell off my shoulder and on to the rainy ground. Urgent suited men passed me as I struggled, some perusing my shape with their gaze, others impervious to my existence.

The mirror in the lift was not kind. Blotches of pink showed through my thick make-up. My shirt was bulging unflatteringly out from where I'd tucked it in, and my hair was damp and flat on my head. I pressed the button for the fifth floor and turned to face the doors.

'Hi there,' I said to the receptionist. 'I have a meeting with Pamela? My name's Joan—'

'Take a seat, please.'

The waiting area was filled with women: some young, some old, all carefully dressed – hair tied back, matching brown pant suits, simple crucifix necklaces. I took my place among them on one of the plastic, municipal-issue chairs. The tall girl sitting next to me had terrible body odour, the kind only induced by nervousness or stress. She smiled at me as I sat down. After a while, the receptionist called my name and led me to another room filled with more women and some men, all hunched over, frowning at computer screens.

'You have twenty minutes,' she said.

First, there was a spelling test. It was simple enough. At the end, the computer informed me that I had scored ninety per cent. Next, some basic maths – eighty-five per cent. Then I was asked to complete a series of technical tasks using the computer itself: *Open Excel. Create a spreadsheet five columns wide. Without using the mouse, insert another column. Use column C to calculate the product of Columns A and B.* This was not my field of expertise. The tasks became more complicated. I became aware of the sweat on my back. The computer told me I had scored fifteen per cent. For the last test, I had to complete some image sequences (sixty per cent). Afterwards, I went back to the waiting room. Maybe it didn't matter I was such a luddite. The job I wanted was in the British Library, making sure people were quiet and placing returned books back on their shelves. I would wear cardigans and wide-legged corduroy trousers, and buy myself an enamel lunchbox for my sandwiches and fruit juice. Apparently, I wanted to work in the 1950s.

'Joan?' A thin woman with a smoker's face stood in the doorway to a side room.

'Yes, hi, that's me.' I got up and followed her into her office. Her name tag said 'Pamela Higginbottom'. I bit the inside of my cheek.

'Right,' she said, eyes on her grey PC. 'You've done well in spelling and maths, OK?'

'Yes.'

'And you're fine in critical thinking, but your IT skills are severely lacking, OK?'

'Sorry,' I said. 'I have a MacBook. I'm useless with Microsoft anything.'

'You should probably take a course to remedy your poor understanding.'

'Oh, right.'

'I'm not going to be able to find you a job if you can't use a computer. OK?'

'OK,' I said. 'Sorry.'

'Go away and take a course. You can ask Diamond at reception for more information on that, OK? I'll send you what comes up in the meantime, but I can't promise anything with your paucity of knowledge, OK?'

'OK,' I said. 'Is there something I can do that doesn't involve a computer? I was looking at jobs at the British Library. I rang them to ask if they had anything and they sent me to you.'

'The British Library are going to need staff that are tech-literate, OK?'

'Oh, OK.'

'OK?'

'OK.'

'Thanks, then,' said Pamela, with a smile that told me it was time to leave.

I passed the tall girl on my way out.

'Good luck!' she said, in a Yorkshire accent.

'Thanks,' I said. 'You too.'

I took myself to the nearest pub and asked for a shot of vodka.

'Tough morning?' said the old barman.

'Yep,' I said, necking it in one.

'On the house.' He winked at me. I nearly cried.

Henry found me in the bath when he got in from work. I'd emptied a three-quarter-full bottle of shower gel into the water, and was lying in the bubbles reading *Macbeth* from a heavy leather-bound copy of *The Complete Works of Shakespeare* I'd found in the flat, having got it down to look at *Hamlet* and wandered off-piste.

'Oh, hi,' he said, coming into the bathroom in his suit and coat.

'Hi,' I said. 'How was your day?'

'Er, fine, yeah. You?'

'Crap,' I said. 'That recruitment agency place was bullshit. Everything's so bureaucratised now, it's ridiculous. What happened to just handing in your CV?'

'What did you have to do?'

'A bloody spelling and maths test, like I was a kid. And then they tested me on my non-existent computer skills and the woman totally shamed me about it.'

'Right. So you failed the aptitude test?' said Henry.

'What? No. I didn't *fail*. She just said I should probably take an IT course or something.'

'Are you going to?'

'God, no.'

Henry went out to the hallway; I could hear him looking through cupboards.

'What do you want to do for dinner?' I called. 'There's a few things in the fridge. Could just knock something up with some veg. Or do you wanna go out?'

He didn't answer.

'Henry?' I called again.

Eventually, he came back in, coat still on.

'Where are you going?' I asked, seeing the umbrella in his hand.

'I've got drinks with some friends.'

'What friends?'

'Old school friends. Haven't seen them in ages.'

'You didn't tell me. Anyone I know?'

'Maybe. I don't know. Do you remember Harry?'

'No.'

'I won't be too late,' he said.

'Bye then,' I said, once he was already out the front door.

The old copper tap spewed a splash of unwelcome water into the bath. I dried my hands and picked my phone up off the floor. Maybe I'd invite Jess over – she'd just be finishing work now, and her offices weren't that far away. I had a new message from *Rich Olivia*. For a moment, I had no idea who this was. Who the fuck was Olivia, and why was she rich? Then I remembered – the dad from the playground.

Hi, Joni. Hope you're well. I just wanted to let you know Olivia just had Jem round for a play date, and he said some very nice things about you. Rich x

I smiled to myself and wrote back,

Hi, Rich. I'm fine, thanks, how are you? Thanks for letting me know. What did he say then? x

Straight away I could see he was typing. I watched with excitement as the ellipsis rippled on the screen.

Well, I might have been asking about you . . . He said you were the best nanny ever, and his new nanny is so boring. x

My heart sank. New nanny. I looked up at the last message Rich had sent me before today.

That's a shame. I was hoping to see you again.

Definitely flirting.

Awww. Thanks for telling me. I miss him (and Clara) a lot.

I sent. There was no reply.

Jess agreed to come over – *But can't stay late. Got a junket tomorrow fml.*

We shared a bottle of rosé and some beans on toast. I told her about Paddy's show, how brilliant he was and how she must go – I would happily go with her. I told her I hadn't been able to get hold of Dyl, and she said she hadn't heard from him. I told her things with Henry were a little strained, as I had nothing to do all day. I cried a little when I told her about T. C. Recruitment.

'Hey,' she laughed, cupping my cheek in her soft, manicured hand. 'Fuck 'em. Don't let the bastards get you down.'

'Thanks, babe.' I hiccoughed into my wine.

'I can teach you PC basics if you want?'

'But I *don't* want, that's the point. I want to do something I love. And if it involves fucking around with Excel, I'll put my head in the oven.'

Jess laughed. 'Right.'

'What?' I said, a little tipsy.

'It's just, most people know how to use a PC, babe. It's not rocket science. But it's fine. You do you.'

'Do they actually, though? I feel like it's one of those grown-up things no one talks about.'

'It's fine. I get it: classic Joni. You've had a slight setback and now you want to stay away from the mean computer.' Jess laughed again.

'What?'

'Come on, I'm just teasing.'

'But I don't get it?'

'Mate, you know. Rejection. Not really your thing.'

'Is it anyone's thing?'

'No, but you, babe, in particular. You're an ostrich.'

'I'm an ostrich?'

'Yeah. Head in the sand. When you have a break-up, or get fired, or, I don't know, you just don't enjoy something, we all have to pretend it never happened.'

'Christ, babe, heavy read for a school night?'

'Sorry, sorry. It doesn't matter. Ignore me, I've had too much wine.'

'God.'

'Look. What do you *want* to do?' she asked, sitting taller.

'Um . . .'

'Come on,' she said. 'I know you have an answer.'

'Well, I want to write, don't I?' I said. 'I was always going to write. I don't know when that stopped being the plan.'

'OK. What sort of writing do you want to do?'

'I don't know,' I said.

She looked at me, and I could see she was making an effort to look cheerful. 'Well, apply for some writing jobs. Copywriting, content creation, anything. Just get the ball rolling. See if there are any creative writing competitions you could enter.'

She made it sound so simple: Just get a job! A writing job! Just make some money! Just be a writer! It almost sounded tangible, coming across the table from her – with her silk pussy-bow blouse and shiny hair. It struck me that she was the antithesis of the tall girl from the waiting room.

I remembered that the deadline for the *Chronicle* competition was today.

'Fuck!' I said, pouring us each another glass of wine. 'How are *you*? Sorry – I feel like I've just been talking about myself.'

'Babe, I've got zero news. Just been working. Got this

junket tomorrow for smug-cunt-Sara, the clean-eating chef I told you about.'

'Oh yeah.'

'So that'll be tedious. Listening to her enthuse on the miracle of Swiss chard or whatever.'

I laughed. 'And who do you fancy?' I said, smirking at the childishness of the question.

'Mate, no one!' She threw up her hands. 'My love life is comprehensively arid.'

'Like the Kalahari,' I said.

'Yep. The Gobi, even,' she added.

'Fuck, not the Gobi?'

'It's getting there.'

'Well, we should go out!' I said. 'We haven't been out in ages, let's get everyone together and go dancing soon.'

'Maybe.'

'Come on,' I said, slapping the table. 'Please? Let's make a plan. We need to go feral. When was the last time we went feral?'

'Been a while,' she said, smoothing a hand down her ponytail.

'Oh my God! We should go to the Spinning Wheel!'

The Spinning Wheel was a vast nightclub south of the river, housed in what used to be a textile factory. It was comprised of four large 'halls', each with a different euphemistic name for what drug you were taking. It opened at 10 p.m. and closed at 10 a.m.

Jess carried our plates over to the sink. 'Christ,' she said. 'Don't you think we're a bit old for the Spinning Wheel now?' She began to wash the dishes.

'I'll do that,' I said. 'Leave them, babe.'

'I'd better head home, then, my love. Adore seeing you.'

We hugged in the hallway, and she told me she'd send

me some links for job applications tomorrow. 'I'm going to be bored shitless, honestly. Gives me something to do.'

After she left, I served myself a bourbon over ice and finally tackled the last suitcase I had yet to unpack. This one contained the contents of my shelves: my jewellery box, wooden bookends in the shape of swans, a couple of china trinkets I'd bought at Portobello market, some old notebooks. I opened one, and out fell a dried-up daisy chain; the one Jem had made me the day I lost my job. It was barely recognisable – withered and colourless. I crawled over to the paper bin and let it fall from my palm. It somehow reminded me of the dead ants.

The grandfather clock in the hallway struck eleven. Cross-legged on the floor, I went through the notebooks. Poems I must have written in Edinburgh – one had a reference to the Auld Toun. Another was an elegy to my youth that made my toes curl with shame. A few fuller pages towards the back caught my eye – a short story. I lost track of time completely as I dived deeper and deeper into the scribblings of my younger self.

*

'Hi,' said Henry.

I jumped out of my skin.

'Sorry,' he said, stumbling into the room. 'I called out, but you didn't answer. I saw the lights were still on from the courtyard.'

'What time is it?' I asked, snapping my notebook shut.

'I don't know, like, half one?' He rubbed his eyes. 'What you doing?'

'Reading some old stuff,' I said, tossing the notebook back into the suitcase.

'I'm knackered, I need to go to bed,' he said.

'OK,' I said. 'Did you have a good time?'

'Yeah, it was fine.'

'Where did you go?'

'Just the pub, and then on to another bar in Soho.' He visibly heaved, and then swallowed.

'Drink a bit?' I said.

'A bit.'

He staggered through to the bedroom. I followed him, watching him pulling off his coat and tie.

'Who was there?' I asked.

'Me.'

'Who else?'

'Tom.'

'And?'

'Rusty came.'

'Cool.'

'I saw Dyl on the street,' he added, clicking his fingers like he'd only just recalled this detail.

'What?'

'We walked past each other, it's so weird when that happens in London.'

'Did you talk to him? Did you ask him why the fuck he's not answering any of my calls?'

'We only spoke very briefly.'

'What did you say?'

'I don't know, just hi and stuff. He was on his way to some club.'

'What club?'

'How should I know?' Henry flopped into bed. 'Joni, I need to go to sleep, I've got work tomorrow.'

'Maybe you should have thought of that before you went out drinking till the middle of the night.'

'Ugh, don't be a nag. It doesn't suit you.'

I unfolded my arms, and went on, trying to adopt a more amenable tone. 'Who was he with?'

'God,' Henry moaned. 'You're fucking obsessed with him.'

'No, I'm not.'

'You bloody well are. And it's doing you no favours. What's he doing, out and clearly off his face on a week-night?'

'I could say the same thing about you.'

'Fuck off, I haven't seen my friends in months. I'm allowed to let off some steam.'

'Well, maybe Dyl's letting off steam, too.'

'Yeah, right,' Henry murmured into the pillow. 'From all his responsibilities. All his demons.'

'How dare you? You know about what happened with his brother.'

'Twenty fucking years ago, Joni. When are you going to get it? Dyl's toxic.'

'Don't say that.'

'Whatever. I'm going to sleep.'

I was still fully dressed and a little tipsy. I got up and went to the dressing table where my make-up was scattered, gave my hair a quick brush and put some kohl around my eyes, and grabbed my phone.

'I'm going out,' I told Henry as I left the room. He didn't reply. Maybe he was already asleep.

People were queuing down the street to get into clubs. Girls in skimpy dresses, drag queens in skimpier ones. I made my way down Old Compton Street, and texted Dyl. *CALL NOW. URGENT.*

The gay pub on the corner seemed like the safest place to get a drink by myself at this hour. I went in and ordered a double vodka Red Bull, and then another. I was invisible here, and I liked it, sitting on a bar stool benignly eaves-dropping on others' conversations. The PVC-wrapped men next to me were leaning in very close to one another. I could just make out their voices – pitched above the Diana Ross remix on at full volume.

'It does scare me, though,' said the taller of the two.

'Me as well,' said the other.

'But I heard that giving up red meat offsets your carbon emissions more than not having a car.'

'Oh, girl, I became vegan years ago, before it got you dick.'

Dyl was calling me.

'Hello?' he answered, as if I had been the one ringing him.

'He's alive.'

'Hi, Phil!' As tipsy as I was, I could hear that he was wasted.

'Are you out in Soho? I'm in the Ship.'

'We're at the Trap. Come!'

I didn't ask who 'we' meant. The Trap was a thirty-second walk away, down one of the narrow warrens that tunnel between the busy streets. There was a queue so thick it had lost shape and order. Everyone seemed too drunk to remember what they were there for.

'My friends are inside,' I said to the bouncers, smiling. 'Can I go in?'

'Aw, Billy No Mates,' said the one closer to me. I didn't mind; if he was bored and wanted a bit of banter as the price of entry, fine.

I laughed. 'I was supposed to meet them outside, but I had a fight with my boyfriend and got held up.'

'Dump him, gorgeous,' said the other bouncer.

'Alright, alright – go find your friends,' said the first one, and I was in.

The Trap was like any other nightclub. It had a burlesque parlour design: a stage at the front, booths along the walls, gold-and-mirror bar at the far end. On the stage tonight there was a tall performer, completely naked bar a pair of lethally high heels, doing some kind of dance involving hula hoops. The room was so crowded I could barely move, let alone see Dyl. I edged my way towards the bar, the sticky floor gripping at my shoes with each step. From here, I could scan the room a little better without being in the midst of any kind of thoroughfare. At one booth, I saw meaty security guards blocking the way of revellers who were trying to get selfies with its occupants. At another, the girls were standing on the benches, dancing, providing the men at the table with a clear view up their negligible skirts. Someone asked me if I wanted some cocaine; I declined. A man hit on me; I politely batted him away. I decided to do a lap of the room. *Where the fuck was Dyl?*

'Hey, hey! Joni!' said a girl's voice behind me.

I turned. It was Cecily Simmons.

'Oh, hi!' I said. 'You here with Dyl?'

'What?'

'You here with Dylan?'

'Oh!' She laughed like it was the funniest thing. 'No, I'm here with some friends. Is he here?'

'Somewhere,' I said. 'See you later!'

I went out to the smoking area. No sign of him. I wanted a cigarette, but couldn't face standing out here alone for the length of one, risking being approached by pervy inebriates. *This is bullshit. Why am I out, anyway? Leaving*

Henry sleeping on his own. On a weeknight. I need to get my shit together.

'Phil!'

And there he was. Shirt unbuttoned to the waist, a week's worth of patchy stubble, eyes almost comically bloodshot and out of focus. His whole appearance was a caricature: The Rake.

'About time,' I said. 'Was about to scarper.'

'Nonsense,' he said, pulling me into his chest and squeezing my head. He smelled different; bad. 'D'you bring Henry with you? I saw him earlier, with some awful Sloaney hairband.'

'A girl?' I said.

'Among others, Phil. Nothing like that.'

'I want to dance,' I said, stealing his cigarette.

'You've come to the right place.'

'Who are you here with, anyway?'

'Some people.'

I rolled my eyes at him.

'You'll like them,' he said. 'They're good fun.'

'If by "good fun" you mean "in possession", then I'm sure I will.'

We danced. I got high. Dyl's friends were Poppy and Otis. I realised – once we were grooving against each other, sweaty and euphoric – that I recognised them from the band of misfits at Marla's funeral.

'Dyl,' I shouted into his ear on the dancefloor. 'I know you stole that money.'

It suddenly seemed so silly that I hadn't told him before. He nodded. But he was nodding anyway, in time with the beat. He held me close for a moment, both of us still dancing.

'I'll pay you back,' he yelled. 'I promise.'

He would pay me back. It was fine. All was well; we were us again. We smiled hazily at each other. We smiled at Poppy and Otis, and they smiled back.

At 4 a.m. the lights came up. We were spat out on to the streets. I suggested we move on to another club – I wanted to dance off the rest of the chemicals in my bloodstream – but Poppy insisted we all decamp back to her place. It wasn't far, a fifteen-minute weave up through Fitzrovia, past the outlet boutiques and old Indian restaurants.

'This is all yours?' I said, as we arrived at a four-storey townhouse.

'I share it with my brother,' said Poppy. 'It's our parents', but they live in Switzerland most of the year.'

'Sure.'

'It's a bit of a mess, sorry. We've had so many people staying round.'

The place was sorely bohemian; filled with books, paintings, pretty jugs, raw *objets d'art* and huge Afghan rugs, a light coating of London dust over everything. We settled around a large, cluttered table in the kitchen, where Otis immediately began to cook ketamine in a pan on the stove. It smelled rancid and sweet. Poppy carried on in hostess mode, offering us toast and tea, which we declined, both still rushing and appetite-free. There were dog hairs all over the place, but no dog appeared. Otis and Poppy inhaled the ketamine fumes through a plastic straw, then lay back on the shaggy sofa, glassy-eyed and skeletal.

'Come on,' said Dyl, taking my hand, leading us out of the room and down an old wooden staircase to the basement. We went into a bedroom, stark and filthy. It was filled with what I recognised as Dyl's possessions: his books stacked on their sides in precarious towers, a hula-girl lamp he'd bought in Edinburgh.

'How long have you been staying here?' I asked him.

'Oh, a couple of weeks,' he said, climbing over the mattress on the floor without removing his shoes. He emptied his pockets, searching for tobacco, then flopped over the side of the bed and retrieved a large hardback from the floor, carefully balancing it to keep the paraphernalia on top from falling. He placed the book on his lap and started rolling a joint. I toed my boots off, one by one, and got into the bed beside him, pulling the squeaky synthetic duvet over me. There were several shattered panes in the sash window that someone had attempted to patch up with gaffer tape.

'Jesus, Dyl, it's a bit grim,' I said, shivering.

'You can go home if you want,' he said, sparking up.

'Alright, keep your hair on. Just saying. You have a perfectly nice room in Camden.'

'I got kicked out,' he said.

'What?'

'They kicked me out. I don't live there anymore.'

'Why?'

'Does it matter?'

'Fuck off, tell me.'

He sighed, as if I were very stupid. 'Just an irreconcilable dispute with my housemates,' he said, exhaling.

'Well, obviously,' I said. 'Over what?'

'Nothing.'

'Dude—'

'Just drop it.'

'Fine. Jesus. Just making conversation. I'm not gonna be able to sleep for at least an hour,' I said, picking at my cuticles under the covers.

Dyl said nothing, but continued to pull hard on the joint, blowing out pillowy fumes which filled the room. It made me feel sick.

'That shit stinks,' I said.

'Yeah, it's cheesy as fuck,' croaked Dyl, with an irritating pride.

'I got chucked out too,' I said. 'I mean, not chucked out, but Fiona's daughter's back from Australia, so I had to move out.'

'Shit. Where you staying? Henry's?'

'Yeah.'

'How's that?'

'Alright, I guess. It's jammy as fuck, but we're getting on each other's nerves.'

'Yeah.'

'Yeah. I haven't actually asked him if I can live there officially. But I was staying there pretty much every night already, so it's not like anything's changed.'

Dyl laughed. 'So you've moved in together and he doesn't even know about it?' he said, choking. I laughed, too. It did seem very funny, all of a sudden. We descended into a long and breathless fit of giggles.

Once Dyl had finished his spliff, he got into bed properly, pulling off his coat and trainers.

'What's Poppy's deal?' I said, nestling in to reap some of his body temperature.

'She's cool. Her parents are mad rich. The brother's a bit of a dick. He gets wavy with the rest of us and then has these big freak-outs, shouting at Poppy, saying how she's fucked her life up and when's she gonna sort herself out. I'm like, mate, you're a fucking trustafarian white boy with daddy issues, back off.'

'Christ.'

'Yeah.'

'Does Poppy do anything? For work, I mean?'

'She's a painter, but I think she wants to design sustainable clothes or something. She's got a lot of Instagram followers.'

We lay in silence for a while, teeth clenched, bodies pressed close to stay warm. I couldn't help but think of the last time we had been in a bed like this, at my parents' house. It felt like years ago. A different world.

'Dyl,' I whispered.

But he'd passed out. I clung to the back of him: bone and heat.

The light was golden and treacly when I woke; it was already the afternoon. Dyl wasn't there. I checked my phone to see if Henry was wondering where I was. There was only a message from Paddy, in our group chat, with a link to a review of his play.

'Fiercely astute and alluring.' GET IN!

The room was even colder now than it had been last night; leaving the warmth of the bed was like plunging into freezing water. I scoured Dyl's mess for a warm jumper, pulling drawers open to no avail, and finally going through a threadbare rucksack that lay on the floor.

I knew it was heroin as soon as I saw it. I pocketed it, planning on throwing it in a public bin somewhere along Oxford Street on my walk back to the Albany.

Dyl was pouring thick, dark coffee from a percolator in the kitchen.

'Want some?' he said, as I hovered in the doorway.

This house was the very thing I thought I was after. A total suspension of reality from the outside world. A crucible of creatives: drinking and drugging and coming and going, sharing meals and possibly lovers, reading an old book, legs draped over another body reading another book. Matisse's studio. Perhaps I could stay here – Henry didn't want me living with him, not really. Dyl and I could coop up in one of the upstairs rooms, write all day till it was time to open wine in the evening. Poppy seemed like a nice girl – a true hippy at heart. I was sure she would let me stay, if I asked. We could take it in turns to cook, to share bottles of booze and extracts of our work. It was a seductive fantasy. Trust Dyl to have found it first.

'I'm fine,' I said. 'I should get back.'

Poppy was lying on the shaggy sofa in a pretty Victorian nightie, smoking a cigarette. The cotton was so light and thin as to be slightly transparent; I could see the darts of her nipples poking through, and make out the dark triangle of her pubic hair between jutting hip-bones. I wondered if Dyl was fucking her.

'Thanks for letting me crash,' I said.

She smiled a dazed smile. 'See you soon,' she said.

The doorman at the Albany stopped me as I approached.

'Evening, miss. It's Joni, isn't it?'

'Yeah, hi, hello.'

'Didn't know if I'd be seeing you,' he said, unlocking the gate for me. 'I have a message from Mr Taschen for you, miss.'

'Oh?'

'He said to tell you he's gone to the country to see his mother, miss, in case you were to come back.'

'Right. OK. That's fine. Thanks for letting me know.'

Henry could just as easily have told me this via text, or he could have called. Maybe I should have stayed in Poppy's fantasy house after all.

I got up to the empty apartment and texted him.

Got your message from the doorman. Guess I'll see you on Sunday.

He replied, a few minutes later: *We need to talk.*

17

Making love with Rich was like losing my virginity all over again. It cast all the sex I'd ever had into sharp – and unfavourable – relief. He made me come several times over the course of our first night together. I felt almost guilty. I nearly told him I loved him, which I didn't – I just couldn't find a way to vocalise how he'd made me feel. But it wasn't about orgasms – lovely as they were – it was everything else. Previous partners had made me come before; some more easily than others. And I'd always been so grateful when it happened, whenever it happened. Rich made me see how hard-fought it had always been. It had embarrassed me, asking specifically for what I needed in order to get there, and I'd felt slightly ashamed afterwards; not just at the intimacy of the act, but as if there was something shameful about having to instruct, to inform your partner that their own methods were ineffective. I realised, too, I had never been that far from performative – whether literally faking it or simply feeling the need to throw various glamorous-seeming shapes with my body, assuming an acceptable facial expression, making the right noises, wanting them to have a better time than I did. It dawned on me, not without mild hysteria, that I'd never truly let go. Rich took that choice out of my hands. It was entirely unembarrassing, natural, easy. Like having a conversation with our bodies. We talked a lot – a practice that I had secretly laughed about in the past, giggling incredulously with Mila over coffee about the pseudo-pornographic utterances of our lovers. Did they really think it was sexy? Rich and I conversed. We asked each other if things felt good, un-rhetorically. To say he was 'good in bed' would be too cynical a reduction. 'Good in bed' implies someone who has deliberately honed their techniques; there's a vanity to it, a panache. He simply made sex feel right, for the first time. *So, this is how it's supposed to be.*

I had packed my things as soon as I got Henry's text. At first I thought of going back to Poppy's, but the prospect of that freezing bedroom again made me want to cry, and I couldn't cry. I could have gone to Fiona's, but Jenny would be there by now. There was, of course, Mila and Jess's place, but I couldn't face them, with their organised fridge and their organised lives. Some chaotic impulse made me text Rich. I was not yet sober from the previous night. The weird non-hangover of pills: my body floaty and lips swollen.

You busy?

Nope.

Can I come over? Sorry. I'm in a bit of a crisis, don't know what to do.

Sure. 38 Cinder Road. x

He lived on one of the pretty, tree-lined streets between Fiona's and Terry and Raf's, a stone's throw from the Italian deli where I once bought my fortune-chocolates. My old neighbourhood. There was an odd sense of familiarity between the two of us – not quite like old friends, but perhaps akin to seeing a teacher on the street after you've left school, a sort of fond irony. He answered the door in jeans and a T-shirt, his feet bare on the painted floorboards.

'Hi,' he said, with an informality that suggested we had just seen each other a few hours ago.

'Hi,' I said, and laughed.

He fed me leftover Bolognese, and we drank a bottle of good, grown-up red wine while we talked. To my relief, he didn't ask me anything about my 'crisis' or why I needed to be there. Mostly, we talked about him. He had gone to law school, but was now a graphic designer ('I didn't possess the requisite level of pedantry to be a lawyer'), which is how he'd met Alex, his ex-wife. They had divorced almost three years ago.

'Fuck,' I said. 'I'm so sorry.'

'Thank you,' he said.

He told me about the painful experience of trying to explain what was happening to Olivia, who had been just a toddler at the time. He told me that Alex had been particularly cold in the meetings with the lawyer. He told me how he had cried when she got primary custody of their daughter. I got the impression he hadn't told the story in its complete form, from start to finish, to anyone before. He seemed to cast around for his words, like he was fishing them out from some deep, still lake. Our anonymity to each other was heady – how open and free it made us, the lack of agenda or judgement.

'Do you mind if I smoke?' I said. The craving to have a cigarette with my wine had been increasing for the last forty-five minutes, but it had seemed rude to interrupt him.

'If you must,' he said. 'But let's go outside.'

He slipped on a pair of felt hybrid slippers – the kind you can wear both in and out of doors and that cost the best part of a hundred quid. I mocked him openly. He took it well.

'Try them on,' he said, kicking them off towards me. 'You'll be a convert, yet.'

I did. They were extremely comfortable.

'Shit,' I said. 'But wait, I've heard it's dangerous to be this bourgeois all at once. I'd better put down this giant glass of organic wine if I want to keep wearing them.'

'Ha, ha,' he said.

The garden was small and pretty: rosemary bedded in an old Belfast sink; an olive tree in a galvanised-steel planter. We sat on two rusty chairs either side of a round table, and I felt disappointed that he wouldn't be able to kiss me from this distance. I smoked and sipped my wine – that superlative combination.

'Would you like to stay the night?' he asked. It wasn't lascivious or assuming, just a gesture of generosity. I wouldn't have been surprised if he'd shown me to the guest bedroom.

'If that's OK,' I said, 'I'd love to.'

He nodded and bent down to pull out some weeds that were sprouting between the slate, chucking their remains over to the single square metre of lawn. It touched me, this small act. It seemed such a grown-up thing to do.

He lent me a toothbrush and a towel. I cleaned myself and came to his room in just my T-shirt and pants. He pulled the duvet back for me to get in. The walls rippled with our shadows in the low, warm light. He stroked my hair from my face.

'You can stay for a while if you need to,' he whispered into a kiss, a few hours deeper into the night.

'Are you sure?' I said. 'I don't want it to affect Olivia, you know, to confuse her or anything.'

'She'll be OK,' he said, his hand gently on my throat. 'I only have her one week out of the month. Shit, I haven't had a woman here since me and Alex split up. It'll probably be nice for her to have another girl around.'

He had referred to me as both a woman and a girl in the same sentence. He kissed my eyelids goodnight.

*

Hey, came the text from Henry on Sunday night. I was curled on the sofa with a hot chocolate, snuggled under a fleece blanket, an old musical on the TV. Rich was next door in the kitchen, making us food. I waited for more. I let a big, jazzy number start up and finish again on the telly, but still nothing came. So I responded, *Don't worry. I'm gone.* X

My phone was ringing; it was him. I didn't answer. He rang again.

Hang on, I texted.

I poked my head around the kitchen door to tell Rich that I wouldn't be long, I just needed to make a quick call.

'Are you alright?' he asked, looking up from a bubbling pot.

'Yeah, yeah, all good,' I said, swallowing.

He looked at me, thoroughly, as if the word help were written somewhere in tiny letters on my face and he was trying to locate it.

'OK,' he said. 'See you in a sec.'

I put on his expensive slippers – though they were much too big for me, their open-backed mule style meant I could walk in them comfortably – and headed out the front door. Leaves crunched under my feet as I strode away.

'Hello?' Henry answered after just one ring.

'Hi,' I said, taking in a lungful of the crisp October air.

'Where are you?' he said.

'Staying with a friend.'

'Dyl?'

'No.'

'Mila?'

'No.'

'Who?'

'No, no one you know, Henry. Just a friend.'

'Right. OK.'

'You OK?' I said. 'How was your mum's?'

'Not great. Losing Dolly appears to have opened the valve on Marla. She barely speaks. Doesn't eat.'

I stopped myself from pointing out that she never ate in the first place. 'I'm so sorry. That must have been really tough.'

'Yeah. It was.'

'I'm sorry.'

'Thanks,' he said, impatient. 'So, look, I thought we should talk because—'

'It's alright, Henry, you don't have to explain. I've packed up my shit. You don't have to say it.' I was gripping my thumb in my fist to stop myself from picking the raw skin of my cuticle.

'What do you think I'm going to say?' said Henry, calmly. It disarmed me. Maybe I was wrong.

'That you don't think it's working. That you don't want to be together anymore.'

He didn't answer for so long that I stopped walking to try and hear his breath on the end of the line.

'Are you still there?' I said, pausing at a traffic light.

'Yeah.'

'Well?' I said, the green man flashing. I crossed the road.

'Well, yeah,' he said. 'That's pretty much it.'

'Thought so,' I said.

'I'm sorry, Joni, you're really wonderful—'

'Not that wonderful, obviously.'

He sighed, exasperated. It made me feel worse.

'It's just,' he said. 'It's all so tangled up. You, Marla, Dyl, Dolly. This year. Your friends, your lifestyle and stuff . . .'

'What the fuck are you talking about?' I said. I was walking without knowing where I was going. Onwards, onwards.

'I mean, I wish I could be more like that still. But I have responsibilities to my family. I can't keep doing this. I have work, obligations . . . it's just not sustainable.'

'Wow. You make it sound like an investment.'

'Sorry. Investments are what I know; I'm not good at this.'

It was my turn to sigh with exasperation. 'It's fine,' I said. 'I get it. Don't worry.'

'I'm sorry,' he said again. 'I really am. It's hard for me to say, but I still, you know . . .' He drifted off.

'Yeah,' I said. 'Me too.'

We were both quiet then. All I could hear on the phone was the sound of my own panting as I marched. He spoke first, and I finally stopped walking. I had ended up round the corner from Terry and Raf's.

'I'll see you around then, I guess,' he said, unable to hide his relief.

'Yeah. Bye, Henry,' I said.

I wish I had had the strength to hang up, but I waited for his 'Bye, Joni' before I did.

Buses and cars crawled their way slowly past; people going home for work tomorrow morning. The weekend was over.

*

Rich had Olivia for Halloween this year. Keen to make a good impression, both on him and his daughter, I decorated the house while he was at work. Steady, light rain tapped against the kitchen windows. I carved one smaller pumpkin into a decent grimace, scooping out the pulpy, rot-sweet flesh, and saved two more for me and Olivia to do together later. I found the stationery drawer (every household with a child has one) and cut out paper bats to hang from the ceiling. I dyed caramel with red food colouring and made 'vampire' toffee apples. These kinds of simple, practical activities usually called for music – something easy, Van Morrison or Paul Simon – but instead, I found myself just listening to the sound of the rain, gentle and tuneless. I took a coffee out to the garden and smoked a cigarette in the rain, then took myself up for a bubble bath. The indulgent, frothy foam thick above the surface, like a blanket.

Since being here, I had become more connected to my body: more *in* my body. The attention Rich paid it had stirred my own awareness: my toes, my elbows, the dimples in my sacrum – like his kisses had the power to wake each part of me up. A corporeal sleeping beauty.

I hadn't left the house in days. It had been so natural, wrapping myself up in the arms of this man and his life – a life as warm and comforting as the tub in which I was currently soaking myself; the world outside those Edwardian sash windows slowly drifting further and further away. A lot of my belongings were still in my car, totems of an old life I no longer felt was my own. After years of wanting Henry Taschen, he had finally been mine – and I'd fucked it up, as was my custom. I was jobless, homeless, single again. These facts were easier to ignore here: playing house with Rich, my mind scrambled by this new-found relationship to my own body, convincing myself that sex this good had to mean something. *How are you?* was a question I didn't fancy considering in any depth, and I avoided my phone as I avoided writing.

I was looking forward to taking Olivia trick-or-treating later. The only time I had ever been, I was already much too old for it: Mila and I had dressed up as some kind of slutty mammals and gone from door to door demanding sweets. Some people obliged, looking rather terrified, and others told us that the sweets were only for the little children, at which point we'd get lippy, call them paedos, and run giggling from the scene. Not quite the fun and festive experience I had planned for Olivia. I wanted it to be magical for her; just the right level of scary to be thrilling, like a rollercoaster or a ghostly cartoon.

Hi, love, Rich messaged. *Meeting running late. Can't get out of it. Could you pick Liv up?*

Rich had done so much for me – letting me stay here indefinitely, pleasuring me nightly till I was exhausted and fell into the softest of dreamless sleeps. All the housework I had been doing was partly my way of trying to thank him, to earn my keep. Of course I could pick Liv up; of course I could. I just didn't want to bump into Clara and Jem.

I hated that I'd been forced to leave without saying goodbye, that I'd never been able to explain myself. The thought of Terry's version, whatever she had told them, plagued me. The knowledge that it was kinder to let it be my fault, not hers. It would be simpler if they never saw me again, if they forgot all about me. What if I bumped into Terry herself? Or Raf? What explanation would I give them – that I was working for Rich now?

Of course I can, I sent.

You're an angel. I'll let the school know.

It wasn't against the rules for me to see them. I wasn't banned from setting eyes on them just because I was no longer employed by their parents.

*

Jem saw me before I saw him.

'It's Nanny Jo!' I heard his voice exclaim, my heart lifting at its raspy exultation.

I turned to find him standing a few feet away with a woman I didn't recognise. She must be the new nanny. She put a protective hand on his shoulder, his arm raised, pointing at me. He was dressed as a pirate, elastic eye patch loose around his neck.

'See?' he said. 'It is her!'

I gave an olive-branch smile to the new nanny and went over.

'Hi, Jem-a-lem,' I beamed. 'You OK?'

'Yeah!' he said.

'I haven't seen you in ages,' I said, unable to resist crouching down and pulling him in for a hug.

'I haven't seen *you* in ages,' he said.

'Sorry,' I said, standing back up, addressing New Nanny. 'I'm Joni; I used to look after Jem and Clara.'

'Hull-oh,' she said. 'Maria. I work for the Kaurs now.'

She was a lot older than me: middle-aged, practically. Her mousy hair was striped with wiry streaks of grey, tied back in a plait that went all the way down to her waist. She wore a thick jumper with a waterproof gilet on top, a tiered skirt and brown knee-high boots. She looked bucolic, like she'd just walked over from the stables to feed the hens. She had faint crow's feet around each eye that made her seem like she was smiling, though she wasn't. She was a sensible person, a sensible nanny. Maria.

'Like *The Sound of Music*!' I said.

'What's that?'

'Like Fraulein Maria.'

'Oh, sorry, I don't speak German,' she said. 'Is this one yours?'

Olivia had appeared in a Jasmine outfit, crumpled and falling down a bit.

'Hey, Olivia,' I said. 'Remember me? I used to be Jem's nanny.' I avoided looking at Maria. 'I'm picking you up today. We'll see your daddy at home.'

'OK,' said Olivia. Jem pretended to stab her with his pirate sword.

'Argh!' she said. She loved it.

'We don't hurt people, Jemmarcus,' said Maria.

Clara was approaching cautiously, having spotted me. 'Hey,' she said, holding out her schoolbag for Maria to take.

'Can I help you, Clara?'

Clara rolled her eyes. 'Can you carry my bag, please, Maria?'

'Certainly, because you asked me nicely,' said Maria.

'Clara, look! It's Nanny Jo!' said Jem, continuing to slash at Olivia.

'Don't call her that,' said Clara. 'She's not our nanny anymore.'

'Hi,' I said. 'How's it going?'

'Fine,' said Clara.

Her trust in me had been broken; she was protecting herself. I was so proud of her I wanted to cry.

'Fun day?' I asked.

Clara looked round over her shoulder. She was dressed in head-to-toe denim, with a red paisley bandana on her head.

'What are you dressed as?' I asked.

'Lil Speaky.'

I had no idea who or what that was.

'Cool,' I said. 'You look wicked.'

'Home time!' said Maria in a sing-song voice. She really was Fraulein Maria. Except without the figure. I hated her. 'Say bye-bye, children.'

'Bye, Nanny – I mean, bye, er, er – Jo!' said Jem.

Clara didn't say anything.

'Nice to meet you,' I said.

'Goodbye,' said Maria.

I watched them walk off to a safe distance, Olivia waiting docilely beside me, before I said, 'Come on then, darling.' My voice was thicker than I had expected. I took her tiny hand to go home.

We walked most of the way in silence, at Olivia's measured (very slow) pace, stopping a couple of times for me to turn up the hems of her harem trousers, which kept slipping down and getting dirty on the pavement.

'When *I'm* sad,' she said, imperious above me as I stooped once more to her ankles, 'I think about cute tiny kittens!'

It wasn't bad advice. I took her into the deli and got us both a chocolate.

18

A Saturday. I couldn't breathe, and woke up gasping for air: a bad dream. It was 6.02 a.m. The room was warm and pitch black, Rich far away in his unconsciousness. As quietly as I could, I tried to steady my breathing (in for four, hold for four, out for four) but my body was so filled with adrenaline that I knew staying in bed would be futile. I put on Rich's parka and went down to the garden for a cigarette. It was still dark. The endless whooshing tide of wheels on wet tarmac nearby.

I arranged myself on the chaise longue in the kitchen and read a Korean cookery book. I thought if I could imbibe a general grasp of the patterns (which turned out to be almost the same as Mediterranean fundamentals: herbs and spices, then booze, then meat, then tomatoes), I could make something off-book later and it would appear impressive and domestic to Rich. It all looked so good: chicken fried in gochujang; thinly sliced beef bulgogi; deep, hearty bowls of bibimbap.

Rich came and joined me in the shower. I marvelled at how different his body was to mine. He had almost no body fat – something which would normally have made me self-conscious (my own body wobbly and soft in some places I liked, and some places I didn't), but his sacred venerating of me had gifted me new confidence.

'I didn't wake you, did I?' I said, sliding some suds off his back.

'Yep.'

'No? Shit, I'm sorry. I tried to be so quiet.'

'I'm kidding,' he said, kissing me on the nose. 'You didn't wake me.'

This was exactly the sort of non-joke joke he liked to pull on me:

'*Do you want ketchup on your chips?*'

'*No thanks!*'

'*Tough.*'

Cue Rich handing me a plate of chips, *sans* ketchup, grinning. I suppose it was the type of lame, inoffensive humour you had to develop as the parent of a young child. *I fooled you!*

We dressed and drank coffee over the weekend papers – Rich reading the actual news while I flicked through the colour supplements for the opinion columns. I laughed at a funny writer's description of recalling her first mammogram.

'Shall we do something today?' Rich said.

'Like what?' I said.

'I don't know. Something proper, like go look at some art or whatever.'

I laughed. We decided to visit the Natural History Museum.

The bus was packed and muggy. Filmy-eyed old women with their plaid shopping trolleys chatting to each other; kids on the brink of puberty going into town to hang out by shops and pubs they couldn't enter. I got out my phone. Three missed calls from Mum. No thanks. I'd been blithely ignoring contact from everyone. There were fifty-three unread messages in our group WhatsApp. A missed call from Jess, another from Mila. A voicemail from T. C. Recruitment. Fiona had called me a couple of times and left messages. My phone screen was dotted with accusatory little red numbers, like digital chickenpox – they itched, reminding me that I was evading something.

In the queue outside the museum, we watched a homeless man feeding the pigeons, his expression peaceful and benign. St Francis of Assisi on the Cromwell Road. I didn't tell Rich that I had never been here before. I was never taken as a child and, unlike *flâneur*-ing around art galleries, it felt embarrassing to go alone to a science museum. I stepped into the vast atrium with awe; the monumental Great Blue Whale suspended above us, her bones arranged so beautifully as to evoke motion, like she was flying through the air. The place smelled of old stone, like a church.

Rich and I wandered hand in hand through the rooms, manoeuvring through crowds of tourists. I tried to drink in everything I was seeing in this basilica of knowledge. A roaring T-Rex, dreamlike marine invertebrates, a taxidermy kangaroo, poised with a joey in her pouch. We watched a short film about ancestry that featured an arbitrary assemblage of celebrities, talking straight to camera about the history of their DNA. I wondered whether I, too, was one per cent Neanderthal. Rich said he was starving – we'd only had coffee for breakfast – and I told him I'd meet him in the café; I wanted to peruse the rest of the exhibit. I stopped in front of a brain. A real human brain and entire spinal cord, floating upright in formaldehyde. Whether formaldehyde was naturally yellow or they had dyed it such a sinister colour, I don't know. This person must have been very tall – a man, surely. A man who had donated his central nervous system to science, like those who donate their skulls for productions of *Hamlet*, as Paddy had told me; immortalising themselves for learning and art. Attempting to cheat death in one way or another.

Rich bought us each a Bakewell slice that was much better than a museum café pastry had any right to be. I made a mental note of it as some sort of permission to come back here by myself.

'What do you fancy for supper?' he asked me, yawning.

'Oh, I thought I could do it tonight. Bibimbap?' I said.

'Sure,' said Rich, mildly surprised. 'Yum.'

*

Rich went up for a nap when we arrived home. I opened a beer and set about preparing the food. I still had no idea how to make bibimbap. I decided to get the recipe up on my phone, so if Rich came in, there would be no open cookbook and he wouldn't suspect a thing.

The number of missed calls from my mother had gone up to twelve. There were others: from Paddy, Mila, Jess, Niall. Lots of them. Messages:

Joni, call me back please.

Babe, you need to call back it's urgent.

Hi Joni, please give me a ring when you get this.

Babe what the fuck

CALL NOW

A nameless dread engulfed me. I emptied the bottle of beer into myself and dialled Mila.

'Hello?' I said, when the phone was answered but no one spoke.

Wailing.

'Babe, what's up? What's going on?'

The sound of her crying made my heart fall through the floor. Had Niall betrayed her? Had her biggest fear come to pass? Surely not . . .

'Mila? Tell me what's happening.' I couldn't make out a word she was saying. 'Mila, what the fuck is going on?'

The sound of the phone being passed to someone else, Mila's sobs moving further away, like she was drowning. Niall's voice. 'Joni?' he said.

'Please, tell me what's happening. Is she OK?' I found I was stuttering.

'You haven't heard anything? We've all been calling. I thought maybe you'd spoken to your parents—'

'Niall?'

'Oh, Christ.' His breathing was ragged. 'Are you sitting down?' he said.

The next sequence of words made no sense. Just noise. I flew upstairs. Car keys. Rich dozing on the bed. Don't look at him. Out the front door, back into the freezing rain. I drove, paralysed. Shivering. Silence. Someone had pressed mute. I caught my reflection in the rear-view mirror and saw a face, ghostly white. I had to get to the others. There was a grenade in my hand. If I could just get there, surely one of them could defuse it. Over the bridge. Second gear, third gear, indicate. Keep left. Right here, into the car park. Up in the lift, the ghost in the mirror again. It was only when I was inside Niall's apartment that the sound came back on.

There they all were: Niall, Mila, Jess, Paddy – and now me. One missing.

My mouth was wide, wide open. I couldn't breathe. Animal sounds I'd never made before were coming from me. On the floor, my knees apart and body bent forwards. My head was on the ground. Pressed into it, like I was praying. My lungs hurt and I didn't stop. Without warning, a fresh wave of pain. A scream. Banging my fists on the floor. On myself. Niall held me. He held me so tight like he was squeezing the pain out of me. Someone gave me a pill and some vodka. I couldn't see the room through my tears. Up, pacing like a caged lion, raw panic. *We have to do something.* Down again – a broken pile of limbs. Niall just kept holding me, *shh, shh,* until everything went soft.

*

'Is it my fault?' said Paddy, head in his hands. 'Do you think the play pushed him over the edge?'

'By that logic,' said Jess, the bottle of gin in her hand almost empty, 'it's Shakespeare's fault.'

Last night, Dyl had been to see *Hamlet.* According to Paddy, Dyl seemed happy and well, if a little chaotic – but wasn't he always like that?

Paddy was still in costume from his matinee, a neon puffer jacket thrown over his tunic.

Mila lit up another spliff.

'Fuck,' I said, murkily remembering. 'My mother. She's been ringing me.'

'She knows you've heard the news and that you're safe,' said Niall. 'I told her you'd call her tomorrow.'

'Thank you,' I said. More tears. Dry throat. Vodka.

I was lying with my head in Jess's lap, her fingers running through my hair, which I think was more soothing for her than me. I felt nothing. All of us – bar Paddy, who was meant to be going back on stage in a couple of hours – had worked our way through Niall's drinks cupboard. Everyone had cigarettes. A thin, lazy layer of smoke hung throughout the apartment. Jess distributed Valium from a supply she kept for her especially neurotic clients. Occasionally, someone would say something in disbelief. It wasn't real, he was probably just off with some girl, we'd catch up with him tomorrow. *Tomorrow and tomorrow and tomorrow.* Wrong play.

I kept wanting to call him. This was the kind of earth-shaking news that I would habitually call him before anyone to share; my mind hadn't yet caught up with that irony. Just one more conversation. *Wait, wait, wait! I have more I need to say, more I have to tell him.* My thoughts were like a ghost train at some ramshackle funfair: abruptly jerking round corners in a new direction, sudden drops that made my stomach turn, the occasional horrific image jumping out at me. His parents. Now childless. There would be a funeral. Dyl's funeral. No, that made no sense. Nausea now. I closed my eyes.

'Right.' Paddy stood. 'I've got to go and be the lead in a play.'

'You can't,' said Mila.

'Call in sick,' said Jess.

Niall stood up, too, and walked him to the door. 'Come back here after, alright?' he said, hugging him. 'Will you get through it?'

Paddy nodded, his face stricken. 'I think so,' he said. 'It'll be one hell of a show tonight.'

*

I spent the night clinging to Jess on the vast sofa. The hours felt stuck in a loop of darkness. I would wake up, cry, Jess would comfort me, I would fall asleep, wake up again. It seemed the sun would never rise, that I would spend the rest of eternity in a cocoon of blackness, weeping until I was blind. Jess asked if I wanted her to call me 'Phil', and I said, 'Go on, then,' and it sounded so strange and wrong in another voice that I cried again.

On waking in the morning, that inevitable brief candle of hope shone before me: *did I dream it?* Snuffed out the second I opened my eyes. There I was, in Niall's mono-chrome apartment, my face bloated, my hangover exquisite.

Paddy came in from the guest bedroom and, without saying a word, got under the duvet at our feet, top-to-tail on the sofa. We three lay there for a while, clinging on to each other's limbs like lifebuoys. Presently, Niall and Mila appeared, holding hands. We all seemed to need to be physically touching one another at all times. Gripping on to warm flesh; connected, unbroken lines of contact.

*

'How did it go?' Niall asked Paddy some time later. He was sitting on the armchair opposite us, Mila on a cushion between his legs, his hands on her shoulders.

'Well,' said Paddy. 'It was either a total masterpiece or a total disaster.'

This would normally have made me laugh.

'How so?' asked Mila.

'Ah.' Paddy sounded close to tears again. 'Well I didn't plan it. But, after yesterday, it was the first time I've played Hamlet not wanting to die.'

No one spoke; we were all watching him.

'Night after night, I go out and I pretend to contemplate suicide. It makes you think, you know, about death, a great deal. Forgive my pretension, but inexorably, you spend enough time being someone else – they start to seep into you. Collide. Osmosis. Call it what you like.'

Niall nodded.

'I have felt, first hand, that Hamlet wants to die. He really does. He's just too . . . not scared . . . too neurotic. Too in his head. But last night—' He let out another hybrid sigh-sob. 'Last night, I really didn't want to die. No, I thought, not this time. Tonight, I want to live.'

Someone sniffed. It seemed to snap Paddy out of his reverie.

'Well. I'd never played it that way before. I shouldn't think I will again.'

Mila went and made a pot of coffee, coming back with paracetamol for us all. I lit a cigarette. On that first, sharp inhale, something dislodged within me and I broke down again. Jess's turn to squeeze me. I screamed, guttural howls buried into the duvet. It felt, despite my wails of protest, like my soul was being ripped apart. Keep smoking, steady the breath, cauterise the wound. Mila came over, too, and sat down on the other side of me, rubbing my back.

'Anyone else think they'd dreamed it all?' she asked.

I nodded. Everyone muttered something in agreement.

'Has anyone told Henry?' I said eventually, stubbing my cigarette out and skinning up another.

Exchanged glances.

'No,' said Niall. 'I haven't spoken to him.'

'Negative,' said Paddy.

'Wait,' said Mila. 'You weren't with him when we called yesterday?'

'No.' I exhaled. 'Me and Henry, that's done.'

No one, me included, had the capacity to react to this.

'But I think I should be the one to tell him, right?'

'Yeah,' said Jess. 'If you can face it.'

Henry. Rich. My parents. Three phone calls. I could manage that, surely?

'Might need another half a pill, Jess,' I said.

'Of course.'

I swallowed it with my coffee, and settled myself on the balcony with four pre-rolled cigarettes; the duvet wrapped around my lower half like an old man with a rug. The rain had paused, but the sky was still a baleful pewter. The city was quiet. Sunday was always the most hollow day of the week. My hands were shaking.

'Look what you're making me do,' I said to Dyl. 'Look what you're putting me through, you fucking prick.'

Mum first.

'Hello?' Her voice was thin, taut – like a string that might snap.

'Hi, Mum.'

'You've heard now, then?'

'Yeah.'

'Well.'

'Yeah.'

'I must say, it didn't help matters that I couldn't get hold of you. Had no idea if you knew or not, if you were safe.'

'Please don't tell me off, Mum. Not now.'

She huffed. 'Well, if I can't tell you off, what can we talk about?'

I let out a single laugh. She did too. We exchanged details of what we knew at our respective 'ends'. His parents had been to formally identify his body. They were already talking about moving to Israel. I told her I'd seen him recently. I didn't tell her about the drugs.

'He always seemed like rather a lost soul,' she said.

I promised to keep her posted, asked her to do the same.

We said goodbye.

Henry. He didn't pick up. I sent him a message.

Call me. Not about us. X

Third cigarette. Rich.

'Joni, Jesus. What happened?'

I didn't cry when I told him. The guilt of abandoning him with no explanation somehow took centre stage for a moment. It was a relief to feel something else. I apologised a lot.

'Fuck,' he said.

'Yeah.'

I waited for him to say something else – to offer me condolences, or even tell me off for behaving as I had. I could hear him exhaling through his nose. There was a beeping on the line.

'Shit, I've got to go, my friend's calling me. He doesn't know yet.'

Rich again said nothing. I ended the call.

Henry: 'Hi. What is it?'

'How are you?' I asked instinctively.

'Fine. You?'

'Not good, actually.' Then came tears again. Heaving sobs.

'For God's sake, Joni, what's wrong?'

'Are you sitting down?' I said, borrowing Niall's words. I think I phrased it exactly as Niall had to me, twenty-four hours earlier; the words making as little sense now as they did then.

'For fuck's sake,' Henry said, breaking down. He began to stutter apologies.

'Don't,' I said. 'It doesn't matter now.'

It really, really didn't.

We stayed on the line, both crying. I looked over the river in his direction.

'Where are you?' he said.

I sat up, as if he could suddenly see me.

'Niall's,' I said. 'Are you – I mean, I'm sure, if you wanted to—'

'No, no, it's OK,' he said.

I was relieved. If he came over, I would have wanted to sleep with him.

'Love you, sweetheart,' he said.

'Love you too.'

I had the fourth and final cigarette out there by myself.

19

I went to see Fiona before setting off. Thankfully, Jenny wasn't there. For the first time, we sat in her front room, where Fiona saw her clients; earthenware mug of tea balanced in my lap, box of tissues on the coffee table before me. The room did have a uniquely calming effect – the large, enveloping armchair and muted colours creating the illusion of being held. Upon opening the door, Fiona had given me one of her signature, slightly-too-long hugs. I found I was impervious to the comfort these embraces had always promised.

Fiona was at ease with my despair. Like a doctor with even the most gruesome ailment, this was nothing she hadn't seen before. It was a reprieve from the company of the others, who, despite nursing their own wounds, had begun to operate around with me a strained caution, constantly offering me hot drinks. I remembered how Henry and I had dealt with this discomfiture after Marla's death by making love endlessly. I remembered how Dyl had told me that death made people copulate.

'How are you feeling?' asked Fiona, across from me.

I shrugged. 'I don't know.' I said. 'I haven't really got my head around it. I keep thinking I'll wake up one day and things will be normal again.'

'Are you angry?'

'It comes and goes,' I said. 'Yes, sometimes. I want to shout at him. I want to fucking punch him in the bollocks.'

She smiled sadly. 'I don't need to remind you that the so-called five stages of grief are never linear, and are often repetitive. Depression, denial, bargaining, anger, acceptance. You'll move through each of them, and between them, and back again.'

'Yippee,' I said.

'Are you sure it's wise to be going back to your parents'?' she said, neutrally.

'Isn't it?'

'Our childhood homes can be triggering; I wouldn't want you to add to the maelstrom of feelings you're already having.'

'It's not my childhood home,' I said.

'Oh yes,' said Fiona. 'Apologies.'

I longed to be told what to do: not just about where I should go, but everything. The minutiae of life now seemed so utterly pointless – brushing my teeth, eating – that part of me just wanted to go home in order to alleviate some of the responsibility.

We sat without speaking for a while. The clock above my head – positioned so that Fiona, and not her clients, could track the start and end of her sessions – ticked laboriously on. I felt as though I could sit here forever, sinking so far into the armchair it would swallow me up, the ticking dragging out ad infinitum.

'How is everything else, hen?' Fiona asked. 'What was life looking like before this happened?'

'Don't ask me that,' I said.

'Why?'

'Because it was a mess.'

'Was it?'

'Yes. I was staying with this man, this total stranger.

Hijacking his life. I had no money, no job. Nowhere to live. Henry and me – it didn't work.' I laughed, realisation dawning on me. 'All I wanted since I was sixteen was to be Henry's girlfriend. As if that would somehow complete me, as if I'd suddenly become someone else – the kind of girl he dated. Like it would finally prove I was good enough. I was so obsessed with being someone's girlfriend that I've completely lost track of *me*.' I found I was standing. 'I've lost my job, lost being with those kids I fucking *loved*, I've lost Mila to Niall. I don't know how to use a basic fucking computer program. Everyone's getting on with their lives without me.'

It felt good, juicy and excruciating, feeling so sorry for myself.

'And I've lost my best—' I choked. 'I've lost—'

Fiona handed me the box of tissues. I ripped one out violently.

'Why didn't I see it coming? Everything I thought was just a drama was a warning sign. And I ignored it. He was all alone – I wasn't there to stop him, I didn't catch it, I couldn't—'

Something had given way inside of me. I felt as if I were both floating and falling at the same time.

'Why didn't he talk to me? Why didn't he tell me? God, I'm so fucking selfish. He was all alone. He must have felt so entirely alone, Fiona—'

I was shouting at her.

'Joni, suicide is never anyone's fault. Ever. The only person responsible for their actions is them.'

'But why didn't he try harder?'

'I don't know. The almighty darkness one feels in those moments—'

'Everything I thought that mattered . . . it was all so stupid. So fucking naive. My God. What's the point, now? I honestly don't see the point.'

Fiona stood up. She wanted to hold me, I could tell, but she was caught somewhere between her roles as friend and therapist.

'You might not be able to hear this, hen,' she said, 'but, in time, that perspective will be one of your biggest strengths. When the worst thing you can imagine happening happens, you're bulletproof. All those little niggles and worries pale in comparison. Ultimately, great peace and wisdom can be born out of tragedies such as this, if you let it.'

'Fuck off, Fiona,' I said. 'Not everything's a lesson. Sometimes life is just unspeakably terrible.'

She allowed herself the hint of a smile. I felt a tiny, tiny bit lighter.

'I'm sorry,' I said. 'I'm appalling. I'm literally the biggest selfish cunt on the planet.'

'You aren't, actually.'

'I am. I hate myself.'

I groaned. I was tired. I felt physically sick so constantly it seemed the nausea would never lift; this was my new normal. And now there was a big drive ahead – alone.

'How long will you stay at your mum and dad's for?' she said.

'I don't know.'

'Alright. Well, before you go, I've got some things for you.'

She went to go, but doubled back on herself and gently took my face in both her hands. 'I'm so sorry for your loss, darling,' she said, and kissed my forehead.

Her care package included chocolates, Scotch, a book on grief, and a crisp, blank new notebook.

'Try and journal,' she said. 'Get everything out on the page. It helps, I promise.'

'Thank you,' I said.

Outside, the dappled clouds were fluorescent with the sun fighting to break through.

'You take care of yourself,' she said, her fingers on my chin, eyes searching mine.

'I'll try.'

Once again, I drove the artefacts of my existence away from one place to another. Out through the grey tower blocks and warehouses, the pollution-stained terraces of the ring road giving way to fields. Back to Ely, where I hadn't been since Dyl and I came together to collect this damn car.

Unpacking in the purple guest room, I found the clear plastic pouch of heroin. I put it in the bedside drawer.

At dinner, my father says how selfish he was, his poor parents.

On my laptop, a window pops up for the Samaritans.

At night, I try masturbating.

My mother lifts the smoking ban, but only in the kitchen with the French doors open.

A text from Rich: *Thinking of you.*

Fiona's book tells me that grief is the price of love.

I go for a walk, in search of water. The Ouse is a river as ugly as its name.

'Why did you never get a pet?' I ask my parents, watching TV. Too needy, they say.

I lie in bed and read.

I say things out loud to him.

My mother comes in and puts a hand on my back. When she leaves, I see she has bought me an advent calendar.

*

On the day of the funeral, my father drove: Mum in the front and me in the back, utterly empty.

'Don't forget to indicate, Mike!' said Mum.

'Oops! Sorry, love,' said Dad.

Henry was there, sitting with Rusty, who was wearing sunglasses despite being inside on a winter's day. In their anguish, it seemed Dyl's parents had leaned hard into Judaism. Ben's funeral had been at the smaller prayer hall down the road, but today we were in the grand synagogue. It smelled of candle wax. The entire service was conducted in Hebrew. It was easier in a way, not understanding what was being said. I rested my head on Mila's shoulder, my new oldest friend, and allowed the unfamiliar sounds to wash over me, studying the ornate chandeliers. They were all the same, really – synagogue, church, museum: musty and reverential. Dyl's casket was made out of crude wood, unvarnished, with rope handles. It didn't do to look at it, much less to contemplate him being inside it.

The cemetery was a short drive away. I shared a taxi with Jess and Paddy, all three of us jammed into the back seat.

'How are you?' said Paddy.

I shrugged. 'I thought today would make it feel real,' I said. 'But no.'

'No,' he agreed. 'I half expected him to show up today.'

'Me too,' I said. 'I keep thinking that. That he'll show up. Can't he just come back now?'

'I'm reading a book about grief,' said Jess.

'Me too,' I said.

'Are you? Mine says that it won't feel real until we've been through a rotation of all four seasons.'

'Mine says that grief is the price we pay for love.'

Dyl was buried next to Ben.

There was no reception afterwards. Dyl's parents were going to sit shiva with some members of their extended family; everyone else went home.

We smoked in the car park.

Mila huddled into Niall's coat. 'Are you coming?' she asked me, squinting into the cold wind.

I could go with them. I could go and sleep in Niall's clean, warm guest bedroom. Surround myself with people, pull them tightly around me: a barrier. I could get drunk, cry, eat pizza, watch sad films and smoke. And do it all over again. Again and again and again. And then what?

'I think I'm going to go home,' I said.

Everyone nodded, a little lost for words.

'Love you,' said Jess, giving me a squeeze.

'I love you, too. So much,' I said. Then I said it to Mila, to Paddy, to Niall, making sure I said the 'I' each time. We said it so much, those two words – 'love you'. As blasé as hello and goodbye. Something about making it three felt deeper, like I was planting it, storing it safely within each of them. It felt important.

Finally, I went over to speak to Dyl's parents. I looked into David's eyes, which are Dyl's eyes, and they were empty.

20

There is only one useful phrase in the book on grief Fiona gave me: Just For Today.

Just For Today, I can't talk to you.
Just For Today, I can't see you.
Just For Today, I can't hug you.
Just For Today, I can't call you.
Just For Today, I can't tell you about the book I'm reading.
Just For Today, I can't tell you about the funny thing that happened.
Just For Today, I can't laugh at your pithy reply.
Just For Today, I can't complain about my parents to you.
Just For Today, I can't go to Theodore's with you.
Just For Today, I can't share a beer with you in the sun.
Just For Today, I can't tell you to fuck off.
Just For Today, I can't touch you.
Just For Today, I can't see your face.
Just For Today, I can't see your mouth fighting to curl into a smile.
Just For Today, I can't steal one of your cigarettes.
Just For Today, I can't read the latest entry in your cryptic handwriting.
Just For Today, I can't smell your musty boy smell.

Just For Today, I can't hear your voice say your
    special name for me.
Just For Today, I can't hold you.

Because, Dyl, the idea that I can never do any of those
things, ever again, for the rest of my life, is too much to
bear.

*

After all the sleeping, there was writing. It was all I could
do. Pages and pages, until my hand ached. Letters. I wrote
an apology to Henry. A thank you letter to Niall. One to
Paddy, telling him how proud I was of him. Near-identical
letters to Mila and Jess, telling them how much they meant
to me.

And then you.

Everything I wrote was to you. It started with reams
of furious block capitals, scratched in so hard I tore the
paper. You can guess what they said. Then I started writing
because it felt like talking to you. Asking you why. Telling
you I didn't care about the money you stole from me, and
the drugs, I just wish so fucking hard we'd talked – and
I'm sorry, I'm so, so sorry we didn't talk. Telling you what
songs I was listening to that reminded me of you (Bob,
obviously, and Nick Drake). I filled you in about the great
sex I'd been having before you did this. Thanks a lot, by
the way, you really cock-blocked me there.

Something happened on the wet drive back to Ely.
The car got muggy and I turned the heater on. Do you
remember? Months ago, after we went to pick up the car,
you kissed my window as you got out at the traffic lights.
It left a mark. Driving away from the city, three days after
I heard you were gone, there it was. Your kiss was on my

window; the steam breathed it back to life. This spectre of you sitting next to me the whole way home.

And you kept your promise. You paid me back, sort of. Your parents wanted me to have the prize money you won for your short story. The one about the man who becomes fixated with the mould on his wall. First prize. You bastard.

Maybe there's a parallel Us, our doppelgängers on Primrose Hill when we were sixteen, who did things differently.

Dyl. I feel completely divided. I am a cuckoo, a parasite. I feel like parts of me were left in Fiona's attic. Parts of me are still with the kids. At the Albany. Frozen in time on that Cornish beach when Henry told me he loved me. Crying in your arms at the train station. Screaming Bowie from a roof. Cocooned in Rich's arms. Scribbling in a notebook in the woods. I am all over the place.

These are parts I might be able to recover. They may weld together again, like birds migrating home.

But the part you took, dear friend, I shall never get back again.

It's with you. I hope it shines a light, wherever you are.

Acknowledgements

Thank you to Zoë Aston, who introduced me to the amazing team at The Soho Agency, where the journey of this book being published began. Thank you to Marina de Pass, my wonderful agent, whose kindness, support and wisdom have made my life both smoother and richer. I feel extremely lucky to have you as both my cheerleader and guide. Thank you for understanding Joni, this novel, and me.

Thank you to Amy Perkins, my brilliant editor. From our very first phone-call I felt that I was in safe – and expert – hands. Thank you for going through this book with a fine-toothed comb again and again, with as much care each time. Thank you for your extraordinary attention to detail, and your extraordinary support.

Thank you to my dog, Maggie, who sat on my lap for most of the writing process, and forced me to take walks, on which many of my best ideas were able to form.

Thank you to Jake Chatterton, my first reader, for everything. Thank you for your insight, your love, and for holding my hand.

I want to thank my second and third readers, to whom this book is dedicated: my parents, Charles and Cressida. You were the most nerve-wracking recipients of that early draft, as your opinions mean so much to me. But I needn't have worried. As ever, you were beyond kind, beyond thrilled, and beyond supportive. Thank you for sending me a bottle of champagne the second I finished typing – a moment I will never forget. Thank you for not just letting, but encouraging me to be an artist. Thank you to my sister and brother, Violet and Gabriel, who came next of the early readers. I love you both more than I can say. To my whole family: thank you for being my permanently available sounding board and panel of experts.

Thank you to Alexandra Dudley, who persisted in getting me to send her my manuscript, and was then filled with kind things to say about it. Thank you for always being there for me, through everything.

To Alice, Orion, Jack and Ali, my WhatsApp gang. Thank you for sending flowers when I first heard this book would be published, and for keeping me sane throughout one hell of a crazy year.

Thank you to Oliver Slinger, Natalie Day, Humphrey Hendrix and Ruby Phetmanh, AKA Team HORN, my acting agents at Independent Talent, for all your support.